BOOK ONE

ERIN GRAMMAR

Midnight Tide
PUBLISHING

For everyone searching for the hearts to call home.

AUTHOR'S NOTE

Please note that this book depicts issues of grief, depression, parental death (off page), anxiety (social anxiety, thought spirals, overthinking), bullying and harassment, mild gore and medical body horror, violence-related PTSD with symptoms on page, features a romantic crush (not acted upon) with a slight age gap, briefly mentions organized crime and illegal substance abuse, and deals with mistaken identity surrounding sexual orientation (not demonized or judged negatively in any way). I've tried to approach these subjects with as much care and sensitivity as I can through the lens of a somewhat unreliable narrator, but please be advised if such content is triggering.

WEDNESDAY

1

WORST BIRTHDAY
EVER

Chocolate icing stained my dress an hour before I got drenched in blue blood and a pinch of magic. When we stood to leave, I saw the blob and shrieked. Every head in the fancy Italian restaurant spun to gawk at me as I ran for the back with my best friend close behind. Distraction gripped me. That's why I'd dropped birthday cake on the cream-colored skirt of my favorite dress. And I had no trouble blaming the creepy old woman for my mistake.

I shoved my bangs up with my big headbow, and dunked the fabric near my knees into the bathroom's only sink.

Chi Ho juggled my belongings, swatting and snarling at the socialites invading our space. Her beauty drew them like bugs to a Venus flytrap. No one knew she'd snap until they got too close.

I scratched at the thick layer of butter and sugar with the rhinestone manicure she gave me. Chunks dissolved to reveal the print beneath—golden ballerinas on marionette strings.

Two soft hands tapped my shoulder as Chi Ho held hers on top of the fuzzy white paw of my designer purse. Usakumya, the white rabbit with crimson eyes whose name I'd kept from his Japanese manufacturer, bounced a sympathetic glance against the mirror. He nuzzled my cheek with the help of his mischievous puppeteer.

She sang a squeaky question for him. "Are you sure you're okay?"

No. I hadn't been since we left Visions of Serenity Nails and Spa, because that's when her grandmother latched onto my elbow by the door.

"*Tonight,*" her warning rasped. "*Don't go through the alleyway!*"

The amateur psychic thought wrong when she assumed cryptic advice made a good present for someone turning eighteen. I expected a card, or a handful of confetti. Not a verbal smack in the face and the devastating unease that followed. Instead of a star on the cats in hats calendar by the front desk, perhaps she'd written a secret message in characters I couldn't read: *Third Wednesday in October, be sure to ruin Holly's big day.*

"What Nai Nai said…" I mumbled.

Chi Ho's face replaced Usakumya's. She rolled her eyes. "Are you still stuck on that? I love her, but she's kooky. Stop worrying about it."

I shut off the faucet. "I know, but—"

"Look." She reached for the wall dispenser and handed me a gigantic wad of paper towels. "If she could really see the future, don't you think she'd be playing Powerball numbers instead of running a nail salon? Who wants to work? Are you spacing? We live in San Francisco now. It's not like the Midwest. Telling you to avoid alleyways is like saying stay inside when it's raining, or don't pay too much for coffee. It's bullshit. Impossible. Even if you asked exactly what she meant, you know she'd never tell you. That's her shtick."

The food in my stomach churned like cement in a mixer. I dried off, spritzed myself with the free perfume sitting on the counter, and tried to hide my uncertainty. Adopting a brave face, I puffed out my chest, locked eyes with my reflection, and reminded myself fortune tellers weren't real. Superpowers didn't exist, except in the mushy minds of people who believed in Elvis conspiracies. Or that trees had souls.

"You know what she says about me. All that crap about destiny." She mimicked her grandmother's prophetic trance. *"You will be the seeing eyes of a great soldier.* Yeah, right. I wish my life was that interesting."

Nai Nai being full of it didn't make me feel better. I'd known Chi Ho since kindergarten, and her personality never strayed far from outgoing, protective, kind when it suited her, and independent to a fault. No one but her grandmother would've described her as *perceptive.*

I swallowed my doubt and forced a smile. "Well, at least we know that isn't me."

She laughed as we wheeled around to leave and found a crowd waiting to wash their hands.

They blocked the door with arms crossed. The woman in front gave me a nasty once-over and sneered.

"About time, princess. Don't you know it's not Halloween yet?"

Chi Ho bared her teeth. The bloodthirsty twinkle in her deep brown eyes crackled as I pulled her away before she could defend me.

The same question pelted us from speeding cars once every five minutes on our walk to the restaurant. A few brave drivers even leaned out their windows to get a better glimpse of me as they flew by, and then promptly slammed their breaks at the next red light. My shy and anxious nature meant she always spoke for me in social situations, but I wasn't in the mood for a fight. I didn't blame the stranger for her mean remark. I'd have heard it anyway, hogging the sink or not.

I chose my fate by adopting the over-the-top Harajuku style that transformed me from another boring white girl in sneakers to a cross between Disney's Alice and a Rococo debutante. People assumed I wore cosplay since I looked like a powerful magical girl. My favorite dresses waltzed into my life when I found a Japanese fashion magazine in my old school's library. Pouring over its glossy pages became my reward for finishing mountains of homework each night, and I never returned the sacred text.

Fierce women designed brands like Angelic Pretty and Baby the Stars Shine Bright for others like them. Instead of dressing sleek and sexy to find an office job and someone to marry, devotees dedicated themselves to rebellion with their old-fashioned gowns. In the early 2000s, new shops opened internationally to spread the whimsical spirit of punk. The fashion's feminist angle few saw or understood felt like a fantastic secret, and I adored the layers of chiffon and soft lace that hugged me like a friend. My doll-like appearance facilitated my ultimate goal. I wanted to keep the world at bay to shield my porcelain heart from more pain, loss, and grief.

I let go of Chi Ho as the door swung shut behind us, but she yanked me in again to navigate the winding path to the lobby.

She elbowed me playfully. "You're getting soft. I could've taken her. If you keep being so nice, the next thing you know you'll be making friends. Traveling the world. Falling in love."

"No chance, *Lee*," I teased.

4

She'd been going by the last half of her name forever—mostly because she could never hear the first without the distant echo of her mother's voice.

Chi Ho made a face and pushed me out the front door. "Don't call me that!"

A chilly pumpkin spice-flavored breeze knocked the breath from my lungs. She gave Usakumya and my parasol back to me. The decorative umbrella's steel frame set it apart from the plastic kind sold to children at summer festivals. Its sharp tip scraped the pavement when I hung it from my elbow. My biceps retained the firmness of room temperature cream cheese when I flexed, but overconfidence told me I could stab someone with it if I ran into trouble on my way home.

It was an extension of my arm in the perpetually rainy city. I'd taken it with me to protect my fair skin from the elements while shopping in Japantown before heading to Visions of Serenity. I spent my days browsing and buying online or in person, and sometimes I socialized with the local J-Fashion community. That Saturday we planned to celebrate the holiday that prompted extra rude questions with a fairytale tea party at an upscale hotel. The girls throwing it both owned small IT companies. They had even more money to blow than me.

I started thinking about potential outfits when Chi Ho pulled me in for a hug.

She rocked on the heels of her worn combat boots, ready to set off for Chinatown and the apartment she shared with her extended family. One of the conditions of our cross-country move left her in the care of her grandmother and cousins rather than living with me. Her parents thought I was a bad influence.

They were probably right.

"Thanks for dinner." She squeezed my bony shoulders and leaned back. "Do you want me to walk you home? If you're still freaked out, I mean. I don't mind."

I lied to save her the hassle. "No. It's way too late. You've got work in the morning. I don't. If I bug out halfway there, I'll get a taxi. I promise."

"Okay," she said, letting go with lukewarm conviction. "But text me in the A.M.!"

I told her I would—barring any magical accidents.

She waved and I watched her go in trendy jeans stretched threadbare by plus-sized thighs, a men's flannel jacket, and the work polo she usually wore twice in a row. She hated laundry, and she wouldn't let me buy her new clothes. We looked like Marie Antoinette and Kurt Cobain when we stood side-by-side, but despite our differences, I loved her more than anyone.

A drizzle started and I pulled my long pink coat tighter. The midnight crowd in Union Square parted for me to walk through it toward Pacific Heights. As I went, I noticed couples first, but I always did. Every time, without fail, and never without an absent tugging near my heart—like a sweater snagged by the first loose strand, threatening to unravel.

Their happy permutations seemed endless. Pairs of men and women, men and men, two women, and groups made up of other magnificent genders floated by. Their feet played cozy melodies as they squashed wet yellow leaves. I tried to distract myself from the persistent itch in my chest by guessing *just friends* or *maybe more*. I wouldn't let myself have what I could pretend they did. That was too dangerous. But spinning something as trivial as a glance or matching outfits into an epic love story was a harmless hobby. It allowed me to live their lives without worrying about mine.

When I rounded the corner into my rich, quiet neighborhood full of colorful Victorians, I stopped where the sidewalk spit me out at the corner of the park. If I turned and continued for another half-block, I'd cross the lane and head for the rear entrance to my building. On any other night, I would've gone straight through the vacant backstreet, but Nai Nai's warning rang in my ears as I even considered it.

"Don't go through the alleyway!"

She was nuts. I knew that. No stars, ghosts, or tea leaves whispered her secrets that said I'd get hurt if I didn't change my ways. But when I tried to move, my feet stayed put. A trickle of slushy dread traveled down my spine. It froze the tips of my toes. When they thawed, I took a deep breath, pressed the button, and waited for the stoplight to change. Nai Nai's unflinching gray eyes invaded the rational part of my brain. I shuddered and decided to take the long way home based on her hunch I might get murdered.

Or worse.

When I arrived on the other side of the road, I looked left and right and stepped onto the cobblestone path. The ten minute jaunt across the sea of fiery trees dipped up and down. During the day, the park's miniature hills and valleys sparkled under a dense canopy of burgundy leaves, but at night the lush landscape cast sinister shadows.

I clung to my parasol, absolutely unprepared to use it as a weapon. Nail gems carved craters into my palm. The cloak of terror weighing me down lifted when drunken laughter drew my eyes to two tall figures approaching. I wasn't alone anymore.

Before I got a good look, I assumed they were businessmen coming from the local sports bar. If they catcalled me, it'd fortify the emotion slowly replacing fear—the smug knowledge I was better than old people who got hammered watching football on weeknights.

I didn't realize how wrong I was until they came closer. The nearer they got, the more I saw. The horrifying impact of their ugliness slammed into me when they wandered into a pool of flickering lamplight. They weren't wearing Halloween costumes. They were creatures come to life. Enormous muscles with bulging atomic blue veins undulated beneath their stretched skin. The monsters lurched forward and I stiffened, awestruck and paralyzed like a child trying to avoid the detection of hungry dinosaurs.

The two giggled as they took uncoordinated steps and plucked medical tubing from weeping orifices on their chests, arms, and legs. They wobbled on their feet like marathoners crossing the finish line of a fun run from Hell. The mysterious periwinkle goo running through their circulatory systems seeped through their tattered athletic wear and oozed onto the leafy ground.

Invisible glue on the bottom of my Mary Jane shoes immobilized me. My thrumming heart inched into my throat, ready to choke me if I didn't take a breath. I looked for a place to hide, and quietly shoved my parasol under my arm to shake off my purse when I didn't find one. After what seemed like years of rooting around inside Usakumya's cramped stomach, I found my cell phone to call 911. As I frantically dialed, the behemoth on the right turned to his friend and stroked his tan, keg-sized forearm.

"Hugo, you're so strong." His thick, heavy voice rumbled like a troll's. "So strong now. Such big gains."

The beast next to him bobbed along, a head shorter than his partner. He reached up and clasped him on the back.

"Big muscles." His brown eyes sparkled in uneven sockets. "You, too. I don't remember your name!"

A few rings later, the operator answered.

"Hello?" the disembodied voice greeted me as my arm hung limp at my side. "Hello, 911. What's your emergency?"

My synapses must've short-circuited because, instead of saying anything to my potential savior, diving for cover, or fleeing for my life, I actually laughed. The startled sound rang out, splitting the otherwise still night air. When it reached the ears of the monstrous beings, it caught their attention like dogs hearing a can of food opening. They stopped and shared a slack-jawed gape when they saw me. The lips of the first twisted into a crooked grin.

"Peeeeep." His drawn-out shout made me cringe. "Bo Peep!"

The other repeated after his friend as they came toward me with more speed than nature intended for massive legs.

I screamed and dropped my phone as the urgent demands of the dispatcher called to me across a vast universe of space.

The slighter one started chanting, his boom brimming with glee. "Peep, Peep. Where are your sheep?"

"Sheep!" His humongous twin wheezed, clutching his stomach like someone who wholeheartedly believed they'd heard the world's funniest joke.

Irony rose like bile to drown the incredulous scream on the tip of my tongue. I was going to die as I often lived: Mistaken by meatheads for a storybook icon.

The smaller of the two—who was at least the size of an upright minivan—landed in front of me. The second crept up behind.

He lifted my skirt and petticoat like a multicolored field day tent—curiously, without a hint of malice. "Sheep under here?"

"Get away from me!" I spun around and shrieked.

I grabbed my parasol from under my arm and held it between both hands. Even though he looked strong, a quick blow to his slimy chest knocked him backward. The one I couldn't see advanced over my shoulder. His voice dripped with the enthusiasm of a possessed child.

"Just like a doll. I want to play."

The other agreed, laughing as he lunged for Usakumya. He yanked the bunny from the crook of my arm—snapping his thick cotton strap as easily as dental floss—and tossed it with a ground-shaking guffaw to his friend.

"She dances!" He clapped when I jumped to reach him.

I choked on spit mid-scream when he scooped me by the armpits and swung me into the air. He almost dropped me when my foot smacked the shin of the tormentor clutching my purse. The walking tumor I hit tripped, closing the space between us.

My parasol slipped from my fingers when walls of flesh mashed together and sandwiched me in the middle. Though the hulking beings worked hard to get a better hold on me, neither possessed the motor skills it took to do it. If they meant to hurt rather than harass me, they were doing a pitiful job. But I couldn't take chances. I had to get away. They lumbered against gravity like twisted baby deer as their glowing limbs trembled.

Their bulbous heads collided. The one grasping me reeled back and let go. I dropped to my knees and scraped them as I tried to roll away from the feet stomping around me. The other abomination took a step and stopped my progress with his thick calf and an outstretched hand.

"Dolly!" He scrunched his sparse brows, unable to comprehend my attempted escape. "Hold still. You're getting dirty!"

I dodged in time to latch onto my umbrella lying in the mildewed grass. Then I made the stupidest decision of my entire life.

I'd fight the horrible creatures.

They weren't as dangerous as they looked.

Shaking my way to standing, I closed my eyes and whipped my sole means of defense around with every molecule of strength in my core. I opened them when its silk-covered rods hit shoulder with a dull *clank*. My target yelped, lost his balance, and fell on the lawn.

The remaining villain roared as he glanced at his partner. I braced for impact again and thrust my pink parasol upward, aiming the metal spoke on its end like the tip of a spear. The blow landed with a wet crunch. I looked up, gasped, and let go of my weapon. Half of it hovered in mid-air with bio-slime dripping like blueberry syrup down the handle. The other disappeared through the paper-thin skin stretched over the mutant's ribs.

His eyes bulged as he sputtered and slapped at his chest. Viscous, cyan blood flowed from his open mouth like lava. I scrambled to my feet, squealing as the shocked brute I'd toppled did the same. We couldn't tear ourselves away from the terrible metamorphosis taking place in front of us. The skin, sinew, and muscles of the thing I stabbed vibrated unnaturally. His flesh bubbled as it swelled and his face contorted in anguish. An inhuman cry tore from his throat to imprint

itself forever on my memory, accompanied by the unforget-
table image of his huge body as it exploded.

A blue tidal wave of liquefied organs and bone submerged
us while we screamed. Without daring to look back, I took off
running for my apartment, grabbing my sopping wet
Usakumya as I went. I ran as I'd never run before. My heart
hammered, pushing a whoosh of adrenaline through the capil-
laries in my ears.

I felt for my keys as I finished the race for my life. My
eyes watered and my vision blurred. The heavy front door of
my building slammed behind me. I rushed through the lobby
and took the stairs two at a time to my floor, not daring to
slow even though I face-planted several times. I didn't stop
until I threw my deadbolt shut. As far as I could tell through
puffy lids, my pastel pink home looked the same as when I'd
left: Perfectly adorable.

But not me.

I didn't.

I was covered in gore.

I wiped my face, limped into the bathroom, and
approached the mess of a girl in the mirror. Mud, leaves, and
guts camouflaged my birthday outfit and coated what was left
of Chi Ho's custom charms glued to my nails. Usakumya
slipped from my grip onto the toilet lid. Our gazes met. His
once-playful orbs shone flat, glazed with the spoils of war. I
looked at myself next, and took in the scrapes and bruises that
meant nothing to me. Not compared to the worst of it all.

Though maybe I was just in denial.

Killing a man only bothered me a little. He struck first. He
was a monster. I did what had to be done. But the most awful
part of it all sank in as water from my showerhead blasted my
trembling hand.

I'd ruined my favorite dress.

I stepped into my tub. Fat tears flowed down my cheeks. Puppet Circus—an ultra-rare and expensive print from 2006 —was gone from me forever. Or at least until I found it for sale on the secondhand market again. And who knew—I lamented as I sobbed beneath the near-scalding stream—how long that was going to take.

2

OH NO HE'S HOT

I fell into bed exhausted and didn't open my eyes until the sun crept past my gossamer curtains. For the first time since I'd moved in, my noisy neighbor hadn't made a peep all night. I begrudgingly belonged to our homeowner's association despite only knowing—and kind of caring—about Kyle Lambert. He was another emancipated minor. Whenever I saw the tiny redhead he always had a heavy textbook about biology or contract law and a bag of shredded newspaper in tow. He never entertained guests, but that didn't keep the bizarre soundtrack of his life from waking me up long past midnight.

My heavy eyelids parted as I greeted the new day with a smile that fell when my other senses turned on. The traffic and city sounds outside buzzed louder than usual. A heart-stopping shiver ran up my spine. My satin sheets encased me like a pile of dead fish—cold, slimy, and damp. I felt them along every millimeter of my body.

Because I was completely naked.

Unlike when I fell asleep.

I bolted up on my elbows and let out a mangled squeal, flinging off gooey covers stained blue. Shreds of my nightgown stuck to me like tar to unlucky ducks trapped in an oil

16

spill. I stumbled through my bedroom and walk-through closet to the bathroom. The haphazard pile of crusty clothing on the floor tripped me, and I cracked the sink when I used it to catch myself.

Usakumya blanked at me from his perch on top of the toilet, his thousand-yard stare boring into my skull. I examined myself in the mirror and breathed a loud sigh of relief when I saw I was still human despite contradicting evidence. Actually, I looked better than usual.

Maybe even better than ever before.

My smooth skin glided beneath my fingertips, as unblemished as a porcelain doll. An elfin pale—more cool-toned and plastic than peachy—replaced the imperfections of my cheeks. Loose, long blonde curls cascaded past my shoulders in waves rather than tangles. My blue eyes sparkled in the glow of my marble vanity like tiny white Christmas lights sat behind each bright hollow. The way my Dad used to describe the low budget aliens from old episodes of *Star Trek* popped into my head: Pretty-ish, mostly human—just *wrong*.

I winced.

A battle destroyed my sheets, but my body remained as clean as when I'd crawled beneath my comforter. I concocted an explanation for the discrepancy and continued my head-to-toe check. The blood of the creatures I'd encountered didn't even clock a one on the normalcy scale. Despite washing, some invisible bits must've gotten stuck in my pores. I'd sweated onto the area around me as I slept. The particles oxidized overnight and turned that hideous, industrial shade of blue that made me nauseous when I saw it. Okay, duh.

No other logical explanation existed.

I went over the rest of my limbs with scientific precision, searching for the injuries I swore I'd glimpsed the night before. When I didn't find them, I considered how to address the disaster in my bedroom. My bed set needed an immediate replacement. Maybe I'd even need a new mattress and headboard. I glued my lips together in a solid frown. The cost wasn't prohibitive, but I never wanted to spend money on necessities rather than clothes.

I arrived at my feet, dead set on getting dressed, gathering up the mess in large trash bags, and disposing of it stoically in the dumpster behind my building. After that, I'd suck it up, push past my cashier-fear, and journey to the nearest home store. Forward motion fed progress. I needed to look ahead, not back.

In less than twenty-four hours, my knowledge of the known universe flipped upside down. Monsters were real. I couldn't dwell on that useless fact. No one would believe me if I told them, except maybe Chi Ho. She'd want to track down the one who ran to take a video and become internet famous. No, I'd continue life as I knew it and let whoever else wanted to delve deeper into the unthinkable deal with what I didn't want to.

I'd rid Usakumya of the evidence of slaughter coating his fur. The idea of a clean slate promised to make us both good as new. He'd survived the supernatural brawl with me, and I'd save him no matter how many hours of work and gallons of color-safe bleach it took. I couldn't abandon my friend to the dump after all we'd shared.

I worked my way back up my body, going about the motions until a glimmer on my knees stopped me. The neon blue, crosshatch pattern where my scabs should've been disappeared when I looked twice. When I found nothing, I melted to the floor next to my bathtub like a Popsicle left on a hot sidewalk. My head spun as every detail of my fight with the mutants came rushing back.

Oh, God. Oh, God.

The uncharacteristically religious refrain repeated itself in my head while I reached for the toilet. I knocked my dirty companion down with nanoseconds to spare and broke the lid off its hinges to spew into the bowl. Practical concerns surfaced as I sprawled across the crunchy evidence of my lethal deed.

I moaned in agony. "What am I going to do?"

A man was dead, and I'd dealt the finishing blow. He wasn't really human, or at least that's what I rationalized as I wiped my mouth with my forearm. I gazed into the mosaic of last night's dinner, willing the stinky globs to form letters and provide the much-needed answer to my prayers. That didn't happen, but I pulled back from the fumes with a comforting thought. No living soul—of the human variety—could connect me to my crime.

I flushed, brushed my teeth, and tiptoed back into my disgusting bedroom. My hand flexed unconsciously as I reached for the doily sitting on my bedside table. I had to text Chi Ho, just like I did every morning, but my fingers closed around air. The place where my phone always slept was empty. I blinked at it as the gears in my mind came screeching back to life.

The parasol I left behind was too generic to condemn me, unlike the cell phone sitting in a puddle of organ soup. Dialing 911 seemed like the most reasonable thing to do in the face of certain death, but calling for help and hanging up when I didn't ask for it put me on the San Francisco Police Department's radar. I'd become their prime suspect if I didn't find it before them. Turning eighteen meant they could try me as an adult. *For murder.*

I tore into my closet and grabbed the first thing I saw: My pink Milky Way cutsew dress, a casual piece with a giant bow near the soft neckline and layers of starry black and pink chiffon. Even without a petticoat, it puffed out in a halo above my knees. I didn't bother with bloomers or safety shorts over my striped underwear.

In and around my desk, I found a bejeweled black head-bow, matching shoes, a tote bag embossed with a carousel, and a pair of ankle socks. A simple tug from me tore the toes of my first foot through the seam of the lightweight fabric. Heartbroken, I exited my bedroom and flopped onto my velvet couch to don the other with more care.

My luck turned sour once more when my butt connected with the cushion. Wooden legs buckled beneath me as a split second earthquake rocked my apartment. Cute figurines and stacks of fashion magazines on the shelves of the entertainment center hugging the front wall shook. The contents of my open kitchen rattled behind me. I cried out as a special edition plate from Angelic Pretty printed with sugar cookies leapt from a wire rack to my left. It shattered when it landed on the hardwood between the rug and the wall. A depressing pattern dictating the fate of my possessions was beginning to emerge.

I gently rolled on my other sock and buckled the ankle straps of my shoes. An uncontrollable slideshow of future misery reminded me I'd wind up in federal prison if I didn't find my phone. I imagined my brand, seized by the state to rot in an evidence locker until the next ice age. Worse yet, maybe they'd give it away to charity. I couldn't bear the thought of my prized wardrobe being ripped, warped, and reused by grubby children for Halloween costumes or school plays.

I ran, picked up my keys, and pulled my front door open. The brass knob came off in my hand with as much lightness and ease as though I'd plucked the decaying Styrofoam nose off a vintage clown sculpture

But I had no time to react to that.

As the wooden frame crashed into the wall, the fist of a knocking visitor smashed into my forehead.

"Ow!" I cried, more startled than anything else.

The blow didn't actually hurt.

"Son of a bitch!" A young man with short brown hair in a wrinkled black suit and white shirt cradled his hand.

His shout chased mine down the hall as my heart fell through the floor. Even though I rarely watched crime dramas, I didn't have to in order to figure out who and what he was—a detective. One sent by the government instead of the city.

I hatched a new plan when I saw the badge peeking out from his inner pocket. The scheme screaming between my ears sang simple, tried, and true.

Lie.

Lie because your life depends on it.

Lie like a televangelist cheating on his pregnant wife, or a New York businessman running for office. Lie until my tale manifested a vibrant life of its own and I actually believed it. I'd do it all in the name of protecting myself and my cherished collection of Japanese dresses. Their lives—the longevity and care of every delicate thread and row of lace—depended on it as much as my own. I braced myself for his first question as the man straightened.

"What the hell is your head made of?" His baritone grumble marked him as someone who'd grown up on the East Coast.

"Meat? I mean, technically speaking."

"Feels like fucking steel." He rubbed his knuckles. "Must've hit just right."

I paused and sputtered as our eyes met. His moved on to the interior of my apartment, and when they did, his masculine brows pulled together. The plague of pink afflicting my body and home proved off-putting to most, but it intrigued rather than fazed him. He looked at the doorknob clutched in my right hand.

His gaze swept past it to the mess behind me. When he inevitably came back to the hole in my front door, that's when I truly saw him for the first time.

I'd only seen faces like his in Calvin Klein advertisements. Even the red slice on his cheek couldn't mar his oppressive handsomeness. He wasn't my type, I reiterated as the nothingness in my gut tumbled faster. I usually liked androgynous men and masculine-identifying people, and feminine goddesses who looked like entire nations belonged kneeling at their feet. Not slightly older versions of the football players who made fun of me in high school.

His tan skin caught the sunlight, revealing undertones of clay and burnt umber he shared with the Cherokee foreman who once worked with my parents. My mouth contorted into a grimace I couldn't suppress. The man in front of me was my enemy.

But also really, *really* hot.

Tiny wrinkles creased at the edges of his moss-colored eyes as he offered me an understanding quirk of a smile. "You sure you're okay?"

"I'm fine." I rushed to recover, adjusting my grip to hide the keys striped with blue blood.

"Really? You must have a thick skull."

I cut him off at the pass before he got tired of faking the

role of clumsy, doe-eyed public servant in favor of going in for the kill. "So, what's your name, and who are you?" I blurted out. "You know I'm a very busy person, and I—"

If I sounded official enough, maybe I'd convince him to leave. After that, I'd hurry downstairs and across the road to find my missing phone. With any luck, it wasn't already being bagged and labeled by underpaid crime scene techs. I tried to reverse my uncertain expression as he jumped back in.

"Special Agent Michael Brannon." A swift, unreadable flash of the credentials in his pocket accompanied his answer. "I'm here helping local law enforcement. Last night—"

I stopped him and adopted the look of a frightened damsel. "Surely, you can't think I had anything to do with what's happened."

I didn't catch my mistake in time. Although he tried not to show it, cogs clicked as he calculated the math of my guilt behind his otherwise placid exterior.

I had to correct myself. Fast.

"I mean. What *has* happened? Something bad? I hope not! I'd be happy to—"

"That's why I'm here, Miss. Last night, an altercation occurred in your neighborhood at approximately the same time an emergency call was received."

"How can I possibly help with that?" I imitated indignant shock as storm clouds gathered in my abdomen.

"You see, the call came from a phone registered to one Holly Kristine Roads. The listed occupant of this apartment. I'm assuming that's you. Am I right? You're kind of young to be on your own. Shouldn't you be in school?"

"I graduated early."

I wanted to slap myself for being so candid. As Agent Brannon's smug smile widened, I decided I hated him.

"We could keep doing this all day," he said, "but the truth of the matter is you know and I know that I'm right. So you might as well go back with me to headquarters to answer a few simple questions. I promise it won't take too long."

I didn't get the chance to say no and slam the broken door in his face before a loud buzz interrupted me. The first garbled bars of a patriotic anthem by a Disney Channel star I'd loved in elementary school blared from his pants pocket. His face turned firehouse red as he held up a hand, spun around, and flipped his outdated phone open.

"Yeah, Nuñez. I've got her." His tone didn't change, but his ramrod posture crumpled. "Are you almost done down there? Ready to head for breakfast?"

As he juggled more affirmations and several inquiries about the other task force on scene, a light bulb went off in my brain. I'd have to play along to a degree if I wanted to weasel my way out of his clutches. With the help of a little creative storytelling, I'd cast a rosy hue on the horrible event that compelled him to arrest me. But I got sidetracked from concocting my tale when his voice dropped to a manic whisper.

He thought I couldn't hear him.

"I told you to stop changing my ringtone. Change it back!"

His partner snickered. "Dude, it's your favorite—" He didn't get to say *song* before Brannon hung up on him and faced me with his tough mask hanging off-center.

I had a million questions, but one consumed the rest.

Who the hell is this guy?

I buried my curiosity to take my last shot before I lost my nerve. "You know what?" An awkward laugh broke my stream of consciousness. "I did see something strange in the park last night. It slipped my mind until now. You know how it is, right? Wacky San Francisco!"

"Uh-hunh." He blinked, totally unconvinced.

If I didn't elaborate, I'd lose him. "There were these two guys. Big guys. Must've been coming from some sort of nightclub. They were covered, in, uh, maybe highlighters? It could've been paint."

That caught his attention.

"Was it blue?"

"You know, I think it was." I hit my stride. "They startled me on the path as I was walking home. It's hard being a girl all alone at night. You've always got your hand on your phone or your keys."

For a minute, I thought I had him. That perhaps my luck was changing and my new version of the truth would satisfy his investigative requirements and send him away. I kept going, emboldened by what appeared like a dim glow at the end of the tunnel of my unfortunate morning.

"Maybe I *accidentally* hit the shortcut button with my thumb. The one that calls 911." I feigned sheepishness. "I was holding onto that sucker really tight."

"Accidents happen," he said.

"Right!" My muscles relaxed and more semi-truths spilled out. "Anyway, they were being a bit rowdy. Pushing each other and roughhousing. Drunk stuff. Probably too much hard cider. But I went past them and got home fine."

My one-man audience didn't say anything.

"I'm so sorry for this terrible mix up. I hate to have wasted your time. I truly hope nothing awful happened to them or anyone else after I was gone. But that's really all I know. So have a nice day!"

I moved to shoulder my door shut, a maneuver made more

difficult by full hands and the effort it took to keep my fake smile plastered on. I knew if he had my phone I'd already be in handcuffs. I'd just have to wait a little while longer. When they all left as he'd promised his partner, that's when I'd go to retrieve it. My idealistic view of the future vanished as Agent Brannon stuck the arm attached to his swollen right hand out to stop the closing slab.

He sighed, showing the first hint of exasperation as he pushed it back and reached down to pluck the doorknob from my grip.

"I'm afraid it's not that simple." Without breaking eye contact, he lobbed the hardware onto the couch where it landed with a soft thud.

"T-that's my property," I stuttered.

His proximity warmed the air between us and sent my system into shock. I wasn't used to having anyone invade my guarded personal bubble. When he took my empty hand, his palm hot and rough against mine, all my mental faculties malfunctioned.

He led me out of the safety of my apartment before letting go to hook one puffy finger through the hole in my door to pull it shut.

"I get it. Don't worry," he said. "You're having a shitty day. Your apartment's falling apart. You've got to deal with that. Then a federal agent shows up on your doorstep and conks you on the head before asking you questions you'd rather not answer. But you've got to be straight with me now. Okay?"

I nodded as the hypnosis of his touch wore off. He looked relieved.

"Good. My partner and I are starving. How about you come with us to eat? After that, we'll go do an official interview. You cooperate fully, and we'll send you on your way. Does that sound like a plan?"

I locked my deadbolt, resigned to the likelihood that I didn't have a choice. My stomach spoke up with the roar of a starving beast when we reached the top of the stairs and started our descent. At least I'd get a free meal by playing a cooperative witness. I tried to look on the bright side of things, though the next words from Agent Brannon obliterated my optimism again.

"By the way." He smirked as he slid his uninjured hand into another hidden compartment in his jacket and brought out a little baggie with my cell phone in the center. "You can have this back."

My world shuddered to a stop as I took it from him. Its custom case—a bejeweled bi pride flag Chi Ho spent weeks making—shimmered pink, blue, and purple beneath layers of gunk. It matched her yellow, white, purple, and black one. An autopilot press of the home button revealed a voicemail I'd have to listen to later—if I had the opportunity before getting thrown in jail. As I held the last nail in my coffin like I'd break it, the sad farewells of my dresses floated down from the floor above us. And that's when I knew it.

I was totally freaking screwed.

3

MURDER, AGAIN

By the time we arrived at the bottom of the stairs, I'd already bypassed denial as the first stage of grief.

I was angry.

A wet floor sign and the weary janitor next to it nearly tripped me as I stared daggers at the broad back of the demon leading me to doom. I wasn't going to let Brannon get away with stringing me along. He'd stood in my doorway like he actually felt sorry for me, listening to me blabber on for fifteen minutes when he'd pegged me from the start as a crappy liar.

My brain rebooted from our brushing encounter in the hallway. I didn't care who the hell he was, what agency he worked for, or what terrible consequences I'd face for opening my mouth.

I let loose on him.

"You jerk!" I screeched, startling the sleeping night watchman behind the lobby's desk. "You had it this whole time, and you didn't just tell me?"

Brannon breezed through the front door without looking back. "I thought I'd give you the opportunity to be honest with me, but we can try again later."

"Why torture me?" I demanded as we glided down the

drying, power-washed stoop toward the damp sidewalk. "I'm not admitting anything, but you obviously knew way more than you let on."

Swift paces carried him ahead. He hit the button for the intersection that led to the corner of the park. The walk sign illuminated within seconds.

"I'm a citizen. I know my rights." I galloped after him. "And you're a dirty rotten trickster!"

A crowd gathered by orange barriers and caution tape on the opposite side of the street turned to stare at the small ball of poof screaming at the man in black. The rage coursing through me bubbled to the surface in goosebumps when the cool fall morning nipped at my naked arms and legs. Hurrying out the door meant I hadn't grabbed a jacket. Brannon stopped near the edge of the nosy onlookers and scowled at me. When I caught him, he bent down with a gruff whisper.

"Can you stop? You're making a scene."

He stood straight and kept going.

"Answer me!" I barked at the back of his head.

Brannon wheeled around and grabbed my forearm. He winced as he squeezed it.

"Don't make me put you in handcuffs."

I squawked at the return of his touch, too stunned to try wrenching away.

"Don't worry!" A new voice called to me. "He doesn't have any."

My captor let go, grumbling and rubbing his fat, swollen hand as the person who torpedoed his macho display came bounding up to us.

The newcomer was younger than Brannon and several inches taller, with a thin frame easy to attribute to lots of fast food and energy drinks rather than exercise. A crooked nose claimed the middle of his face between tawny beige cheeks scarred by teenage acne. The wind lifted his shaggy black hair out of dark brown eyes. Although he wore khakis, a navy jacket, and an untucked gray shirt, I immediately knew he and Brannon made a pair from the same set.

"Diego Nuñez." He offered his hand—which I shook for politeness' sake. "I like your dress."

His partner shot him a dirty look. "You didn't have to tell her that." He came at me with a brand new threat. "If you run away, I'll tackle you. Got it?"

Images of us tangled on the concrete as he attempted to subdue me sent my brain spinning. I jostled it from side to side, trying to banish the thoughts by jettisoning them out both ears.

The newest addition to our crew sucked in a breath when he saw Brannon's throbbing fingers.

"Dude, what happened to you?"

I answered. "He busted his hand trying to beat down my door. And he punched me in the head!"

"Whoa," said the stranger I already knew I liked better. "You hit a girl?"

"Wait, wait," said Brannon. "That's not how it happened. I went to knock when she yanked her crappy old door open and I slammed it against her big, hard skull."

"Ouch! That hurts." Nuñez made a fist and rapped his thin knuckles against my forehead. "You must be tough. You look fine."

We both laughed—though his was real and mine wasn't—as Brannon sulked. Our instant rapport disturbed him. For a moment, he looked at me as if he wanted to stick his tongue out like a petulant child. But he didn't.

"It doesn't matter," he said. "Are you done here, or what? Are the locals satisfied enough to go home?"

"We're all set," said Nuñez. "They wanted to take samples for their own lab, but I told them that'd be too complicated and that we'd take it from here. It wasn't easy at first, but a little bit of science mumbo jumbo convinced them they really don't want to deal with this post clean-up. You'd be surprised what happens when you start throwing big words around—coupled with the certainty of federal involvement. It helps most of them already wrote this off as some elaborate Halloween hoax."

Brannon's shoulders softened. "Good. So, you want to go get breakfast?"

"Oh, hell yeah." Nuñez jogged a few paces back to pick up a large tackle box labeled *FORENSICS* in bright yellow letters. "If you're not in a hurry to get Holly back."

He knew my name without asking. My alarm bells stopped ringing when I took a second to guess why. One of them waded through mutant guts while the other went to find me. Nuñez got stuck with the gross job, but at least Brannon kept him in the loop. The two seemed more like friends than coworkers, anyway.

I doubted most techs got away with playful teasing in front of potential murder suspects.

"She might as well come with us." Brannon beckoned to me as they started their journey down the sidewalk. "I already offered."

They let me walk a few paces behind. Nuñez checked on me occasionally, hiding his backward glances by flipping his hair out of his face.

The neon sign above our destination popped up over swaying trees when we reached the next corner. We made a beeline for the small market I often went to for midnight snacks, a family-run business serving bagels twenty-four hours a day.

When they judged it safe to whisper, I leaned forward to pick up every word they said.

Brannon started. "Have you heard from Laura again? Is the kid awake yet?"

So there were at least two more of them? And one was hurt? I kept listening.

"I missed her call, but she left a message," said Nuñez. "He woke up when she shook him, cross-eyed and bawling, so she knocked him back out with a sedative to give herself time to dust off the MRI and send him through. Only way to check for injuries without him flailing around. Looks like the little guy got hit pretty hard."

Brannon tensed and glanced at me. I looked down, busying myself with inspecting the shiny surface of my patent leather shoes. I didn't want him to catch me eavesdropping.

He lowered his voice even more. "Until we get the whole story from him, we won't know what we're dealing with. I'm not sure if we'll get much more than we already know out of her."

He jabbed his grotesque, blood-filled thumb at me.

Nuñez flinched. "Mike, that hand looks really bad." He accidentally bounced back to normal volume. "You should have Doc look at it when we get back to the lab."

Lab? I puzzled, the corners of my lips twisting south. *What lab?*

An anxious moment passed between them as they weighed the likelihood I'd overheard an important secret. I thought we were headed to some boring government building for the rest of their unit to bombard me with questions.

Why lie to me? Did they plan to take me someplace else? I needed the answers I sought to inform my next move. Nuñez backtracked after a look from his partner.

"Err, I mean office. The office. Where we're working remotely. HQ."

Brannon frowned as we slowed and waited for the bright white walking man to wave us across the street.

That's when my good sense caught up with me.

The entire situation stunk. What kind of feds let a not-yet-convicted criminal walk unescorted? Neither of them bothered to treat me like danger lurked beneath my cute exterior.

I tried to think back to when Brannon whipped his badge past my nose at the speed of light. I couldn't remember the emblem or the acronym on his credentials. C.I.A.? F.B.I.? Nuñez looked more like a stoner than someone who worked in law enforcement, though perhaps his casual disguise lured suspects into lazy confessions.

The fact I'd failed to ask more thorough questions before agreeing to breakfast and a formal interrogation made me feel like a gigantic idiot. Still, I kept my mouth shut. Maybe the mismatched men really were secret agents sent to destroy my idyllic existence.

I'd find out soon enough.

I resolved to continue my assessment of the situation as we entered the combined corner store and delicatessen. If they went to use the bathroom at the same time, I'd run away to hole up in Chi Ho's apartment if I remained unsure of their intentions. Eventually, Brannon, Nuñez, and their unknown bosses would get tired of looking for me. I remembered the alert on my cell phone and my fingers itched to answer it.

We made our way to the register. Brannon stopped halfway and waited for me.

"What do you want to eat?"

I considered the menu although I already knew it by heart. I wanted him to think we stood on even ground.

"Turkey on wheat." A thoughtful pause completed my ruse. "No pickles, extra tomato, and a bit of cream cheese."

"Anything to drink?"

"Just water." I smiled.

A better attitude might get him to lower his guard. More crucial tidbits could slip.

"You got it." He and Nuñez mulled over their orders. "Go ahead and grab us a seat."

Grinning like a good hostage, I pulled an extra chair up to one of the dining sets close to the front window. Witch silhouettes and Frankenstein heads decorated the glass. Brannon nodded, satisfied I wasn't going anywhere. He turned to address the college student behind the counter.

I dove into my bag and removed my phone from its cellophane prison. I had to send Chi Ho an emergency text. If the agents really were bad guys—like goons from some Marvel knockoff engineering supersoldiers for world domination—I wasn't going to let them take me quietly. I pressed the shortcut for voicemail.

"Hey!" said Chi Ho, her tone disconcertingly chipper. "I guess you're still sleeping. No big. I wanted to call and check on you..." She trailed off there, as though unaware of whether or not her next thought belonged out loud. "It's just that— you're going to think I'm being silly. I woke up this morning and I felt like I should call you. Getting those bad vibes. Anyway, I think it's just the weather. This cold shit sucks. Hit me back when you're awake so I know you're not dead. Okay, bye!"

By the time she finished and clicked off, the clerk plopped

two of our three baskets onto the countertop. Breakfast distracted Brannon and Nuñez for the seconds it took to text her before they came back.

Alive, I wrote. My finger pads zoomed over the keypad with a soft touch. *But trouble. With weirdo cops? I don't know. They're not normal. If I don't answer in a day, call the police. They might do something. Maybe.*

After pressing send, I turned the device off and stashed it in my purse again. I had to keep my one tie to the outside hidden.

The metal tray Brannon held with his good hand brimmed with stuffed bagels, chips, pickles, a black coffee, a bottle of water, and one huge orange smoothie. When they sat down, Nuñez deposited his plastic case by his side and took most of the food. Brannon passed me my order before grabbing his cup of caffeinated sludge, and a ham and cheese sandwich. The tech dug into his meal like a backhoe plowing through loose dirt. He destroyed half a poppy seed tower with the works in less than 10 seconds, and I couldn't help but think of Chi Ho as I watched him inhale her favorite combo.

I worried about how she'd react to my S.O.S. as I picked up my own sandwich and bit it. To find out what my captors wanted, I'd have to up my game.

Brannon started eating as we sat in silence. It felt like he didn't know what to say. Nuñez didn't have room to talk with his mouth full. He ate like an animal, and surprised me when he took a breath. He cocked his head and glanced at his partner for permission to speak, but continued without it.

"So, Holly—" The tomato goop stuck to the corners of his mouth bounced up and down. "What do you do? For a living, I mean."

"I'm an heiress."

The answer I provided established me as someone wealthy who wouldn't vanish without repercussions.

Too bad only half of that was true.

He took a big gulp of his drink. "An heiress, hunh? Never met one of those before. When we looked up your number and apartment contract, I saw your age and guessed you were a child actress or a model living by yourself. Happy birthday, by the way. Having rich parents must be cool. I wish—"

I stopped him there. "We're a rare breed."

As Brannon listened, enjoying a calm moment behind his bagel, I hurried to ask more questions.

"So, Nuñez. Diego, right? I know you both work in law enforcement. That you're assisting the locals, but Brannon never did tell me what branch. Or what it is you're investigating that needs my input. Of course, I *am* happy to help."

The other agent snapped out of his food-induced coma, twitching like a mean nurse jabbed him with a shot of adrenaline.

"Would you two stop playing house and dispense with the pleasantries, please? We're not soccer moms catching up over Sunday brunch. This is official business. There's a system in play. We're going to eat in relative, merciful peace, and then we're going back for our interview."

Nuñez and I both stared at him. If I kept trying to decipher their motives, I wouldn't get far without running into the brick wall that was Brannon. Every. Single. Time.

He stood. "I'm going to the bathroom, and then we're leaving." The scraping of his chair on the floor punctuated his next declaration. "I'm ready for this morning to be over. Eat fast and let's go."

"Whatever you say," said Nuñez with an obvious hint of sarcasm.

Brannon mumbled to himself as he entered the heart of the store. He flew past rows of soda and chips toward the sign designating the establishment's restrooms. When he ducked out of earshot, the other man turned to me with an apologetic look.

"Don't mind him. He's cranky today. I think I'm going to hit the can, too. I'll be right back. Don't go anywhere, okay?"

"Okay," I parroted.

I still wasn't sure whether or not I'd actually be there when they returned.

Nuñez got up and snaked his way through the maze of chairs, but stopped near their edge to face me again. He wore a strained, sad expression—like a farmer charged with the job of putting down his favorite sheep dog.

"I'm sorry you got mixed up in all this, Holly," he said. "You really seem like a nice girl. I know it sucks, but this shouldn't take too much longer. Then you can forget about everything. I promise."

As he disappeared past the artisan packs of jerky and roasted nuts underneath a family of tinsel bats, I took stock of everything I'd learned so far.

Brannon and Nuñez were the active members of a four-person team of unknown origin. They knew their way around the justice system, but they didn't work for any agencies in the habit of advertising their jurisdiction. Nuñez liked to eat, and Brannon liked to annoy me. Neither carried any real means of identification, and they meant to take me somewhere for *questions* about the murder.

They didn't seem shocked to discover a crime scene made up entirely of blue corpse parts. Both let slip a moment of uncertainty on our walk to the deli, but otherwise seemed way too blasé about the whole thing. By connecting the dots, I jumped to a rational conclusion.

Enforcers of an evil empire or not, they'd kill me after I told them what they wanted.

I was a liability who'd witnessed the shambling antics of two superhuman creatures never intended for civilian viewing. The death of one didn't matter on a greater scale. Whether they knew I'd caused it or not, my fate would be the same. I couldn't escape to sell my new knowledge to the highest bidder. They had to dispose of me properly—away from the prying eyes of the public—to make sure the tale of the princess assaulted by mutants in the park never saw the light of day.

Fear for my life dissipated as red-hot fury came chugging in to replace it. How dare they act so nice while harboring such awful plans for my future? What unimaginable cruelty led them to return my possessions, treat me to breakfast, and even bother asking about my life?

My half-eaten bagel mocked me from its home in the flimsy basket on the table. I wasn't going to let my last meal be a crappy, mostly cream cheese sandwich made by a tired university student. Determined to flee, I pushed my seat back and hopped up.

The chair toppled over with a *clank* and the counter clerk jolted. Rather than saying sorry—which was the polite thing to do—I redirected my anger toward Brannon and Nuñez at them. The look I gave communicated *get lost* loud and clear.

With my purse nestled under my arm, I rushed for the front door. And I would've skipped through it and out onto the street if it hadn't been for the bulky man in the black ski mask who came charging through.

He flailed the gun he held like a patriot waving a party

streamer on the Fourth of July. The early morning hour didn't stop the wretch from smelling like he'd already spent hours bathing in a pool of hard liquor and sweat.

I threw myself into the nearest aisle to avoid his belligerent trajectory.

"Gimme all your—" He aimed his weapon at the employee behind the counter and unleashed a burp that smelled like death. "Money."

I'm not sure what caused the flood of pure, unfiltered id that followed. Maybe it was the helpless *save me* look the cashier sent me, like I owed them for all the times they didn't comment on my frumpy nightgown late at night. Maybe the fact I'd already faced the prospect of my imminent death with valor. Or maybe I just couldn't stand the thought of letting one more piece of my wardrobe get splattered with blood of any color.

Not without one hell of a fight.

With a primal scream, I pulled myself off the cracked tiles and lunged for the robber. I soared through the air like a lion taking down a gazelle.

When we landed on the floor, the gun flew out of his hand and careened several feet away. The fall knocked the breath from his lungs, leaving one puff for the pitiful wheeze he let out as he howled in pain. He thrashed, disarmed and incapacitated—but I still wasn't satisfied. I slid from atop his chest and went to grab the firearm.

Waking from his stupor, my adversary roared like an injured kaiju going in for the kill during the finale of a B-rated monster movie. He gathered his strength, rolled over, and latched onto my leg.

Somewhere in the back of the store, I heard a door open as two familiar voices started shouting. Until they came to my rescue, however, Brannon and Nuñez were useless to me. They stopped short of the scuffle with matching expressions of shock and awe. This informed me with one glance that I was—at least temporarily—on my own.

Angrier than ever at their inability or unwillingness to help, I renewed my assault with vigor. I squirmed out of the masked man's sticky grasp. Without a single care as to whether anyone saw my underwear, I picked up my thigh and kicked hard.

What I expected to follow was another cry before our struggle continued. What I hoped—staunch in my role as the reluctant heroine—was that Brannon and Nuñez would run in to take over the fight.

But fate had other plans.

As the tread on my sole made contact with the mesh obscuring the face of my attacker, a wall of flesh and bone gave way beneath it. The man's horrified gaze turned one-hundred and eighty degrees as he went limp and silent.

I stared at his head doing its best Linda Blair impression and shrieked. Bright torrents of blood poured from his mouth and eyes. My skirt and the ruffles of my lace-topped socks got soaked when I squealed and scooted away.

Though cause of death was obvious to those who'd watched his head spin like a top, the coroner would have his choice to pick from. Broken bones protruded like white arrows through the slain man's disheveled clothes.

The sound of someone retching caused me to look up past the avalanche of emotion pressing against my sinuses. Nuñez stood, caved in half and pale-faced above his breakfast.

"Oh, God," he heaved. "I should *not* have eaten." His glazed eyes looked through the leaking body as some new thought transported him far, far away.

Brannon and the clerk both stared at me—the first with amazement and the second with fear. I cried as I crawled along the floor. When I arrived at a table leg and grabbed it, the cold metal between my fingers squished like Play-Doh.

I couldn't stop the tears from coming. Killing one man, or mutant, I could live with. It wasn't like I'd had a choice.

Two was too many.

I didn't feel like myself. That morning upon waking and conducting my full body inspection, I'd known deep down something was different.

Where were my bruises and scratches? Why'd it been so difficult to get dressed and out the door to find my phone without destroying my apartment in the process? How did my skinny leg turn a man's skull into the movable piece of a ball-jointed doll with a single jab?

I wanted answers. I needed to know. In light of recent events, all I could do was cry as I confessed, searching, perhaps, for redemption.

"I did it. I killed him, too!" I wailed at the black and white blur that was Brannon. "Last night in the park. They both came at me all blue and sticky and huge and gross and I didn't know what to do. So. I. Stabbed. Him. With. My. Parasol!"

He moved closer, gliding through my underwater vision to tiptoe past me to where the gun lay by the door. I knew what came next. Before I could compose myself to utter my final words, I'd hear the trigger pull.

I was a monster.

I had to be put down.

I wiped my eyes and peered at him through puffy lids. He picked up the firearm and looked at me, though what he did next wasn't what I'd expected.

Brannon crouched down and placed his hot, bad hand on my shoulder.

"Everything's going to be okay, Holly."

I sniffled as he stuffed the gun into his waistband and retrieved Nuñez's leftover smoothie from our table. He went to the middle of the room and poured the remainder of it onto the floor, motioning for his partner to help him with the corpse. Together, they maneuvered the dead weight on top of the spill. Nuñez, still dazed and half-sick, stayed put while Brannon crossed to the sandwich bar with renewed fire in his stride.

The worker behind it reached for the company phone, but not fast enough. Brannon took hold of them.

"Settle down," he said. "Listen to me."

They trembled as their eyes darted from me to Nuñez, to the body, and finally to the fierce man in front of them.

Rather than his badge, Brannon pulled a wad of large bills from his jacket pocket and slammed them by the register. "You never saw us. That drunk asshole came in, ordered a smoothie, knocked over your tables, then tripped over his big feet and broke his own damn neck. Do you understand?"

"Y-yes, sir."

"Good." He backed away from the counter. "Wait five minutes and call 911. The police are still hanging out in the park. You'll have to hurry. Take his mask off, dump it before they get here, and erase any security footage. And the back-ups! If you tell anyone what you saw, I'll come back for you."

Nuñez, alert and ready for action again, navigated the disarray to scoop me and his tackle box up from the floor.

"Come on," said Brannon. "Let's go!"

With help, I stood on shaking legs and we hobbled out behind him. The three of us ran for a burgundy sedan sitting at an expired meter about a hundred feet down the road and launched into the car. Brannon climbed into the driver's seat while Nuñez and I sat in back. We pulled out with a screech and sped up while buildings and trees—and a lone sandwich withering on the sidewalk—flew by as we approached Mach speed, hurtling toward the place where my new life would begin.

4

THE MOST DANGEROUS SNAKES IN THE STATE

We'd already veered onto the 101, the crowded throughway leading out of the city and across the bay to Alameda and other suburbs, by the time Brannon collected his thoughts. He turned down the volume of the crackling police radio sitting on the dashboard. An unflattering glimpse of my blotchy, half-purple reflection in the rearview mirror had already convinced me to stop crying.

"You said there were two of them?" Brannon's questions demanded answers before he'd even consider any of mine. "Back in the deli."

"What?" My head was full of cotton.

He repeated himself with more urgency. "You said there were two that attacked you in the park. What did they look like? I need to know."

I cleared the lump in my throat. "Big, glowing, and dripping blue goo."

Nuñez—who'd kept his eyes on me the whole car ride while plastered against his door—slowly leaned forward. He shuffled through the contents of his box and produced a squatty beaker. The container held a few shreds of tissue suspended in slurry made of biological material and mud.

I lurched away as he held it closer for me to get a good look, pressing my shoulders into my window.

"Was it like this?" he asked.

I fought the urge to jump out of the moving car and nodded. "Yes."

Gruesome memories of the sights and sounds of my mutant assailant's explosion crept into my consciousness. I tried to discard them, gritting my teeth against the awful short film playing on a loop.

Nuñez gathered how much the presence of his sample bothered me and didn't hesitate to put it back. He stayed near me instead of returning to his former post.

"Son of a bitch," Brannon hissed. "Two. You're absolutely sure?"

I couldn't answer before the tech spoke up, flying forward to jiggle Brannon's shoulders. He didn't have to unbuckle since he'd never put on his seatbelt.

"Forget about that for a second. Are we going to ignore the obvious here? Really? Holly just turned a guy's face around! Or did you not see that? You don't think that she—"

"You don't think that she what?" Frustration gnawed at my center like a swarm of buzzing, furious wasps. "You know, you haven't told me anything. And I have been very, *very* accommodating! What the hell is going on?"

Brannon shot his subordinate a penetrating glare to keep quiet under the guise of checking his blind spot to cross lanes toward the 280 junction.

Nuñez disobeyed his unspoken orders. "Did any blue stuff get on you? When you, uh, stabbed the guy?"

I nodded and stretched my generosity to give him another important detail.

"All over me. After he—"

"Blew up." Nuñez took over for me. He'd probably exam-ined enough of the crime scene to determine what happened. "I mean, not just on you, but really *on* you. Like, in a cut or a scrape?"

I had to think before I replied. I no longer suspected they meant to kill me after Brannon refused his chance to do it, but telling the truth guaranteed the two agents and their myste-rious conglomerate wouldn't leave me alone anytime soon. Then again—if I was infected with some experimental super juice, I wanted to know about it sooner rather than later.

I gulped, averted my eyes, and said, "Yes."

My travel companion vibrated in his seat. "Holy shit. Holy shit!" He shook Brannon again. "Do you know what this means? Do you think? I mean—there's no way. But look at her! She's totally fine. And you saw what she did! That's not just a freaky coincidence, right?"

"We can't jump to conclusions." Our driver worked to shake his partner off without tearing his eyes from the road. "Laura has tests to run. There are protocols to follow."

Nuñez ignored him. "Screw that! Can't you be happy, for like, a split second? Maybe we actually did it. Admit it!"

My patience shattered. Someone needed to fill me in.

"Brannon," I yelled, finally garnering his full attention. "If you don't start answering my questions right now, I'll—"

Silence fell as they both waited for me to finish.

What I landed on was desperate.

"I'll punch you in the back of the head!"

Nuñez gasped. His eyes went wider than those of a raccoon trapped by an expertly-wielded broom in the corner of a two-car garage.

We changed lanes again and headed toward the exit I knew led to Hunters Point. This dangerous, rundown corner of the world—home to poverty, empty warehouses, and an enormous shipyard—had nothing in common with mine. I got my negative impression from local hearsay since I'd never ventured that far south. Though the unkind auras of the corrugated steel buildings we passed didn't disappoint my bias.

"Not while I'm driving," said Brannon, "unless you want us all to die in a fiery crash."

I groaned as I searched for another meaningless threat to get him talking.

We slowed our speed to make our way through the abandoned streets by the waterfront. Graffiti on the side of a convenience store—Superman's symbol with different initials in the middle—inspired my next move.

Small talk with other geeky J-fashionistas at social gatherings taught me a thing or two about comic book lore. Fate gave my favorite magical girls their powers to fight evil, restoring balance and harmony to the universe. Most superheroes were born exceptional, and others gained their abilities through happenstance. Their lives of duty doomed them to near-constant discomfort and self-sacrifice until death. At first, these people often ignored telltale signs of a greater calling.

I was beginning to understand why.

From what I'd learned in my AP courses, the rules of psychics rendered the limits of the human body finite. Individuals like Spiderman and Wolverine could only exist in the realms of fiction. No mysteries remained in the world, other than what lay beyond the stars and at the bottom of the ocean.

My breakfast lurched. The mounting evidence pointing to

fantastical changes within me demanded immediate attention. I shared my educated guess with the group.

"*You* might," I shot back, causing Brannon to stop a little too forcefully at a dented red sign. "I think—and you ought to tell me right now if you value your life—that I'd be absolutely fine. I could walk away from a wreck without a scratch. What do you think?"

The other occupants of the car erupted in a flurry of emotion.

"Holly," warned Nuñez, "don't do anything dumb."

"I won't," I said, "but I could. Couldn't I?"

The glint of fear in Brannon's eyes betrayed his steady outburst.

"We don't know yet!"

"Let's not try it!" said Nuñez

I leaned into the front seat with balled fists.

"Tell me what I am!"

Brannon pressed his foot onto the gas and sped up, taking the corner on two wheels. We zoomed around our last turn and jumped the curb into a gravel parking lot overrun by weeds, cigarette butts, and empty glass bottles. Before we crashed through the painted windows of a dilapidated reptile emporium, he mashed the breaks and threw the sedan in park.

"We're here." He unbuckled his seatbelt and spun around. "Come inside, let us run some tests, and then we'll answer your questions for you. Okay, princess? Is that okay with you?"

Nuñez hopped out with his box. Brannon exited, walked around to yank my door open, and didn't ask again when I didn't answer.

I was too preoccupied with the spooky building in front of us to say a word. The place fell apart as the wind blew, sloughing spray-painted shingles and chunks of cinderblock that landed in the dirt. I shivered as they approached the door, afraid of what I'd find in an establishment that once advertised *The Most Fearsome Snakes in the State.*

"Who does she think she is?" Brannon complained as they disappeared inside. "Pulling a line like that. Like she's Bruce Willis in that science fiction movie we watched, or something. Wasn't he a janitor? What was it called?"

The door closed. I'd nearly found the gumption to mount the porch of the creepy place when he doubled back and stuck his head out.

"Holly!" He snapped at me.

I scrambled after him.

A dull sliver of midday sun slithered in with me from outside. Brannon's mangled hand hadn't gotten any worse since we'd left the deli, but it was definitely broken. I didn't need a medical license to know that.

A layer of dust and a generous smattering of cobwebs covered the interior of the storefront. Someone once planted a forest of faux foliage to create the illusion of a tropical paradise, but the decaying branches withered with no one to tend them. They hung like moldy ghosts above our heads, casting ominous shadows over the dim showroom.

Brannon and Nuñez slid across the floor and went for a door marked *Employees Only* as I stopped and started behind them. Fake leaves and bits of fallen ceiling crunched underfoot. Serpentine trails crisscrossed the floor down aisles to my left and right. I hurried to catch up, unwilling to discover if the owners of the legless footprints lurked nearby. Brannon charged through the swinging portal with his shoulder, but Nuñez lagged and kept it open for me as I tiptoed into the room.

The breath I was holding sprang out like someone bashed my lungs with a bat.

Sheets of snakeskin as big as my arms hung from metal rafters. Yellow beams dancing through a broken skylight caught the scaly leavings and projected diamond patterns everywhere. I gulped and looked for fanged beasts coiled between shelves piled with old tank supplies. My resolve to push through the house of horrors waned.

"Don't worry." Nuñez gave a friendly wave of his hand. "It's been at least a year since we've found any. Snakes, I mean."

While his review wasn't glowing, it managed to draw me closer to where the two men stood.

They faced the door of a walk-in freezer emblazoned with a no-smoking sticker with an upside down mouse drawn where the cigarette should've been. Brannon approached its plate-glass window and pulled out the badge he'd shown me. He pressed it against the smooth square. The pane glowed green as lasers materialized to scan the contents of his billfold. Satisfied with what they saw, buzzing gears on the other side of the metal gate spun to free multiple locks.

I stared at the feature straight out of a spy movie with my mouth hanging open. Nuñez thrust his arm out.

"Let me get that."

They both looked at Brannon's busted hand. As we stepped into the refrigerator, he caught me with an accusatory frown that made me queasy.

It took me a moment to realize we were in an elevator. Two buttons sat inside a little box on the wall. I punched the lower one.

Where else could we go?

"Nice." Nuñez laughed. "Quick on the uptake. I think you'll fit in fine around here."

"Not sure I'm staying."

An invisible sucker-punch pummeled my spleen when the words left my lips and made his happy smile tighten.

"We'll be the judge of that," said Brannon. We rumbled to a halt at the bottom of the shaft. "Don't get too cocky."

I suppressed the urge to swat at him as the wall in front of us retracted to reveal a small antechamber. The carpeted room was cramped, dingy, and didn't share any similarities with the high-tech government lair I'd pictured on our way down.

A stuffed bag of trash with two-thirds of a gas station cup poking out the top like a crown sat in the corner to the left of another door. To the right, three beaten yellow jumpsuits and helmets hung on a wooden shelf with four hooks. A sign like the kind used to advertise vacancies in cheap hotels flickered above the portal. I fidgeted uncomfortably beneath its glow.

The *No* before *Biological Hazard* was unlit.

They groaned when they saw it. Rather than rush toward their plastic coveralls, Brannon crossed to an intercom as the wall closed behind us.

He pressed the circle underneath the voice grate by the door. "Hey, Laura, what's going on in there? Do we need to suit up, or what?"

The distorted voice of a concerned woman answered him.

"No," she sighed in a rich Southern accent. "It's fine. You can come in. Just make sure you leave your shoes on."

Brannon missed his chance to reach for the door handle before his partner grabbed it.

"Wait a second," said Nuñez. "You're not going to tell her we brought Holly down? You know how much she hates surprises."

"Well—" He paused uncertainly before angling to push on. "She's about to find out."

I wedged myself between them and entered on my own, but stopped moving as soon as I took in the absolute strangeness of the place. It looked more like an aquarium than a military base. Beyond the dropped hazmat gear at my feet, two vats of misshapen fish took up the bulk of the main room. Computers connected to various research stations lined the walls.

On my left, in front of a hallway that led elsewhere, an official looking table ran perpendicular to the specimen habitats. Full beakers knocked sideways pooled their contents on the ground between glittering shards of glass and torn paper. It all swirled together to form a stew kept lukewarm and pungent by a humming space heater.

A medical skeleton wearing a vampire cape stood watch over a gray hoodie on the floor. The ripped fabric sprawled out like a dead body waiting to be outlined in chalk.

In the corner nearest me, an L-shaped counter held aloft by two filing cabinets overflowed with ripped pamphlets and crumpled spreadsheets. The nearest fish tank sported a red smear with bits of hair attached.

Brannon cursed again when he saw it.

Nuñez went white. "This looks bad." He abandoned his cargo and called out to locate the team member who'd spoken to us through the intercom. "Hey, Doc! Where are you at? Are you okay?"

The sound of an unseen door opening and closing somewhere in the back of the room alerted us to another presence. Brannon palmed the gun in his waistband with his swollen hand. He and Nuñez relaxed when a tall woman with deep brown skin appeared.

"Keep it down, please," she said. "He's still sedated. He needs to rest."

A doctor's coat, baggie mom jeans, and floral pajama shirt dwarfed her statuesque frame. She was older than Brannon and Nuñez, probably in her mid-to-late forties, and a thousand times more tired. Her amber mane of hair, tied up with a purple scarf, held coarse locks out of intelligent brown eyes. They locked on me, bypassing her boys entirely.

"Who the hell are you?"

I didn't know what else to do besides answer. "Hi. I'm Holly."

"Hi, Holly." She studied my blood-splattered, cotton candy form before chewing Brannon out. "What the hell is she doing down here?" She didn't let him speak before launching in on Nuñez instead. "I told you to call me if you brought a witness in so I could come upstairs and deal with them there!"

"It's not that simple—" he said.

I gave him a look of utter betrayal. She didn't sound like someone who wanted to ask me questions before we shared a cup of burnt government-issue coffee.

The doctor noticed Brannon's injury.

"And what the hell happened to you? You two leave me here and don't bother to keep me updated at all. You expect me to clean everything up while I'm trying to take care of him." She threw one angry thumb in the direction of their unconscious fourth friend. "All with no guarantee that God knows who or what else wasn't going to come back, trash the place all over again, and kill us in the process!"

"Laura, calm down," said Brannon. "We need to talk. We've got bigger problems."

"What the hell do you mean?" Her gaze glistened with

frustrated dewdrops. "We've got bigger problems? Michael, this is your area of expertise. You're supposed to take care of all this!"

I felt as though I'd intruded on a nasty family feud and tried to slink away from the mess, but didn't get far before she caught me.

"Now you've got me causing a scene in front of this poor girl," she said. "You're going to have to hold her down while I hunt around here for the right drugs to give her. The same ones I would've had ready if only you'd taken the time to warn me on your way back!"

"Change of plans." Brannon placed his imposing frame between us.

I called over his shoulder to her, anxious to know their original plan for my less-than-warm welcome. "What do you mean, drugs? What drugs?"

"Don't worry, honey." She lunged for a group of syringes on a nearby counter. "I'll make sure you don't remember a thing about these idiots, just like the last twenty-four hours are a bad dream. It'll all be over in a minute."

Mind-erasing drugs, I deduced as I leapt back.

Brannon tried to wrestle the needles she held above her head out of her hands, occupying her with a dangerous game of keep-away.

"Will you listen to me for a second, Laura?" He added a string of expletives as he attempted to throw the surprisingly agile doctor into a headlock. "We're not wiping Holly's brain!"

That was my cue to leave. I stumbled over broken glass toward the exit, spurred by my desire to keep the essential organ between my ears in its unaltered state.

"I don't see any other choice. If she saw anything, it's got to be done. We can't risk compromising the project!" She squirmed free and came at me again before Brannon could stop her.

My plan to run for the elevator would've worked—if not for Nuñez.

He secured me around the waist with an elbow, and pulled a knife from his pocket with the fluid motion of a rushing stream.

"Would you two shut up?" he bellowed, holding the blade to my cheek.

I froze, too stunned to move or shake him off. During our short time together, I'd actually started thinking of him as— well—not quite a friend, but someone I liked more than most people. The emotional sting I experienced when he sliced a clean line under my eye hurt worse than the physical one.

That I hardly felt at all.

Nuñez dropped his weapon, kicked it under a desk out of reach, and pointed to his handiwork.

"Doc, stop. Just look!"

He let me go. Brannon regarded the cut that almost matched his. His face settled into grim acceptance, confronted with the reality of an entirely new set of problems he'd already anticipated.

Doctor Laura deposited the medicines she held onto the closest table. She approached me with the reverence of a religious disciple in the presence of a holy shroud.

"Lord, have mercy," she breathed.

I used two fingers to feel my oozing wound as tiny droplets crept toward my jaw.

"Sorry, Holly," Nuñez took my other hand and squeezed. "I had to make them listen."

Flesh knit together beneath my digits as I pulled them

away. The blue blood sparkling back at me shone even brighter than the dead mutant's. That explained why my eyelids puffed more lavender than red after crying in the car.

The shade reminded me of the cerulean color Angelic Pretty dubbed *sax*, but it was anything but cute. It wasn't *kawaii*, a compliment I often heard from Japanese tourists who saw me in bookstores or cafés, but rather *kowai*. When translated roughly, it meant *pants-shittingly terrifying*.

"You sweet, sweet child." Doctor Laura arrived in front of me and placed her warm hands on my arms.

"You see what I mean now?" Brannon acted as though he'd believed as Nuñez did all along that I was no longer your typical blonde-haired, blue-eyed member of the human race.

No one but me noticed the almost imperceptible squeak of the door in the back of the room as it opened. Initially, I ignored it, more interested in keeping an eye on Doctor Laura as she removed herself from my gravitational pull to right the swivel chair sitting behind Nuñez.

She didn't have time to tell me to sit before someone new joined our party.

A familiar, groggy yet nasally voice came from just beyond Brannon. "What's going on? I heard shouting, and I—"

My neighbor Kyle stumbled into view and stopped mid-sentence when he saw me.

I stifled a gasp. He was the fourth member of their team. At exactly the right height, his disheveled head was the likely source of the bloody imprint on the fish tank.

The blue and orange Hawaiian shirt he wore, covered in a multitude of stains, put him in the middle of the one-sided battle that'd turned the laboratory upside down. The usually zombie-like pallor of his face drained as we continued our staring contest. He regarded me like a well-dressed ghost from his past.

Brannon, Nuñez, and Doctor Laura watched us curiously.

"H-hey, Kyle." I tried to sound casual, but my tone faltered and I failed. At least I didn't faint.

I took a deep breath, and started again.

"What's new with you?"

5

N.E.R.D.S

After the shock of finding him in the basement laboratory wore off, I loudly let everyone know Kyle and I were neighbors, and nothing more. God forbid anyone—particularly Brannon—somehow got the impression we were friends. Or worse: Dating. Much to my relief, he agreed we'd only ever met in passing.

We didn't really know each other at all.

Doctor Laura marched us into the lounge off the main hall, a room untouched by intruders but no less messy. She sped ahead to a board on the wall, a podium rewarding good behavior with sparkling Velcro stars. Nuñez lost his minuscule lead when she yanked two markers from his position and slapped them under Kyle's name instead. The silent punishment hit like a bullet grazing his heart, but Brannon didn't even flinch when half his points met the same fate. It didn't matter as much. He didn't have many to begin with.

I sat between Nuñez and Kyle on their musty couch. The three of us got comfortable as the doctor deposited her oldest boy in a dented folding chair beside the card table to our right.

"What happened to your face?" She grabbed his chin and tilted the nick on his cheekbone toward a lamp.

Next to me, Nuñez shifted with his mouth turned down

and eyes on the floor. "He woke me up too fast. I didn't mean—"

Doctor Laura reached over to squeeze his hand, but didn't let him finish. "It's okay, D. You don't have to apologize. He's smarter than that."

Brannon agreed, rubbing the back of his head. "I should've ducked."

They dropped the subject as I subtly scooted closer to my neighbor. I was beginning to get the idea that Nuñez was far more dangerous than I'd guessed.

Brannon flipped on a radio sitting in front of him, and the same station that'd played in the car filled the room with static. In the name of cooperation, or—more accurately—before anyone told him not to, Kyle gave me a rundown of the group I found myself with.

N.E.R.D., or Nanomolecular Engineering Research and Development, got its cheesy nickname from poor planning on Doctor Laura's part. The C.I.A. affiliated defense initiative marked its tenth anniversary in late summer. She left a tenured position at Cornell to come to San Francisco to pursue advancements in experimental gene manipulation and biological adaptations. The U.S. government chose her to shepherd its miracle serum, a magic potion for soldiers meant to make them stronger and faster than their enemies.

Too bad for her, the well of enthusiasm for creating super G.I. Joes dried up when progress ground to a standstill after a few years. Her fellow researchers deserted one by one until she found herself flying solo. During that time, some unknown entity with an absurdly high clearance level acquired the project and allowed her to stay. No one cared if she kept toiling away, so long as she kept her head down and didn't bother anybody too much.

She started fresh with the help of Brannon's predecessor, a field operative assigned from N.E.R.D.'s new Day One to protect her and the laboratory from harm. Nuñez came to her after enough well-written complaints convinced her mysterious overseer she needed someone to fix her outdated equipment. Soon after that, Kyle showed up on her doorstep with a PhD obtained at fourteen—and she took him as an intern because his father held an influential position somewhere in the Capitol.

Doctor Laura's lips thinned when she got to Brannon, who replaced her first guard last Christmas. He stirred in his chair and tried to hide a guilty frown.

A meager housing stipend, prepaid bills, and sporadic supply shipments in unmarked boxes sustained their program. These materials included the blue base of her most recent serum—a strange plant byproduct the color of my blood.

Maybe it was from a plant.

That was her Ivy League guess.

The two scientists spent most days conducting experiments. Nuñez played video games and occasionally tinkered with broken electronics. Did Brannon join his partner in two-player campaigns across virtual worlds when he wasn't busy moping or exercising? There wasn't much else for him to do.

Until that morning.

She finished her depressing tale and went to fetch a first aid kit from the small kitchen across the hall. When Doctor Laura returned, the man in her care sent me a mean look before he told her about our collision in the doorway of my apartment.

I gathered her last name was Baba from the faded patch on her jacket, tinged pink from the stain Kyle's head left near her heart. Perhaps Brannon didn't call her that because he thought it sounded like a toddler's nickname for their grandma. I wanted to ask him later, even if I didn't expect a straightforward answer.

He didn't turn back to the couch before he switched gears to start his briefing, content the three of us would listen to him and remain still like browbeaten children at a fancy dinner party.

"We're going to start from the beginning. Zero hour this morning or before. That means you, Kyle. Go."

His recollection of events spewed out to preface mine perfectly. He'd been in the lab by himself the night before, starting around eleven after Doctor Laura went home, conducting a few unsupervised tests because he felt like it.

"Why didn't you wait until morning?" Brannon prickled, glaring at him. "You know you're not supposed to be down here by yourself. You don't have the proper training for emergency situations like—"

Doctor Laura knocked the flat of her hand against the side of his head, intent on protecting her young assistant from his tirade.

"Turn around and hold still."

Brannon obeyed with little more protest than an *ouch* and a groan. He tensed as she moved her fingers down his forearm to inspect his puffy hand.

"You know we've never had an incident here. I can't think of one. When was the last time we turned the elevator lock on before today? Hell, I figured the whole world forgot about us," she said. "And don't pretend like you didn't, too. It's not like we ever thought he'd need to know how to shoot a gun or to—"

Kyle was foolish enough to talk over her. "Thanks. I know it was—"

"Oh, I'm not finished," she laid into him. "You should've been safe, but I know you know better than to play with lab equipment while I'm not around. I'm angry. Make no mistake. I'm just glad you're still with us."

He slunk back, deflated.

Brannon inhaled sharply as the doctor pressed on his wrist and knuckles to assess the damage I'd done. "Okay, so what happened next?"

"I was here, and, uh—" Kyle pushed past the foggy nature of his concussion. "All of a sudden I heard a huge crash in the lobby. The next thing I knew some guys were coming through the door and grabbing our stuff. I tried to fight them off, but one shoved me into the tank, and I hit my head." He paused to massage the dried blood-covered bump on the back of his skull. "Then it just goes black."

His voice broke as the memory of his terrible ordeal threatened to overwhelm him.

"I swear, that's all I remember."

Brannon wanted more. "Did you get a good look at them? Did they say anything to you? Anything at all?"

"No. They were talking, but it happened so fast. I can't remember a word they said. Not specifically."

"They sounded American," I offered. "At least, the guys I saw did. I heard them speaking English. Bad English, but still. Like, *Me Tarzan. You Jane.* Does that make sense?"

"Yes," said Doctor Laura. She'd moved onto constructing a makeshift cast with tongue depressors and gauze. "Slowed and impaired cognitive function is one of the first indicators of a failed test."

I cocked an eyebrow at her from the couch, in total control of my mind.

She rushed to correct her previous statement. "That is,

before you. And I'm not kidding when I say that's a damn miracle. I still need to figure out exactly how you came in contact with my serum in the first place. Something about the delivery must have gone just right. You're sure you don't feel any different?" She started firing off questions, spraying them like a machine gun. "No difficulty concentrating? No muscle pain, disorientation, or nausea? No lack of impulse control? Unusually aggressive urges? Or lustful ones?"

I looked up at Brannon and tried not to give myself away. Bright, bitter fireworks exploded between us whenever our eyes met, dimming the stars I saw at the same time. Thoughts of his fingers laced with mine in the hallway outside my apartment invaded every pause in the air.

I'd had instant crushes before, but all with specific origins. Like my obsession with the girl who kicked dirt in a bully's eyes in fourth grade, or the boy in AP Calculus who smiled instead of laughing at me the day I wore my first Angelic Pretty dress to school. I couldn't come up with any redeeming qualities for the handsome jackass who redirected the conversation for me.

"You'll get your turn later, Laura," he said with too much bravado for someone at the mercy of a disgruntled medic.

Instead of dealing payback by jostling him, she sighed and kept working as he started again.

"Holly, it's your turn to tell me everything. Don't skip a single detail. What time did you run across the mutants in the park?"

I tried to remember the hour I'd viewed on my phone while dialing 911. "I'm not sure. Maybe twelve-thirty? It was a little bit later, I think."

"Their injections must have been administered almost immediately after the break-in," said Doctor Laura. "But why would anyone perform experiments in motion rather than just staying here? And why leave Kyle as a witness?"

"A smash-and-grab operation has to be executed quickly," Brannon said. "You have to prepare for rapid retaliation from the enemy target. If our security was any better—and they would've planned for the best—then getting in and out in a hurry was crucial. I'm sure they wanted to avoid detection by an armed response team."

"What about me?" Kyle squeaked.

"Honest answer? They probably thought you were dead."

"Yeah." He gulped. "That's what I thought."

Brannon continued. "Leaving was a smart move on their part, but we still have no idea how they managed to make it back up to Pacific Heights so soon. Or why they were headed that way in the first place. We don't even have a complete headcount."

"At least five," said Nuñez. All eyes fell on him as he finally spoke up. "Let's say I'm a mad scientist working on the move. I'd probably want plenty of room. Like a big RV, or something. And, you know, another person to hold my subjects down. If they became, uh—uncooperative."

"The mutants—" I counted on my fingers. "Plus one driver."

"And two agents in the back," said Brannon. "Since Holly ran into them solo, there's a good chance their handlers didn't get very far carrying their rabid passengers. When they got loose, anyone who saw them wandering around probably thought they were in costumes. Nuñez, I'll have you look for strange posts on social media and hack into the city's traffic cam database. You can start digging when we're done here. Look for odd photographs and vehicles with cabs large enough to carry at least two med bays. Concentrate on accidents and unmarked vans."

"Got it," he said.

Brannon didn't acknowledge him before he came back to me.

"You were walking through the park, and then what?"

"That's it," I said. "They saw me and ran over, foaming at the mouth, and screaming insults before they started pushing me around."

Curiosity claimed Doctor Laura. "What did they look like? Deformed?"

The creatures I'd encountered were larger, more ambulatory versions of the blobs swimming in her tanks. They were people, but barely. The question surprised me.

"Don't you know? I mean, shouldn't you?"

She wrung her hands. "It's never been tested on humans before. The furthest we've ever gotten is those fish out front, and they're all a bit—misshapen."

"They didn't look like me, if that's what you're asking. They were huge. Really muscular, but weak and uncoordinated. That's why I managed to get away. I hit one in the shoulder, and he tripped and fell. Then the other went for me again, and that's when I stabbed him."

I had a sneaking suspicion I'd left out a few details, but I couldn't remember which ones. The clothes they wore and the shades of the sparse hairs left on their stretched scalps seemed insignificant.

Brannon nodded, apparently satisfied with my description.

"And let me guess," she said. "That's when he exploded."

I confirmed with a grimace. "It was like a horror movie. I got soaked with blood and guts. I'm almost positive that's how I got infected. I had these fresh scrapes on my knees…"

She sighed. "I need to run some tests, but I will say this. You're very, very lucky. You were probably safe in your bed during the stabilization process. Even the smallest scratch could've killed you then. That's what happens to most of the fish. First they bloat and ooze while the cells of their musculoskeletal systems expand. They're supposed to return to normal shape and size, but that never happens. And if you poke them to take a sample even a second too soon—boom!"

She mimed the action of the noise she made and fury burst within me. I wound up to smack Nuñez before reason kicked in.

"You cut me when you knew there was a chance I might blow up?"

He leapt from the couch and I missed him, but the forward motion of my arm carried me off-balance. My palm crashed down against his cushion and the springs inside the pillow flattened with a bang. He flew toward Doctor Laura and Brannon, yelping like a sorority girl with the misfortune of finding a hairy spider in her favorite pair of boots. The bandaged agent—in better spirits with his hand encased in soft cotton—laughed while his caretaker adopted a worried frown.

"New rule," said Doctor Laura. "Holly, every time you get mad and feel like hitting either of them," she pointed to the N.E.R.D. sitting beside her—whose smile vanished, and the other huddled nearby, "you tell Kyle and he'll do it for you. Okay? I have a feeling it's going to be often, so you'll both get plenty of practice."

We agreed, for safety's sake.

"I just knew you were different." Nuñez crossed back to sit on the armrest, careful to remain a few inches out of my reach. "None of the fish, even the ones that survive their injections, ever look the same when Doc's done. You're totally normal, and you walked away completely unhurt after destroying that robber in the deli. I was sure, after all that, there was no way you'd go nuclear. It wouldn't hurt you. Am I right?"

"I guess not." I touched my healed cheek. "I didn't really feel anything at all."

Doctor Laura looked like she wanted a pen and paper to take notes with. Relief washed over Nuñez.

"You were it. *The Chosen One.*" He made air quotes around the cliché. "That's bullshit, but you know what I'm saying."

The half-smile I used to apologize for attacking him manifested more constipated than remorseful. Embarrassed, I turned back to Doctor Laura.

"So, I'm fine, for right now. It sounds like. Are you sure I'll stay that way until you can fix me?"

Activity in the room fizzled. Brannon and Nuñez waited for the resident science experts to speak.

"I don't know if we can." Kyle kept his gaze on the floor, counting the fibers in his shoelaces.

My heart sank. "What do you mean?"

Doctor Laura took over for him. "Our work has been about finding the solution to make supersoldiers." She twisted her hands, but held eye contact. "I'm not sure I thought we'd ever get that far. After so many years of no success, reversing the serum—like Kyle said—I don't even know if it's possible."

Without a second thought as to whether or not it made me look like a giant crybaby, I started sobbing again. Heavy tears fell on my tulle skirt. I pictured the years ahead of me filled with untold instances of tearing brand, destroying furniture, injuring strangers and friends alike, and various other calamities caused by my new powers.

"You mean," I said between shallow breaths, "I'm stuck like this?"

"Oh, honey," cooed Doctor Laura. The pitter-patter of her feet on the rug atop the concrete floor assaulted my hyper-attuned hearing. "I'm so sorry. You never asked for any of this."

She sat on the damaged couch cushion and wrapped her soft arms around me. Her kind hands found and stroked my hair, taking extra care not to catch the strands matted by bits of burglar blood. This soothing gesture stilled my heaving chest for a second, until Brannon broke through the warmth of her embrace with more coarse practicality.

"You can boo-hoo later," he said without any of the same understanding Doctor Laura, Nuñez, or even Kyle seemed to show. "Now's not the time."

I tried to strike him down with a glare. Maybe if I concentrated hard enough I'd scald him with lasers shot from my eyes. I didn't want to admit it, but he was right. Self-pity didn't help us with another mutant on the run. If the escapee survived long enough to report back to his masters, they might realize my shower in blue guts made me like him—and better.

Even so close to Halloween, I stood out amongst the polyester princesses roaming the streets in search of booze and candy. San Francisco was home to several other girls who wore extravagant Japanese dresses every day, but I knew a group of trained commandos wouldn't have trouble singling me out.

I untangled myself from Doctor Laura, stiffened my upper lip, and packed down the rest of my tears before addressing Brannon again. She'd told the truth earlier.

He was the only one of us capable of running a military operation.

"What do we do next? Are there people we can get in touch with? For help?"

My logical conclusion set him on edge. His knees shook with bottled energy. "No. We've got to take care of this by ourselves. No outside involvement. Not yet. Not at all, if we can help it."

"Dude," said Nuñez, "we might be in over our heads here. Don't you think—?"

"If we make that call, then the people in charge will know just how badly we screwed up." Brannon stood his ground. "And you can bet your ass the minute they're convinced we're a bunch of incompetent douchebags, they'll have those thugs running black ops down here to clean us out. No questions asked. I don't know about the rest of you, but I'm not willing to let some man on the phone tell a ghost to put a bullet in my skull to cover his own damn tracks."

Doctor Laura fidgeted. "I don't follow."

"Think about it. Either we find the missing mutant and track down his makers, or they get to him first and disappear. If they get away with our tech, and intelligence finds out, who do you think that comes back to? As far as I know, we're the only people working on supersoldiers. That makes us the obvious source of the leak. We're fucked coming and going. We've got to work together to make this problem go away."

The others stared at him with transparent concern.

"Because if we don't—" He became more serious than ever. "Odds are we're all dead. Except for Holly. I have a feeling we're going to be stuck together for awhile. Worst case scenario, we lose the thieves like I said. If that happens, and she's with us when the reckoning comes, those grim reapers will take her and stick her in a test tube to study for the rest of her life."

That's when fear crept up on me. There'd be no frills inside a secret prison where I'd be poked, prodded, and experimented on until death.

"We've got one chance. We catch whoever broke in and take back whatever they stole, whether it's in a tube or a person. The easiest way to do that will be to go after the mutant. Now it's a race. I'm sure they'll be out there looking for him, and if they find him first it's all over for us. They'll skip town. Game over. If we succeed and do a good job of handling this quietly, then maybe the big guys will be grateful. They might even give Laura more funding."

No one but me heard what he said next, all too busy exchanging meaningful looks as they considered his extreme proposition.

It didn't help that none of them had super hearing, either.

"And maybe they'll reward me with a position as far away from here as possible," Brannon whispered to himself.

Nuñez exhaled. "Alright. I'm in."

"So am I," said Kyle.

They all waited for Doctor Laura to agree.

"Where do we start?" She gave up all semblance of control. "We need some kind of plan."

My vote hadn't been counted during their summit. Perhaps that meant I was free to go. Lady luck, my greatest enemy, decided otherwise and appointed Brannon to deliver her verdict.

He stood abruptly, picked up his folding chair, and moved it in front of where I sat. As he took my hands in his—a gesture that made my breath catch—I saw past his calm exterior to the distress running deep to his core.

"Holly." My name fell from his lips and reverberated toward me like a beam of blistering sunshine. "Right now you're our greatest asset. As far as we know, that other mutant is still out there. If he's just as strong as you are, we're going to need your help to bring him in. I know you probably don't want to hear this. It's not ideal by any means, but the truth of the matter is this—you're our best shot."

I couldn't believe it. I wasn't cut out for espionage work, but Brannon wanted to deputize me as the fifth member of N.E.R.D.'s elite team. I had no combat training, I'd never held a gun in my life, and I knew nothing about tracking monsters and their fiendish handlers through an urban jungle. The prospect of killing again—even in the name of protecting the American public—made me feel sick. Not to mention, I'd have to work cooperatively and get to know new people.

That put me in more danger than any manhunt.

With my objections in place, I took one last look around the room. Four pairs of needy eyes begged me to stay. The serum coursing through my veins fogged my judgment. A heaping helping of guilt and peer pressure insisted I join up with them. I couldn't refuse in good conscience.

"Fine." I threw up both hands as those around me celebrated. "I'm in. I don't want money, but you'll have to compensate me for my time, and I need to know you'll work on a cure. Or at least try to. Please."

"Absolutely," said Doctor Laura. "We can collect samples and get started right away."

Brannon concluded his briefing by flicking his wrist at Nuñez. "Great. Take your demands up with our treasurer. I'm going outside for some air. I need to think."

He stood and carried the radio out with him as the doctor returned his chair to the table.

She motioned for Kyle to sit with her. "Come on over here so we can get your head cleaned up a bit more. It'll make you feel better."

Doctor Laura's intern obediently followed her to the other side of the room, and Nuñez seized his opportunity to begin. He retrieved an old laptop covered with meme stickers from the floor and took the redhead's seat next to me.

"Let's talk about what you want." He smiled as the computer hummed to life. "Go ahead, hit me with it. I'm your man."

6

D IS FOR DELIGHTFUL

Nuñez made a mistake when he pushed up his sleeves, excited to start hammering out my contract. I zeroed in on the large burn scar on his left forearm surrounded by a smattering of illegible tattoos. He looked thin and spindly beneath his baggy clothes, but the strength he revealed didn't match my first impressions. His taught muscles—smooth and hard like river stones veined with silver ore—twitched when he noticed me staring. He tugged the cloth back down, and I didn't comment on what I saw.

I knew without asking that he didn't want me to.

If N.E.R.D. really needed me, they wouldn't mind fueling my shopping addiction. I usually spent most of my time browsing secondhand clothing websites. Domestic networks, foreign auctions, and small consignment stores provided ample stalking grounds to prowl in search of more designer clothes. For those days when I didn't feel like trekking to Japantown to browse in person.

Doctor Laura disappeared and returned with a new med kit. She asked if she could draw a few vials of blood as we worked. Kyle, freshly bandaged and hot on her heels, looked like a ninja wearing the wrap taming his unkempt forest of hair. His jaw dropped when she successfully stuck my outstretched arm with a needle thicker than a coffee straw.

"Come again?" Nuñez thought he'd misheard my demands.

"A computer program made to research and automatically buy items from my wish list," I repeated as the scientists collected a handful of samples.

I mimicked Kyle's expression when I looked down at the eerie blue stream flowing from my elbow into a tube.

Was I a walking superhuman factory like the mutant who exploded? A talking tank full of toxic sludge? That seemed unlikely since no one wore gloves.

I tapped Doctor Laura with extreme care. "Since I'm infected, does that mean I'm infectious?"

"No. When you came in contact with my serum, it was still active in the test subject's blood. Without a living host, it's harmless. Now that you've stabilized, you can't transfer your powers to anyone else via bodily fluids. But you'll keep getting stronger—which you'll have to get the hang of. Your genetic makeup is no longer compatible with other humans." She attempted a joke. "So, if you're listed as an organ donor, you might want to take that off your license."

Reassured, I returned her small smile. Maybe I'd avoid my terrible cramps and heavy period if it took her a month to synthesize my cure. Once finished, she laid my arm on my lap and dragged a stunned Kyle out of the rec room. I turned back to Nuñez.

"I'll provide you with my payment information. I have it memorized. Is building a platform like I described something you think you can do?" I stood to search the pigsty for a pen and piece of paper as he processed my request.

"Well, yeah. That should be pretty easy. It's just a basic algorithm, but—"

"But what?" I called over my shoulder.

When I found nothing near the table, I rummaged through the bookcase by their ancient TV and a pile of game consoles. On top of a row of textbooks, an open sketchbook revealed a half-finished scene of Doctor Laura, Nuñez, and Kyle laughing while playing cards.

Hidden in a corner, I spotted a notebook with a pencil imprisoned in its spiral binding. When I plucked it off the shelf and flipped through, a picture of Doctor Laura with her arms around a grinning woman with alabaster cheeks and graying brown hair fluttered to the floor.

I picked it up and returned to the couch. It drew my focus away from trying to recall the name of every dress I wanted. I traced my fingers around its sharp edges. Doctor Laura looked years younger—but the movie poster behind her wasn't that out of date. I pushed it between Nuñez and his screen.

"Who's this?"

His long fingers pinched the sides of the glossy paper. He took it from me and placed it in his palm as softly as if one wrong touch would turn it to dust.

"That's Amanda," he said. "She was the agent in charge before Mike got here. They broke up when she left. Doc destroyed almost every trace of her. Of them. But I kept this. I miss her."

Nuñez heard footsteps in the hall before I did. He shoved the photograph under his butt, waking me from the memory that wasn't mine. Doctor Laura leaned into the room.

"Holly, what was your blood type before the—" She searched for the right word, "Accident?"

"AB positive, I think."

She nodded and left.

Nuñez stole another glance at his treasure and tucked it beneath the couch cushion. He pulled up a new program and started typing.

"That's really all you want?" He still couldn't believe what I'd asked for. "A shopping bot?"

I wanted to know more about what happened between Doctor Laura and her girlfriend, but we had a job to do.

"That's right. Of course, for Yahoo Japan, Mbok, and Fril you'll have to translate the search terms to run them in Japanese kana. Maybe Mandarin, to be safe. English is fine for Lace Market. That's like eBay for Japanese fashion. Then there's Closet Child. Wunderwelt. And Maiden Clothing. Rakuten. Taobao. Mercari. Don't worry, I'll write them all down."

I gave him a lot to take in all at once.

"But," he said, "I mean—"

His brows shot up when I interrupted to recite my debit and bank account numbers.

"Heiress," I reminded him. "Remember?"

The bizarre need to elaborate overcame me when he turned back to his screen.

Nuñez didn't make sense. His personality—kind and goofy one minute, rough and withdrawn the next—made him an odd mix between Mister Rodgers and Mister Hyde. Despite that, I couldn't deny how much I liked him.

Possessed by the spirit of camaraderie, I went out on a limb and attempted a reference I thought he'd enjoy.

"I've got that Batman money," I said. The punch line came out a bit strangled. "You know what I'm saying?"

Mischief lit his eyes as he took my joke and ran with it. "That dead parent cash. Am I right?"

This time, the misstep was mine. His innocent reply flew too close to the truth and darted between my ribs like an ice pick.

I should've seen it coming, and got what I deserved for letting my guard down. Normally, I tried to forget about being an orphan. It had to be another mundane fact of life, like green grass or blue skies, if I wanted to live without wallowing in a haze of constant grief.

When Chi Ho hatched a plan at the beginning of her senior year to flee her parent's college expectations for her grandmother's salon, I sped to finish my GED so I could go with her. I'd lived on my own since the start of that summer, petitioning the state for independence that came easily won. The only relatives available to dump me on after tragedy struck lived in a corner of Alaska with no sun, no schools, and no prospects. The court decided I'd do better alone. So, we ran from the rural hometown that held nothing but bad memories for us the day after graduation, determined to never look back.

I recoiled from Nuñez as the vivid imagery of my parents' funerals surfaced.

He pulled his hands up from the computer and held them in front of his chest for protection. "I didn't mean it." He tripped over his tongue. "I—you never said. I'm so sorry. For your loss? If they—did they—*dead*?"

His pathetic emphasis on the last syllable inspired transparency.

I ran through the basics as he listened. "Farming accident. Big insurance settlement. The details are gross. You don't want to hear them."

"That's awful," he said. "When did they—?"

I snapped and cut him off. "A million years ago! Back in Ohio. It's not important."

The blood drained from his face. After all, Kyle might've been within shouting distance to run and smack him, but I hadn't yet tested Doctor Laura's punishment system. With a little effort, I softened.

"Can we talk about something else? Please?"

Nuñez's troubled look evaporated into sheer absence. He remained blank as he thought—I guessed—of all the injuries I'd inflict upon him as the result of misspoken words.

"Go ahead," he said, returning to the realm of the couch. "It's your turn. You can ask me anything you want."

I thought as he brought up a flashing green and black window. His speedy fingers input code that looked more like magic runes than letters and numbers. I'd already learned N.E.R.D. belonged to a real branch of the United States government, but while we juggled the subject of my finances, questions of my own started brewing about theirs. As Doctor Laura and Kyle reentered the room with a final test tube and a handful of long Q-tips, I let one out.

I hoped a new topic might distract us from the tension manifested by our painfully honest exchange.

"I've been wondering, how does this whole operation work, anyway? It seems like they kind of left you guys to rot in this basement, so—" I paused when the woman at my side frowned. "Who pays for everything around here? Chemicals, medical equipment, tropical fish, exotic plant barf. It can't be cheap. I doubt the aforementioned *box of stuff* dropped on the doorstep every month or so is enough to get you by."

Doctor Laura handed the container to Kyle who deposited it in a plastic rack.

With a plaintive glance to my right, I begged Nuñez to chime in before I risked further offense.

"It's a decent question," she said when he didn't.

His face contorted to suppress what I supposed was a humble blush. "That's my job, too," he said without looking up. "I wrote a program that divides and organizes our funds. It's totally boring, though. You wouldn't care."

"Don't be shy," said Doctor Laura. "Holly, make him tell you what he did. It's genius. But first, open your mouth up wide so I can get a swab."

I pressed him as she suggested, gagging when I didn't finish before she poked the back of my throat.

Her praise of his programming skills excited me as I imagined a flood of packages arriving at the front desk of my apartment building. I couldn't wait to watch my wardrobe grow.

"You heard her," she said as she collected a sample of dark purplish earwax. "I wouldn't keep stalling. You don't want to make her angry."

Kyle agreed, shaking a fist gleefully at Nuñez who sighed.

He took a deep breath and stopped working. "It's nothing, really. It's just—we were broke when they left me here. And I'm talking that couch-diving-for-quarters-to-buy-slushies-at-the-gas-station-because-you-don't-have-a-dollar kind of poor. So, I wrote a program. An untraceable bot used to steal bits of cash here and there. From, you know. Stuff."

"Like?"

"Just little things," he mumbled. "Public works. Water and sewer. Nothing important like schools, healthcare, or anything like that. Mostly construction. That's really it."

The way he turned away made me wonder whether or not

he was telling the whole truth. I couldn't think of a reason for him not to.

"Like all those never-ending roadwork projects." Doctor Laura picked up where he left off. "You know the kind in the Midwest that can run on for years and years, but never seem to go anywhere? We figured, better our money than theirs. Have you ever been to Ohio?"

The hiss of their radio and the heavy stride of the man attached to its hip interrupted our conversation. Brannon captivated us with the intensity of his presence and saved me from telling Doctor Laura about my tragic past.

Not that I planned on thanking him.

Ever.

"I've had some time to think," he announced to the room as though we hadn't already figured that out, "and these are our odds."

He set the spitting box on the table and turned the volume so low that only I could hear it.

"As long as our target is in the wind, the people that broke in will be concentrating all their efforts on getting him back. For the time being, I doubt they're interested in us."

"So, what you're saying is," said Doctor Laura, "we're safe as long as they're out there looking?"

He didn't sugar-coat his answer. "Hardly. One mutant supersoldier is great. Don't get me wrong. But if they recover him in one piece and he's everything they've ever dreamed of, that's when they'll come back here. Next time, they'll take everything. Trust me. I've dealt with people like this before. It doesn't matter where they're from or who they work for. Bad guys are all the same, and they only want three things. More weapons. More power. More influence."

"What do we do?" Kyle asked, looking ill.

Our brief encounters at home always painted him as timid and weak, but level-headed. Seeing him tremble made my heart beat faster.

His mentor reached for his hand. "Don't worry. We know they're coming this time, and that gives us a leg up. Am I right?"

"You're not wrong," said Brannon, "but that's not going to make what I'm about to say any easier."

He braced himself.

"For now—and you're going to hate me for this—I'm going to need everyone to stay put in the lab."

7

THE PLAN

The room's occupants—including me—exploded the instant the counterintuitive instruction left his mouth. Except Nuñez.

He merely let out an agonized groan.

Doctor Laura screeched the loudest. "What do you mean, stay here? Didn't you say five seconds ago they're coming *back*?"

I threw my own redundant opinion into the mix. "That doesn't sound like a good plan. That sounds like a bad plan."

"I don't like it!" said Kyle. His voice cracked like an overheated mug in a high-powered microwave.

"Neither do I." Doctor Laura continued. "Are you out of your damn mind? You want us to sit here and wait for—"

Brannon stood up straighter, gathering every inch of his height. "Enough! All of you. Listen to me." His command subdued the crowd. "Laura, I know you're scared. I understand, but you've got to think rationally. This is the safest place in the city for all of you. Until we take stock of what's missing and clean this place up, there's no telling what they might've found on documents lying around. That includes where we live. Kyle, I want you to stay, too. Even though your file doesn't have an address. The rest of us are sitting ducks if we go home and they want to make a clean sweep."

No one said it, but everyone agreed with him.

"There are only two ways in and out of here, and the one they know about is easy to guard. D—"

The modern warlock looked up from his virtual cauldron.

"I want you to take first watch when you're done with the traffic cameras. You'll alternate shifts of five hours each. I'm going to set you up with a defense wall, and a truckload of artillery in front of the main door. In the meantime, I'll keep listening for trouble on the radio and call if I hear anything. Laura, you and Kyle need to gather the remaining vials of completed serum and any samples you've taken from Holly. You have to be ready to run. Lock them in one of my mobile gun safes and put it in the back. I'll take the key with me as an extra precaution."

Kyle squawked in disbelief. "That means you're leaving!"

"We'll cover more ground working with an away team," Brannon insisted. "You three will stay here. Once activated, the emergency system should work well enough to lock you in and keep them out. And I trust everyone here with a gun. Except you." His pointed look made my neighbor slink back, but he continued with a hint of optimism. "Keep in mind, if they assumed Kyle was dead, they'd have to have known someone would find him. It only makes sense we'd redouble our security. Even if they nab the mutant in the next five seconds, it'll take at least another twenty-four hours for them to come up with a better plan for a second assault. It should be a quiet evening for all of you."

"Where are you going, then?" Doctor Laura glanced at me. "And what about her?"

"From what we know so far, our missing subject is headed north. I'm taking Holly with me to set up a second base at her apartment. If I'm wrong—and it all goes to shit here—we can't risk letting them have her, too."

My ecstatic reply didn't fit the general mood. "That means I get to go home!"

"Looks like it." Brannon was nowhere near as relieved as me. "The rest of you, get ready for a slumber party nobody asked for. This one won't be much fun."

Returning to the warmth of my pastel sanctuary thrilled me, but I didn't want *him* tagging along. I cultivated the comforts of my home for one, and the idea of cohabitating with the bossy stranger made me incredibly uneasy. Only Chi Ho ever visited, and she usually stayed in my kitchen, restocking my refrigerator with the few foods she knew I couldn't resist.

The notebook and pencil slid out of my lap as I went for the purse at my feet.

Brannon summoned the others to his side. He didn't notice that I stayed behind while they shuffled out. I turned my phone on and braced myself for an onslaught of missed calls and messages.

As they walked down the hall, Doctor Laura whispered her misgivings again.

"You're sure this is our best course of action?"

"It's all I've got," said Brannon, "but we'll find him, Laura. We'll get the people who did this. I'll fix this mess. I promise you."

Small pats putting her faith in him landed softer than the next thud. Nuñez yelped.

"And what the hell were you thinking, being so reckless?" She scolded him. "Cutting her open? If you died, it'd kill me."

They slipped out of earshot.

I didn't bother to look for any texts from my best friend

before I sent her one. I hoped getting a response from me would keep her from calling the police like I'd asked. She hadn't already, as far as I knew. I doubted she would, unless our options ran out. Chi Ho trusted them even less than I did.

None of the voices chatting over the frequency of Brannon's radio had said anything to make me believe otherwise.

I'm okay. I wrote simply. *Headed home now. I'll call you and explain better in like, an hour. Maybe two. Tops.*

That wasn't good enough.

I hit send and rushed to type a new message. One with a personal touch to reassure her it was really me.

By the way, I should have gone through the alleyway. Your grandma is a wrinkly old fraud.

An icon flashed in the top corner of my screen, a pyramid stacked with empty gray bars. No service. I groaned. What kind of signal did I expect to get several stories underground? Texting Chi Ho would have to wait. I put the device back as Doctor Laura reentered the room.

"Holly, honey, can you come with me? I need to run an MRI while the machine is still on. I'm not sure how long we'll have before it craps out again. Let's find out what's going on inside your body."

I retrieved my purse and my list, and followed her into the main space. We skirted around the mess and made our way toward the door at the back of the lab. Brannon and Nuñez huddled around a computer near it—one of the only ones spared during the break-in. When they shifted, I saw a fuzzy mug shot of the dead man in the deli. They didn't notice us stop to hover behind them.

"I can't believe you lifted his wallet," said Brannon, eyeing Nuñez. "I didn't see you do it."

He shrugged. "I thought we might need it. He doesn't."

The screen pinged. Brannon read from the boxes that popped up.

"Three charges of aggravated battery, one for arson, domestic assault, soliciting a minor. He was in and out of jail for years." He took the mouse and scrolled down. "Plus the hospital. Look at all those corresponding injuries."

A flash of the burglar's backwards head made me flinch, but I exiled the image with reason. Maybe I'd done a public service by dispatching the menace no one else could. Doctor Laura studied the blood in my hair with more interest than before—but no fear or judgment. My neck muscles tensed.

I still didn't feel like a hero.

"I can't say I blame whoever shanked him," said Nuñez. "The universe was really trying to get rid of this guy."

Another picture joined the first. This one showed him younger, clean-shaven, and grinning as employee of the month in his In-N-Out Burger hat.

Nuñez tilted his chin, examining the photograph. "Too bad he was such a scumbag. He used to be kind of hot."

"You think?" Brannon squinted at the screen. "I guess I can see it."

Doctor Laura pulled the door open with one hand and placed the other on Nuñez's shoulder. She chuckled when he didn't move, except to reach for her touch. It was a warm, soft, quiet sound—a familiar tone a piece of my broken heart remembered all too well. It stabbed me as I ducked beneath her arm. Without looking, I could hear the smile in her voice as she followed me into the cavern of shadows.

"Y'all ain't never gonna be the kinds of gays they put on billboards."

I had a millisecond to wonder if she meant they were

86

together. Did that explain why Brannon and Nuñez seemed so comfortable with each other despite their differences in rank? All speculation fizzled when Doctor Laura turned on the lights.

The hallway we stood in would've looked like a TV set— if NASA sponsored *Grey's Anatomy*.

Small rooms with clear plastic walls flanked the long corridor in front of us. Uneven coatings of dust covered forgotten counters and surgical tools that lost their sterile shine eons ago. Large pieces of medical equipment—some I recognized and some I didn't—lived in pods to my left. Doctor Laura led me to the door of the third. She deposited me on a platform attached to a giant white tube after a quick jaunt through an antechamber with a desk and an ancient computer.

When she left to locate a paper gown, I scanned the alcove across the hall. Novelty lamps duct-taped to the ceiling illuminated hospital beds stacked upright in a corner, and the battered ping-pong table that took their place. This had to be the boys' secret lair. They even had their own board. Blueprints for a Rube Goldberg machine designed to feed Kyle crackers with a dart gun sat underneath bold letters spelling *Days Since Last Accident* scribbled over with anarchy symbols.

A bowling set made from two-liter bottles filled with crushed soda caps sat in the empty bay to my left. Bright green toy guns and Styrofoam darts littered the ground. An old wooden desk buckled beneath the weight of a half-finished papier-mâché dinosaur skull.

Doctor Laura returned with the gown and busied herself with inspecting the machine while I put it on. I laid on the platform and let the world fall away, visualizing Brannon and

Nuñez shooting each other as they stalked around their child-like war zone.

The MRI circled my head, clicking like a hoard of cicadas, as we made small talk about the weather and recent Netflix shows over the speaker system. I pretended I didn't hear her more personal questions, and Doctor Laura kindly skipped past them.

An hour or two passed before I finally got permission to redress. We were about to join the others when Kyle appeared in the doorway, lugging a heavy black case in both hands. His boss rubbed his shoulder and took the container to the end of the hallway. She placed it beside the tall vent that blew with the tarry smell of the street above. This had to be the lab's second exit, hidden in plain sight.

I followed them back into the main hall to find a new fixture—a barrier of broken glass and bags of gravel with a window in the center—sitting in the tidied spot in front of the door. Brannon and Nuñez dropped a final sack onto the base. Doctor Laura sighed when she saw the enormous trail of sand coming from a supply closet.

Brannon ground his teeth and shook his bandaged hand, trying to banish the pain emanating from it. As he disappeared into the storage room again, Nuñez looked up. He wiped beads of sweat from his forehead and reached for the paper in my hand.

"That's the list? Let me see."

I hesitated. "It's not done. There's more, but—"

Guilt pricked me when he took it. He'd be busy enough without worrying about my demands, sifting through mountains of traffic footage and tagged photos on social media between stints guarding the front door.

Brannon brought forth an enormous gun. The piece of

artillery wobbled as he balanced its spare parts and a ground mount in his arms. Nuñez helped him maneuver it into place behind the hole it was meant for.

"I'll finish your program as soon as I can," he assured me, assembling the rifle's barrel without looking. "It might be a day or two, but I'll get it done. For right now, just concentrate on staying safe out there. Okay?"

I mumbled that I would, but couldn't quite shake the shame of burdening him.

Brannon replaced the robber's handgun in the waistband of his pants with a new one attached to a matching black holster. Once done, he waved to Kyle who brought him the set of silver keys that belonged to the case that contained my blood and the rest of Doctor Laura's serum. My temporary guardian pocketed them, picked up the leather duffle bag by the door, and slid it onto his elbow.

"Let's go."

He placed his good hand on my shoulder and his body heat sizzled through the thin fabric of my dress. I shuddered, overcome with an odd blend of disgust and—something else. Brannon wasn't shy about pushing people around where he needed them to go.

I didn't like it.

Kyle had one more question before we left. "You're sure you don't want me to come with you? In case Holly gets mad and wants to hit someone?"

Brannon shook his head and pulled him into a careful hug. He reached for Doctor Laura and gave her a few more instructions while she held him tight.

I caught what she whispered near his ear.

"Keep her happy. She's more volatile than she seems."

I didn't mention what I'd heard, though it made me

nervous. I didn't feel unstable. Brannon gave her the slightest nod before he finished saying goodbye.

"You know where to find the rest of the guns and more ammunition. We'll be in constant contact. Stay near the phone. If nothing changes, you can expect us back sometime tomorrow."

He added the word *hopefully* under his breath.

"Until then, keep this place on lockdown. No one goes in or out. There's plenty of food and leftovers in the kitchen. Try to relax, but stay alert." He stepped up to Nuñez. "Let me know what you find on those tapes or online, and keep a close eye on all ingoing and outgoing communications on our network. They might've left a bug."

Their embrace lasted the longest.

"You got it," said the tall man when he let go. "I'll keep you posted."

Brannon gave them one last piece of advice. "This should go without saying—but if anyone else tries to come through that door that isn't me or Holly, you shoot them."

Everyone hugged me, too, before I followed him out into the laboratory's lobby. Three sets of concerned eyes vanished as the door shut behind us with a finite thud. He removed the grate covering the speaker system and input a code on a hidden number pad. The wall hummed as a dozen bolts slid into place.

In silence, we crossed to the elevator, pressed the button, and stepped inside—ready to ascend to the hilly landscape above undoubtedly fraught with peril.

8

KARAOKE
CRASHER

When we resurfaced in the dank stockroom, it was almost pitch black. Dull stars and a piece of the moon peeked past the veil of sunset through the broken skylight. Brannon closed the door of the refrigerator, unzipped his duffle bag, and dropped it on the floor. He produced a plain black t-shirt and a pair of jeans, and handed them to me.

"Put these on."

They were his, judging by their size and the aroma of cheap drugstore deodorant glued to every thread. It'd been a year since I'd worn anything other than dresses or skirts. I imagined myself tripping naked into his arms as I pulled up his baggy pants. A hot tingle wracked my body.

I frantically ignored it.

His jaw clenched. "You stick out like a sore thumb in that getup, whether you're bloody or not. I need you in plain-clothes. We don't want to draw any more attention to ourselves going forward."

I'd almost forgotten during my short time in the lab that I was still a fringe member of society. Doctor Laura didn't notice my dress when we met, and Kyle had never said a word about my clothes during the months I'd known him. Nuñez complimented my coordinate as soon as he saw me, and even agreed to encourage my expensive hobby without asking about the fashion—or why I possessed such unparalleled enthusiasm for it.

I understood why Brannon disapproved of my signature style, but I still didn't want to give up my delicate armor. When he looked as though he'd pounce and strip me himself if I didn't hurry up, I bent down and unbuckled my shoes. I had to prevent the steamy scenario my overactive imagination concocted from taking place.

"Turn around!" My command slapped him hard enough to make him realize he'd been staring. "I'm not going to change in front of you. If you really want me in these ugly clothes, then do me the kindness of not looking while I get dressed."

Brannon grumbled and angled away from me.

I took off my shoes and squeaked as a sheet of snakeskin crunched underfoot. The uncomfortable intimacy of wearing his clothes crawled over my limbs as I buttoned his old jeans.

"Are you done yet?" He turned around as I straightened his dress-length shirt.

I held my legs together to keep my new pants from slipping, and cupped my dirty dress. Its chiffon layers overflowed from my fingers like the soft petals of a wilting rose.

Brannon scanned me, peering across the darkening room with great difficulty. I didn't have to squint to see his eyes narrow as they landed on top of my head.

"That's got to go." He pointed at my offending accessory. "That bow thing."

I plucked it off and resisted the urge to chuck all my garments in his big, dumb face. "Happy now?"

He shook his head grimly as he took my things and stuffed them in the sack he shouldered. "You look terrible. Like a lost kid who raided a construction worker's closet."

"You suck," I hissed.

I traced his steps as he navigated half-full shelves of fake logs and overturned boxes of dried insects. Golden beams cast by streetlights lit our path when we crept onto the main floor to make our way outside.

Brannon skipped down the porch steps and took his keys —which now included the ones for the safe—out of his pocket. The sedan's rusty lock clunked open.

"At least it's better than before." He dropped his bag in the backseat and fired up the engine. "Kind of. But you might want to do something about that hair. Run your fingers through it, or something. It might help hide the—"

I touched my crunchy curls, drilling holes in the side of his head with my unflinching gaze. "Evidence. Yeah. I get it."

He flipped the radio on and the grating white noise of bored police officers discussing their dinner plans filled the air between us.

I managed to pick a few strands of congealed blood from my temples before two beeps chirped from the tote in my lap. Chi Ho called three nanoseconds after my texts sent. I scrambled to snatch my purse before Brannon could stop me.

"Where the hell have you been?" she screamed when I picked up. "Are you safe? Who are you with? Tell me what's going on!"

Her cries bounced around the car like the piercing bleeps of a fire alarm in a cramped shopping mall.

"Chi Ho, wait!" I said in a hurry.

Brannon tore his eyes from the windshield long enough to scald me with a fiery glare.

"Holly, hang up the phone." He tried to push past the moving wall of my arm with his useless right hand. "We can't involve anyone else."

"It's my best friend." I grunted as I carefully thwarted each of his attempts to knock my cell away. "She already knows. I texted her earlier, so there's no use fighting it now! It's too late."

It was a tiny lie since she didn't have a clue about my transformation—or N.E.R.D.—but it made him stop flailing.

Her voice turned frantic. "Who's that? Holly! Say something if you can hear me."

"I'm okay!" I shouted. "Just give me a second. I'll explain everything."

"This is ridiculous." Brannon put his hand back on the wheel with resigned resentment.

I knew he'd feel better if Chi Ho confirmed nobody else had ringside seats to our ongoing disaster.

"Did you call the police?"

"No," she said, loudly disgusted by the suggestion. "You told me not to!"

"Good." My reply managed to iron out some of the concerned wrinkles in Brannon's forehead. "Keep it that way. I'm actually with them right now. Well—sort of."

This confused her more.

"Sort of? What? Why?"

"It's a long story." The phone crackled as we passed through the shadow of a crumbling overpass. "I saw a fight in the park on my way home last night. I took a detour, like Nai Nai said I should. And now I'm—uh—working with a detective to help catch a fugitive. But he's not like a regular cop." I added the important distinction to comfort her. "He's an independent investigator."

Brannon leaned over, his whisper a weapon. "Why not just tell her I'm an officer?"

I covered the microphone and squinted at him. "Because

you don't have a uniform, you drive an ancient red beater, and you're not *that* much of a bastard."

My points penetrated his defenses. Chi Ho forged ahead.

"Like a PI?" she asked. "Does he have a gun? Let me talk to him. I know I heard him a second ago."

"What? You don't want to, really—"

"Just do it," she hollered. "It sounds like you're about to lose me, so hurry up!"

He looked at the phone suspiciously as I put it on speaker and held it between us.

"Okay." I shrugged tense shoulders. I didn't know what she wanted, either. "You've got—um—Detective Brannon."

"Look detective," she said, "you better be nice to my best friend and keep her safe. You hear me? She doesn't know anything about hunting criminals, so you have to do shootouts and stuff by yourself. If she gets hurt—"

Brannon adopted the same fake nice tone he'd used on me during our first meeting. "I assure you, I'll do everything in my power to make sure we catch the guy quickly so she can get back to her daily life. I won't let anything bad happen to Holly. Satisfied?"

Chi Ho didn't get a chance to say whether or not he'd placated her before the call dropped, just as she'd predicted. As soon as the line clicked off, Brannon switched back to his true persona.

"What were you thinking? Who is she? How much does she know? The more people we get wrapped up in this mess, the more dangerous this whole operation gets! Just how dumb are you? Give me that."

He took my phone and stuffed it inside his jacket. I didn't hit him, or smack the dashboard, or stomp my feet through the creaky floorboard to let off steam.

Even though I really, *really* wanted to.

"I'm not stupid." I snapped. "When you took me this morning, I texted her to let her know I was going with weird men for questioning. I didn't know who you were because you wouldn't tell me. You and Nuñez obviously weren't normal cogs in the justice machine, but you sure tried hard to make me believe you were. That act needs a lot of work, by the way. Yours specifically. You reek of fed."

Brannon snorted. "Don't pretend for a second you're not a terrible liar, too. You're lucky I wasn't one of the boys in blue showing up on your doorstep to cart you off for murder. Who the hell leaves their bedazzled nightmare of a cell phone at a crime scene?"

"I don't know." Sarcasm dripped from my tongue. "Maybe someone running away from a big freaking mutant? Excuse me for forgetting to take stock of my possessions before I fled for my life."

It felt like I'd won when Brannon didn't reply. He focused on the road, his temples twitching. Silence reigned as he turned down a different avenue than the one I knew led us back to the main drag.

We passed several cars along the way, although the congestion in the industrial neighborhood remained minimal. The water to our right was ominously still as we wound our way north. When it didn't seem certain we were headed back to my apartment, I spoke up to reconfirm.

"We're not getting on the highway?" I worried I'd pissed my new partner off enough for him to decide he could track the creature without me.

Brannon moved with robotic precision. His cool, dark aura made him the breathing equivalent of the eye of a hurricane. He didn't hold the government's most prestigious position, yet I knew he wasn't someone to be messed with. In less than a day, I'd discovered the natural talent I possessed for pushing his buttons. But—like an unskilled bomb technician working in the field for the first time—I didn't want to press the wrong one and risk the explosive consequences.

Another unfortunate side effect of Doctor Laura's serum reared its frustrating head again. When I transformed into a superhuman, my internal wires must've rearranged themselves into the twisted configuration of a people-pleaser. My anxiety cared most about making sure no one saw past my pastel exterior, but now I also hated the idea of anyone being mad at me. This need to make everyone happy extended to Brannon as well.

Even though I kept telling myself I didn't particularly like him.

Nope. I insisted as I admired the hard planes of his cross features. *Not at all.*

Not one bit.

"It's safer to stick to side streets," he said to quell my unspoken concerns. "Easier to figure out if we're being tailed if I've got the opportunity to stop and check at red lights. Nuñez can track our progress as well. If anyone shows up to snatch us, it'll all be caught on film. Fewer cams on the main roads. Makes them much more dangerous."

"Got it," I said. The start of a halfhearted apology followed close behind. "I didn't mean to be so defensive. About Chi Ho. You're right. Had I known more about the situation upfront, I probably wouldn't have told her anything. She doesn't know about N.E.R.D., not really. Or the serum. Or my new—err—self."

We accelerated out of a row of warehouses into a hipper district full of packed bars and expensive soap shops.

"You promise?"

"Y-yes," I stuttered.

His simple question disarmed me when I'd expected worse.

"That's it. Bare bones. You can't really blame me for getting freaked out after being basically kidnapped. I had to let her know, you know, to look for me. In case you guys turned out to be creeps and my body ended up on the ten o'clock news."

He threw a glance in the rearview mirror to look for cars that might spark déjà vu as we waited for a group of bar-crawling superheroes to cross the road. "We didn't kidnap you. I asked nicely if you wanted to come to breakfast, then go answer some questions. You're the one who said yes."

Brannon was wrong, and I was itching to argue.

"I didn't really have a choice, did I? The second you handed over my phone, I knew what was up. I had to go with you."

"Why? So you could lie to me some more?" He leaned on the horn to part the crowd that kept causing our progress through their midst to stop and start.

"Like you're so innocent. You wanted to pump me for information about the mutants and then dump me back on the street after Doctor Laura got a chance to wipe my memories. The only reason I'm here now is because I'm special and you need me!"

"Would you really want to remember any of this if you didn't have to?" Brannon escalated to match my volume. "Don't tell me for a second you feel lucky. I'm sure if you had it your way, you'd rather be at home, no serum in your veins, pouring tea with your same old noodly arms for a pair of teddy bears. Or whatever it is you spend your precious time doing!"

"Oh, like that's any better than—"

I gasped as we slowed for yet another group of costumed revelers. Something—or *someone*—reached down my throat and squeezed my vital organs. The telepathy attributed to twins by corny YouTube documentaries overcame my senses. My body buzzed as I felt the presence of my mutant counterpart.

He was alive, and *close*.

"Better than what?" Brannon nagged. "Come on, I thought we had a good back and forth thing going on here. You can't leave me hang—"

"Stop the car!"

I didn't wait for him to do it before I rolled out.

The effect wasn't very dramatic since we were only going about five miles per hour, but my departure shocked my travel companion. I removed the passenger's side door from its hinges in my rush to hit the pavement. The hunk of metal bashed against the side mirror and fell with a clank as I charged toward a packed karaoke bar.

Brannon shouted my name as he stepped on the screeching breaks. Curses from a distressed valet accompanied the whine of the old sedan's engine shutting off. The parking attendant yelled at him, but I couldn't distinguish the finer points of their screaming match over the din of pop music booming from speakers on the overflowing patio.

I hurtled past the bouncer to find the source of my fixation.

A map formed in my mind, a path drawn by the overwhelming sensation of nearness. The blue dot blinking on its edge blipped farther and farther away. I chased my elusive ghost like Pac-Man, dodging gray-haired businessmen in smart suits and paper masks waiting to sing showtunes. Because my big mouth could speak, I stopped to ask for directions.

My open hands slammed into the bar to my left. Low lighting hid the hefty dents in the lacquered oak.

"Have you seen a guy?" I asked the bartender, hitching up my pants to take off again. "Giant—but not in a costume. He might still be kind of blue-ish. I don't know. Maybe?"

The elderly man raised his voice to battle the electronic notes of a one-hit wonder from the eighties. "You mean Hugo? Is he your boyfriend?"

A crash came from the back, followed by a grunt tinged with the rumble of sliding boulders. I swept through the waist-high privacy gate and skittered toward the kitchen.

That's when Brannon entered.

The sound of his herald—more concerned and clueless than angry—made me stop and whip around halfway through the swinging steel door.

"Is that your husband?" The bartender's round face imper-sonated a startled emoji as he accused me of adultery.

I hoped I didn't look old enough to be married.

"Holly," Brannon yelled. "Wait!"

I ignored his request in favor of obeying my all-consuming urge. My soul screamed. *Find Hugo!*

I zipped past crackling gas ranges as cooks dove out of my way. Behind me, glasses shattered in a wave of tinkling booms, but I couldn't turn back to find out what happened. I careened into the filthy alleyway without waiting for Brannon.

The scent of vomit, trash, and urine greeted me as I arrived at a high fence. I scaled the see-through wall, using the broken ledges of chain link as footholds as I skipped skyward.

Another pair of huge hands had already carved finger-shaped indents into the pipe I crushed and vaulted over. My mark was closer than ever before. I couldn't begin to explain how I knew, but the prospect of catching him fueled the need within me. If I captured the escaped villain, my contract with N.E.R.D. would be half-finished.

Freedom waited for me.

Asphalt crunched beneath my feet as I took off running again. I shuddered to a halt at the bottom of a rusty fire escape and climbed. Cool drops of joy slid out the corners of my eyes. I was sure the man galloping after me could make quick work of an interrogation to lead us to the mutant's evil cohorts. I broke through the maze of stairs and scrambled onto the rooftop.

The bulky outline of my nemesis sailed by in the distance. He leapt from building to building like a titanic gazelle, silhouetted against the faint glow of the moon in all his glory. He was just as big as I remembered, but not as goopy and grotesque.

The blue gunk that once coated him like icing was gone. His unblemished skin remained as uncanny as mine, but we looked vastly different. The cool-toned blood running beneath my pale exterior gave me the creepy appearance of an antique doll. It turned his once-warm tan the hue of aged burlap.

His broad features claimed his Pacific Island heritage in a way they hadn't when they were too swollen for me to notice. He'd replaced his torn athletic clothes with a pair of white chef's pants with an elastic waist. They hit mid-calf like the favorite trousers of middle-aged moms visiting the beach. His eyes hadn't quite managed to come back together after his skull expanded. Otherwise, his face was pretty normal.

He looked more like a karate instructor wearing a kid's uniform than a devious international spy.

The mutant landed on another roof a block away and our eyes locked, even though hundreds of yards separated us. His changed in our time apart from brown to electric blue. I gasped when I saw what filled them. It wasn't hate, or the intent to kill and dismember I'd assumed I'd find. It was fear. His expression was so readable I could hear exactly what he intended to communicate. We didn't need words.

Stop following me. Rang the sound of his thoughts. *You freak. Stay away!*

I'm the freak? I puzzled. *Have you looked in a mirror lately?*

Murderer. The deep cadence of his silent cry dug at my heart. *Leave me alone!*

My lips curled into a menacing snarl. *No! I have to catch you. It's my job!*

He slipped behind a water tower, punctuating his disappearing act with a ping meant to end our mental tête-à-tête. I denied him the luxury and propelled myself forward to continue my pursuit.

My resolve, however, wasn't strong enough to follow through with my original plan.

Not when I remembered I was terrified of heights.

My impeccable sense of mortality caught up with me before I jumped. I skittered to a stop against the roof's ledge. It crumbled like a piece of cake beneath my outstretched arms. Bricks toppled into the dark chasm between buildings as I reeled back to regain my balance. My foot teetered and my torso swept over the edge. The siren song of the street below beckoned, but its tune ceased when a familiar set of mismatched arms wrapped themselves around my chest.

Brannon grabbed me and pulled me back. Our legs tangled as we fell together in a heap on the cement floor.

That's when I noticed I was freezing. Over the course of my chase, I hadn't observed the one detail that became horribly obvious as I lay next to the man who'd saved me.

The pants he'd lent me were gone. I'd lost them somewhere in the alleyway.

Brannon groaned, unhurt for the most part. I sat up and scooted away from him while yanking his old t-shirt down around my bare thighs.

"Son of a—" He didn't bother uttering the last bit of his favorite phrase.

I knew he'd have questions, like who the hell I thought I was, taking off like that and breaking his car without a word to describe where I was going or why. But he surprised me by reaching for my shoulders instead.

"Are you okay?"

I nodded, but my teeth chattered as I shivered. "I saw him. The mutant. I felt him. I can't explain it, but—"

"I believe you." The steadiness of his hold told me his trust was real. "Which way did he go? What did he look like?"

I shook my head *no* this time. Suddenly, I wasn't so sure the boy I shared my strange connection with was who we thought he might be.

"It's cold." I said, shaking. "I'm so—"

Before I repeated myself, Brannon draped the warm shell of his jacket around me like a cape.

"Here."

He held it gently as I maneuvered my arms through its

sleeves—which wasn't easy to do without flashing him again. I recovered from my brief stint on the verge of hypothermia and shock.

He stared into the distance past my haphazard renovation to the short wall. "I'm guessing he's long gone, right? You can't sense him anymore?"

"No. What was that? How did I—?"

"I don't know," he said, "but we need to find out. I'll call Laura as soon as I can. I need to tell her, anyway. About the car. Technically, Old Red is hers, even if I'm the only one who ever drives. I'd bet money we're getting towed right about now. We'll have to take a taxi back to your place. That'll put another dent in the emergency fund."

I remembered the mountain of cash he'd handed the deli clerk earlier. He probably didn't have much left.

We crossed to the stairs and he slid down onto the first landing. I cringed as I took in how many flights I'd have to traverse to make it to solid Earth. When I didn't budge, Brannon popped his head back up and gave me a comforting smile.

"Don't tell me you're afraid of heights," he said. "Come on. You don't have to worry."

He thrust his good hand out, but I didn't take it.

"You'll be fine. I'm right here behind you."

"So what if I am?" I crimped the railing beneath my white knuckles as we went down. "Everyone is, of something. I'm sure that includes you."

He jumped from the last ladder. "Not much, really. Nothing worth mentioning."

Curiosity wiggled at the base of my spine, but exhaustion prevented me from asking about his deepest, darkest fear. He let me walk beside him without another word as we made our way through the service streets and back out onto the road.

In front of the karaoke joint, about fifty feet away from us, a real squad car and a tow truck sat guarding our burgundy tank on wheels. Brannon's face told me he didn't intend to approach the scene. The flustered bartender entertained onlookers as he gave an animated description of us to the police.

We switched directions and did our best to blend in, linking elbows to stay together despite the pressure of the swirling masses. Angels, fairies, and demons flitted by and ducked into nearby bars. Costumed in normal clothes, I became just another non-descript girl in the crowd. Brannon and I merged into the soup of affluent businessmen and their dates in short black dresses. We huddled on the corner to maintain our cover and keep warm until a yellow cab pulled up.

I sidled in first and gave my apartment's address to the man driving as he leered at my smooth legs.

He gave Brannon a snort of approval, but didn't push the issue when met with nothing but a murderous stare. His stubby fingers input the number I gave him into the GPS.

"Is that okay? We can go home?" I moved a bit closer to Brannon.

"I think we're done," he said, drained from the colossal stress of the day. "For the time being. We'll get the car from impound in the morning. Then we can continue on from there. Before we do anything, we need to reconcile your new ability."

I leaned against the sticky leather bench. A stale stream of hot air wafted through the open window separating us from the front seat.

What happened back there?

If my fellow mutant sensed me too, then why hadn't he taken the opportunity to strike? Surely, a supersoldier trained to live and die for some wicked branch of a rival government wasn't afraid of a fight.

Why? The question haunted me. *Why did he run?*

"Tough night?" Our lecherous driver woke me from the hypnosis of the broken record skipping in my head.

An exceptionally dirty look—one that Brannon and I delivered together—convinced him to keep his mouth shut for the rest of the journey.

9

SLEEPOVER PT. 1

The night watchman jolted awake when we arrived at my building, knocking over the cup of coffee on his desk. He saw me wearing an odd combination of men's clothes and my own socks and shoes, but thought better than to say anything. I smiled at him fraily to communicate that yes—I did look like I'd spent a lurid afternoon with the man walking next to me. And no—it couldn't be helped.

I was grateful when he coughed and picked up his soggy newspaper instead of saying hello.

Brannon climbed the stairs beside me. He stopped beneath the doorframe of my floor's hallway.

"I'm going first," he said, "to check and make sure no one's waiting inside. If we found you by tracing your 911 call—"

"They could, too," I said, more apprehensive than before. "I understand."

We approached my door with synchronized footsteps.

"Is that how you ended up here this morning?" I whispered.

We found a blank work order covering the hole where my doorknob wasn't. The note next to it bore the fastidious night janitor's signature and a warning to keep the floor clean of Halloween *goop*. I tore them both down.

Brannon pulled out his gun.

"A local patrol went through the park around five A.M. and found your big blue mess," he said, barely audible. "I heard it on the radio. Woke Nuñez up and had him hack emergency call logs for the area. That brought up your name. We let Laura know what was happening and went straight to the scene. She insisted on going in even though no alarms pinged either of us. I told her to hold off, but she's so damn stubborn. She found Kyle. Open the door."

My house keys were in my purse—which was still in the car. So I reached through the hole and turned my deadbolt.

Nobody grabbed my hand.

That was a good sign.

My phone buzzed inside Brannon's jacket as he went in first, his weapon held awkwardly in his non-dominant hand. I flipped on the light switch and let him scan each small room for armed strangers. After a whirlwind tour of my bathroom, closet, and bedroom, he reappeared.

"Clear."

I locked the door again and removed my shoes out of habit while he shut the kitchen blinds and curtains. I watched him and frowned when I spotted his dirty loafers.

"Plug up that hole in the door," he commanded, coming at me with a black and white rectangle headdress stolen from my wardrobe. "Not like this rag will do much good, but at least no one will be able to see in."

He finished the job for me before I could object.

"Could you please take off—?"

I wanted to reprimand him for dragging in germs. Until I

saw the bottom of his white dress shirt hanging red and shredded.

Blood. I took off his jacket and held it out.

He whizzed past me as I gasped and let go of it. My floor lamp popped on and the overhead lights went out. Oblivious to his injury, Brannon went to sit on my delicate velvet sofa.

"Don't!" I shouted. "You're bleeding."

He stopped, his neurons firing a bit slower than usual as he tried to take stock of what hurt and what didn't. The answer crept across his scrunched face: Almost everything, and very little. He looked at the slick hilt of his weapon and the blotches smeared over his bandage.

I muffled a strangled cry.

Crimson fingerprints painted every surface Brannon touched during his brief stay in my apartment.

"What happened?"

I inched closer while he fumbled with the buttons of his shirt. My jaw dropped and I pushed it back up, eyeballs spinning to avoid his sculpted chest and the fine trail of hair that ran from his collarbones to his belt buckle.

"Don't know. Probably got cut skidding down the side of that broken fence you hopped. Or maybe sliding across the bar. How bad is it?"

I wasn't fast enough to stifle a giggle when Brannon put his gun on the coffee table and faced the wall. Half-dried sweat glistened on his neck and shoulders, dotting dewdrops on his full back tattoo. The pink lotus nestled in a wavy forest of leaves caught me off-guard.

Suddenly, I remembered what Doctor Laura said before. It *was* too beautiful to belong on a straight man, I decided instantaneously. Maybe that made no sense, but it had to. I finally had enough half-baked notions to cook up a reality that gave me something in common with the grumpy drill sergeant invading my space. If Brannon was queer, too—*and* dating Nuñez—it'd be that much easier for me to be alone with him, to work with him. It gave me the best reason to ignore the goosebumps his touch burnt into my skin.

The details fit—sort of. I could make them. They lived together. They teased each other at every opportunity. The trust I'd observed between them ran deep. They'd hugged for so long when we left the lab—both of them holding on like they didn't want to let go.

Maybe Brannon didn't even like girls at all.

That'd keep me safe.

I didn't need to feel awkward about our impromptu sleepover. It was totally fine. The cold lightning radiating from my core didn't mean I was jealous.

No way. My lips tightened and twitched without permission. *Nope.*

"Still waiting," he said.

I unfroze. "Right. Sorry."

Wide scratches stretched from the middle of his back to his waistband. Rocks embedded in the swollen valleys irritated his broken skin.

"Doesn't look good." I delivered my amateur assessment as kindly as possible. "You've got some pretty big cuts. With dirt and stuff stuck in them."

He sighed. "Can you clean them out?"

"I think so. I've got a first aid kit. Come with me to the kitchen."

He slumped onto a stool beside my island as I pulled the box I restocked with cute Band-Aids out from under the sink. The tweezers I used to pluck stray hairs from my eyebrows sat in a silk pouch inside the bathroom cabinet. Brannon dialed his outdated cell phone as I rounded the corner to retrieve them.

"Kyle?" he called when the intern answered. "I need to talk to Laura. Put her on."

I reentered without a word as he waited for her, and he squirmed when my untrained hands started rooting around in his wounds.

Brannon didn't bother to say hello when the doctor's voice came over the other line. He went straight to business.

"We found the mutant. Holly tracked him to a rooftop behind a bar in North Beach, but he got away. She can sense him. We need to talk."

This revelation sent her into a tailspin. She started rambling, but I didn't gather much from what she said. Phrases like *quantum entanglement, molecular communication*, and *symbiotic pathways* meant nothing to me. Science was never my best subject, and trying to wrap my head around her metaphysical concepts gave me vertigo. I steadied myself against Brannon's arm and he pushed back, holding me up.

From what little I caught, I figured we shared some sort of psychic connection. Each one of us acted as a homing device for the other.

I distracted Brannon with a sharp poke before I snatched the phone from him, worried if I took the chance and asked for my turn to talk he'd flat out refuse me.

"What else does it do? Because out there, on the rooftop, I could hear him thinking. Or not thinking, but—"

His mouth fell open. "What?"

This new bit of information shocked him and Doctor Laura. I pictured her making the same face when she inhaled a croak.

"It wasn't thoughts. Not really," I said. "But I could read his intentions. When he looked at me, I somehow knew what he was feeling. Does that make sense?"

"It's a possibility," she said. "I never anticipated—"

Brannon cut her off. "What did he say? This is important. Word for word. What do you know?"

I pressed the speaker button so she could listen. "*Stop following me.*" I repeated the mutant exactly. "*You freak.*"

"That's it?" He looked unsure. "Name-calling?"

"Are you sure that's what you heard?" asked Doctor Laura. "Nothing about who he is? What he wants? Who he works for?"

"Villain speeches aren't exactly a thing in real life," said Brannon. "They don't open their mouths to announce their grand plans to anyone. Or their brains, I guess. In this case."

I kept going. "The thing is—he was *running*. This guy didn't want to stay and confront me. He didn't have any weapons on him. He couldn't have. He wasn't wearing anything but a tight pair of pants. And—well—he didn't seem evil. Not even a little. He was—I don't know. Scared, I think."

My confession pointed a spotlight of uncertainty on our initial assumptions. Doctor Laura and Brannon fell silent. My voice quivered when I remembered the blue gaze that pierced my soul.

"He called me a murderer," I said. "And he's right, I—"

Brannon interrupted me. "Holly, don't go there. You can't let him get inside your head. You did what you had to do."

"I guess."

I resumed tending to his gashes to keep my mind occupied. He jumped when I grazed his raw skin again.

"Bottom line—" He muffled a hiss to hide his pain from Doctor Laura. "This new ability is bad news. I'm guessing their brainwave instant messenger is a two-way street, and that makes our mission much more dangerous. If she can find him, then he can find her. That's going to make catching him impossible if he doesn't want to be found. I need you to put your thinking cap on and find a way to scramble their reception, pronto. We can't afford to waste time."

She replied after a short pause. "I'll see what I can do."

"Good. Sounds like the lab is still quiet. And safe. You should take the time between watch posts to sleep if you can."

Brannon grabbed the phone to hang up, but stopped to add one last thing.

"By the way," he said nonchalantly, like a brave teenager trying to sneak a bad report card past his mother, "we lost Old Red. I had to park—uh—illegally, to get out and aid Holly during the chase. If you think you can spare him, send Nuñez over to impound when it opens tomorrow morning and we'll meet him there. I'm going to need his help. He's a better liar than I am."

A smug smile eclipsed my melancholy. He ended the call with a beep before she could yell at him, and glared at me in a manner that said he wouldn't hesitate to kneecap me if I dared say *I told you so.*

I finished my job by swiping a tissue soaked in rubbing alcohol over his throbbing stripes. Brannon sucked in a sharp whistle as I blanketed his back with globs of petroleum jelly and unicorn-themed bandages.

"Do you want one for your face, too?" I asked.

He spun to see the rainbow horse between my fingers and rolled his eyes, even though they lingered on it a bit too long.

"No thanks."

I wanted to insist, but my stomach started growling. Then his mimicked its call like a wolf howling in a distant forest.

We were starving.

Without bothering to ask if I'd let him, he got up and started foraging for dinner. He only managed to find a few items before his hunt was over. Half of a bag of jelly beans, a dusty box of instant mashed potatoes, a tin of Belgian waffle cookies, a canister of bacon bits, three eggs, some spices, and a thumb-sized packet of ranch dressing mocked me from the countertop. He shot me a judgmental scowl before setting off on a mission to locate my seldom-used mixing bowl.

My cheeks tingled. "I eat out a lot, okay?"

Brannon concentrated on pouring every powder-fine ounce of potatoes into a saucepan. Guilt writhed within me as I watched him flit around. I had no culinary skills to contribute.

He wouldn't miss me if I snuck away to charge my phone.

Plugging it in on its crocheted bed felt like fitting a missing piece of my sanity back in place. I wanted to read Chi Ho's new texts when it kicked on, but disappearing for too long seemed rude.

Not that studying Brannon from the safety of my bedroom did anything to help him.

Alone in my kitchen, he was relaxed, in his element, and even more disturbingly attractive without his hard shell. I couldn't stop looking at him, but that didn't mean I had to like what I saw. The thin scab on his cheek served as a reminder that he wasn't made of marble. I returned, sat quietly on a bar stool, and blurted out my inside thoughts.

"Not trying to be nosy," I lied, "but you never told me what happened to your face. What's wrong with Nuñez? You said that he—"

He took my lead. "He's got great aim with that pocket knife. The one you saw earlier. If I need to get him in the morning, I find a shield and shout from the doorway, but I was in such a hurry I forgot."

I couldn't hide my astonishment. "He *threw* it at you?"

"Waking up suddenly scares him," he said. "Some agents have bad experiences out in the field."

"What happened?" I asked.

If I learned about his triggers, I could avoid them.

"I've never asked. I don't want to upset him."

He busied himself with flipping patties, eager to talk about something else—or nothing at all. My chest crumpled as I slouched, but he didn't see before I puffed it back out.

If he cared that much, they were definitely together.

I coughed and changed the subject. "It's a good thing Doctor Laura went in when she did, even if it was dangerous. Kyle's head looked really gnarly."

"He's lucky they didn't kill him with that hit." Brannon pulled two paper plates from my cabinet. "He shouldn't have been there in the first place."

Tainted memories of Sunday breakfasts brought me back to Ohio as he assembled our dinners. I shook them off before they stuck.

"No use holding a grudge against the kid." I focused on Kyle. "He was just trying to get more work done. I think that's sweet."

He took the seat to my left. "More like stupid, but you're right, I guess. I'm glad he's okay."

The bizarre sandwich he placed in front of me was unlike anything I'd ever eaten. A tower of potato-egg disks, candy, and hunks of dried bacon dripping ranch dressing wobbled between two lightly blackened cookies.

Brannon mistook my awestruck pause for disgust and shoved the plate at me.

"Eat it."

Since he'd been so quick to judge, I traded the mean look he gave me for one of my own before I took a bite.

We ate in suffocating silence until I filled it to avoid thinking about my parents. Even forced conversation was better than misery.

I circled back to recent events. "What happened when you got to the crime scene? The cops just let you take my phone?"

"We found it," said Brannon, chewing with his mouth open. "Nuñez convinced the locals to let us work with them before they suited up to wade through the carnage. He nabbed a crime kit and took samples while I scanned the area. I came to get you after the evidence confirmed we had a witness to deal with."

I finished my last morsel. "I get that, but I don't understand why you were listening for trouble in the first place. Do you always have the police scanner playing in the background?"

"I keep up with what's going on with them."

"Why?" I asked.

"I still want to make a difference. I can reroute sensitive calls to safer, socially responsible agencies, or rescue small animals from trees," he said, growing gloomy again. "That's about it. I wish I could do more, but—with where I am now— that's what I've got."

I went with the flow of our conversation before I realized its current swept me dangerously off course.

"Is that why you want to leave N.E.R.D.?"

Brannon recoiled. "What? How did you know?"

"I —" I tried to recover. "I overheard you muttering something. Back at the lab. You know, about what happens if we find the mutant. That you might be able to leave—"

He backed off when he saw me shrink away like a frightened rabbit. Even with ninety-nine percent certainty he and Nuñez were dating, I wasn't sure if he cared about any of the N.E.R.D.s enough to stay in their dank basement for the rest of his days.

I couldn't keep a tight lid on my curiosity any longer. "You don't like it there?" I asked. "You don't like them?"

"It's not that." Remorse penetrated his low voice. "You've got it wrong. Holly, you've got to understand. I don't belong there. Babysitting scientists is for has-beens. Wrinkly old men retired to desk jobs. I was handpicked from basic training by the C.I.A. for an elite program halfway through my first year. Most people don't enter until they're at least twenty-five, unless they're amazing with technology or Einstein-smart. I was never meant to be here. That's not how my career was supposed to go, and—"

A wistful sense of mourning for another life lurked beneath his flat expression. In an effort to be supportive, I attempted a display of empathy in Doctor Laura's wheelhouse —even though it fell completely out of mine. I slid my hand clumsily across the table and set it on top of his bandaged one.

This was neutral enough. I knew whatever butterflies I felt whenever we touched would never flutter within him as well.

"D, Laura, Kyle—," he said. "It's not that I don't like them. It's this job. Don't you see? I'm supposed to be their protector, and that's just—not a good fit for me."

His fingers twitched beneath mine as he leaned closer.

"Promise me you won't tell them. We still have to work together. At least, until this thing is all over."

The sound of his plea ignited a spark between us that threatened to engulf me in flames if we stayed in contact. I withdrew and stood, taking three steps back to escape the imaginary heat.

"Fine!" I wanted to run from the intimate nature of the darkened room that reduced him to a real person with deep thoughts and feelings. "Whatever. It's cool. None of my business, anyway. I—uh—I have to pee."

My awkward confession snapped Brannon out of his funk. "Yeah. Yeah, okay. Me, too. Can I?"

He mirrored my trajectory up and away from the island while messing with his hair. I wondered why he hesitated, since he already knew where my bathroom was.

The answer hit me like a bus.

Though his manners were suspect at best, Brannon was actually asking permission to go before me. Chivalry wasn't dead in the odd man with a heavy heart and full bladder.

"Fine," I repeated louder. "Just don't take forever."

Brannon bowed, surly once again. "Certainly, your highness."

When he strode out of the kitchen I turned on the faucet, grabbed a crystal decanter full of white wine, and took a swig of alcohol bought with the best fake ID money could buy.

The whooshing sound of running water helped distract me from overhearing the business going on in the next room. I wondered—with my enormous drink in hand—if now I'd always feel like a total sleaze within earshot of any restroom. I downed more as my new roommate flushed and returned.

"Your turn." He pointed at the container near my lips. "Give me that. You're too young to drink, anyway."

"What are you going to do, arrest me?" I took another sip. "You're not a real cop."

He snatched the shimmering glassware and upended it over his chin. When the fruity elixir hit the tip of his tongue, he choked like a child tasting a favorite dish riddled with microscopic vegetables.

"That's not vodka!" He thrust it back at me. "What the hell is this shit?"

"It's Riesling, you Neanderthal. What did you expect?"

Betrayal soaked his gaze. "You're supposed to keep spirits in those things. Riesling is a kind of wine, right? Doesn't it come in bottles to begin with?"

"All alcohol does. I think it looks nicer this way. It's cute."

"It's ridiculous," said Brannon. "Why would you do that? Do you want to make people throw up?"

I flounced past him to continue our argument from the peaceful interior of my bathroom.

"Oh, I'm so sorry, Mr. Bond," I hollered in my best foreign accent, "that I don't drink gasoline, or whale piss, or whatever else it is you think is *cool*."

I made air quotes he couldn't see.

Usakumya, who sat on the floor next to the ruined clothes I'd been too busy to fix earlier, laughed at my witty remark. We exchanged looks, his patient and mine remorseful. I'd forgotten the plight of his bloodstained fur until then.

His limbs crunched while I dug inside him for my wallet. After depositing the billfold on the back of the toilet, I placed him in the sink and plugged the drain to run his bath. A triumphant grin spread across the cheeks of my reflection. Brannon's abrupt silence meant he'd failed to find another comeback. I poured a mishmash of soaps over my bunny, massaged his body, and watched ecstatically as the water turned blue.

I caught another glimpse of my matted hair in the mirror. "You know what," I called out, "I think I'm going to take a shower."

I opened the door, retrieved a long flannel nightgown, and raised my voice again to make sure Brannon heard me. My shower's hum enveloped me with white noise as I refreshed Usakumya's bathwater, undressed, and stepped in. The day sloughed off my discolored arms and legs.

But the dirt and grime muddying my tub wasn't enough to distract me from the uncertainty of our sleeping arrangements.

I had one unusable mattress and a couch. A pile of extra blankets and pillows—old family heirlooms I couldn't bring myself to discard—sat on a shelf in my closet. Faint rustling sounds told me my guest might've already located them. I shut off the water and dried, finishing with my spirits somehow soggier than my towel.

I'd had boyfriends and a secret girlfriend in high school, but spent stolen afternoons with them instead of whole nights. And no one but Chi Ho slept over now. Frustration curled my fists.

Brannon didn't like me, and—with a little effort—I could convince myself he was the last person on Earth I wanted to fall asleep next to. My traitorous brain only entertained the fleeting notion of something more because he was so stupidly hot. I wrung out my now cool-toned Usakumya and hung him in the shower. I'd try to be a good hostess by offering my annoying roommate the couch.

When I went back to the living room, I found Brannon lounging on the floor as he flipped through one of my fashion magazines. The coffee table wedged against the front door between the entertainment center and the wall served as a makeshift desk for most of his possessions. He hadn't touched the plate shards from my morning accident, but his gun snuggled up with them near the decorative cushion cradling his head. His humble habitat lacked even a blanket, but the couch was made up with a bottom and top sheet, three pillows, and a knitted afghan folded neatly on the end.

He saw me and stiffened as he shoved his booklet back onto my shelf, fumbling with it like its contents were infectious—and on fire.

"I don't know how you can read this nonsense," he said, flustered. "Come on. We should get some sleep."

I nodded, glad he hadn't taken the opportunity to make fun of my frumpy nightgown, and burrowed into the couch.

"Get that light," he instructed. "It's going to be another early morning."

The pitch darkness appeared as twilight to my well-adjusted vision. I let go of the distinct city sounds and listened to the cadence of his even breaths. He rolled so his back faced me.

Before drifting off, I couldn't help but air the primary concern I'd tried unsuccessfully to bury after my second superhuman encounter.

"Brannon," I whispered, "Can I ask you one more question?"

He turned over. "Yes."

His voice wasn't the tiniest bit gruff.

I could see the outline of his eyes as they searched for mine. Staring into them felt far too invasive. The top of his head—rather than his naked shoulders and hard stomach littered with faint scars—seemed like the safest place to look.

He waited patiently for me to continue.

"I was just—I keep going back to how scared the mutant looked. Of me. If he isn't who we think he is—if he's not part of some plot to take over the world or—well, whatever—then I guess what I'm asking is, who is he?"

"I've been wondering the same thing," Brannon admitted.

His facial features morphed until they gave way to the calm he wore only in private. "I'm starting to think there's more to the story than we know."

"Do you think Kyle lied?"

I couldn't come up with a better explanation for the discrepancies in our knowledge of the break-in, even if I didn't suspect him one bit. The unsettling, oppressive silence emanating from his side of the wall actually made me miss him. Without Kyle's customary bangs and curses, I'd have to rely on the mellow tone of Brannon's soft and deliberate words to lull me to sleep.

"No," he said. "I've been hit that hard. I get it. Really screws with your head. I'm sure he told us everything he could."

"Yeah," I agreed. "You're probably right."

I feared if I shut my mouth too long my partner might float away down dreamland's river. He'd arrive at a point where I couldn't reach him again until morning.

And I didn't want to be alone.

My limbs grew weak. One arm tumbled off the couch.

"So, what happens next?" I murmured. "For us."

Brannon yawned. "It'll all be okay. We'll find him again, and we'll catch him this time. As long as we work together— all of us—then we'll be just fine."

I tried to let him know I heard him as my heavy eyelids fluttered. I couldn't keep them open any longer. That is, until I felt the nub of his middle and index fingers close around my dangling pinky.

He gave it a light yet reassuring squeeze; the best he could do with the swollen hand creeping out from underneath his thin pillow.

An unspeakable thrill consumed me when he let it rest

there, too tired to pull away. My waking thoughts chased each other down the drain near the base of my skull. I'd temporarily borrow him from Nuñez, if only to pretend I was lying side-by-side with someone who cared about me.

"By the way," he slurred, sure he'd finally found the best way to win our latest argument. "White wine—is for girls."

Even as he teased me, his hold never wavered. It was as strong and steadfast as ever.

As the veil of sleep crashed down on my head like a wave over the sands of a lonely white beach, I thought that perhaps —just maybe—I could sense Brannon smiling as I did the same.

10

TOO MUCH PINK

I woke up to the smell of coffee and no companion to my right. The absence of rough fingers around mine pinched my heart as I wondered if I'd invented N.E.R.D. and the mutants in a hyper-realistic dream. I peered toward my kitchen, sure I'd find Chi Ho pouring over a stack of paper menus as she figured out what to order for breakfast. Maybe after my birthday dinner we came home and drank enough wine to scramble my brain. I vibrated with relief when my vision focused and I saw Brannon pacing in front of a pot of boiling water.

He muttered to himself, but I was too groggy to think anything of it.

"There's no way he's involved. You're being paranoid."

His gauze cast was clean again. He wore the same white shirt as before, damp and untucked around the edges but mostly free of stains. Steam coming from the bathroom lingered like fog. The floral scents of my favorite soap and shampoo on someone new confused my nostrils. My stomach did a magnificent flip. I never knew lilac and vanilla could smell so manly.

Apparently, I was wrong.

Brannon struggled with the other half of his internal

monologue, clicking his stubble-covered jaw. He sucked the chocolate coating off the last espresso bean from my secret stash and crushed it with the side of the empty tin. Sandy bits slid from his palm into the roiling saucepan. His attempt to brew the world's saddest cup of coffee deserved some kind of medal.

"Hey." I spooked him with a phlegmy croak. "That's gross. Does it work?"

He dropped his makeshift pestle and glared at me as he chased it into the living room. The tenderness I'd witnessed in him as we fell asleep was gone, replaced by the rigid half-frown he wore in perpetuity.

"It's better than nothing. I refuse to drink that leafy tea you keep in those tins on the counter. It smells like fruity mold."

He went back to dig through drawers for a strainer as I emerged from my blankets.

Chi Ho's unanswered texts called to me. I rubbed the gunk from my eyes, snatched my charged phone, and took it with me to the bathroom.

Flecks of soap scum coated the inside of my tub and shower curtain. Short brown hairs sat in a satanic circle around the drain, performing some arcane ritual to summon more filth. The sink hadn't fared much better. A balled up towel, pile of rubber bands, and the hot pink Angelic Pretty shopping bag Brannon must've used to protect his cast sat beneath the toothpaste-splattered mirror. At least my tooth-brush looked dry.

I wrinkled my nose. "Why are boys so disgusting?"

I gazed up at Usakumya, hanging from his perch at a slightly different angle than where I'd left him.

Beats me. His red eyes twinkled with a mischievous secret. *He's got a really cute butt, though.*

I pursed my lips and tried to abandon the mental image of Brannon wet and naked as I devoured Chi Ho's messages.

You're so lucky! Read the first. *Nothing cool like this ever happens to me.*

I doubted she'd feel the same if we switched places.

He sounds hot. Your new bodyguard. Brannon? That's his name, right? The subject of the next made me groan as I looked back at Usakumya.

He grinned.

You should bring him by the shop tomorrow if you guys have a minute.

I didn't really want to introduce my boisterous and nosy best friend to my cranky partner, but I needed to see her. Regaining some sense of normalcy had the allure of a clear pond to a traveler in the desert dying of thirst. My stomach rumbled as I seriously considered how I'd convince Brannon to make a pit stop at Visions of Serenity.

Nai Nai wants to apologize for scaring you. She says she'll make dumplings and everything.

Chi Ho knew how to bribe me. Her grandmother's excellent cooking drew me out of my apartment on my worst days, even when I didn't feel like eating.

I'll try. I typed lightly. *Give me an hour or so.*

After combing my hair and brushing my teeth, I launched into my closet to find an inoffensive coordinate. Brannon hated attention-grabbing patterns and bows, which made my job almost impossible, but I eventually found a dress that fit the bill.

I paired my pink Pop'n Rock jumperskirt—a plain knee-length piece with no sleeves and a motorcycle collar—with a scalloped white turtleneck, matching over the knee socks, and pink rain boots decorated with subtle blue stars. A fuzzy pair of shorts underneath it all would keep me warm. Color palate aside, I looked like a Hell's Angel dipped in fairy dust.

I stashed my phone in one zippered pocket and ran back to the bathroom to grab my wallet. Then I secured my bouncy waves in a high side ponytail with the nearest pastel bow. When I emerged to show off my new outfit, I found Brannon on his bar stool like he'd been waiting.

He appraised me, swirling the speckled brown liquid in his crystal mug. "Nope. Not this again. Too loud. Too much pink. Not going to work."

"Really?" I whined. "I worked hard on this. It's subtle. Just look at the lines. There's hardly any poof. You don't like it?"

"Not at all. Change."

I bristled as he took a sip of his chunky tonic. "Into what, pray tell? I'm really trying to work with you. If you haven't figured it out by now, let me fill you in. I don't do oversized sweaters, and I don't own a lot of denim. Our options are kind of limited. And I'm not putting your dirty shirt back on!"

"I wasn't going to ask you to," he grumbled, "but let's see if we can't find something a little more age-appropriate."

He set his drink down and intentionally bumped my shoulder when he walked past.

I followed him into my closet. "What do you mean? Don't tell me you're one of those bigots who thinks a girl has to start wearing tight skirts and all black the second she turns thirteen."

"Yup, that sounds about right," he said, flipping through my hangers. "That's what a normal person does."

I snatched a pink polka-dotted skirt out of his coffee-stained hands and shoved it back onto the rack.

"You're a swine with no taste."

"No. I'm a realist. This whole queen of the candy kingdom bullshit you've got going on here is too flashy. It really doesn't work for a manhunt." He squinted like looking at me hurt as much as staring into the sun. "Besides, don't you feel weird? Going around in this kiddie stuff? Is it supposed to be sexy?"

The needle on my invisible rage-o-meter sailed off the charts. I'd heard the same stupid question a million times before my emotional control vanished in a tidal wave of mutant blood. I lunged at Brannon to shake some sense into him. He dodged out of my crippling hold with catlike dexterity and retreated into the bathroom. My fist made contact with the door as it closed, shattering the board beneath it.

"You big, ignorant asshole!" I locked eyes with him through the hole. "Lolita fashion is a Japanese reinterpretation of Rococo and Victorian garments made for modern women."

I cringed the second I said the name I tried to keep hidden. Although my favorite Harajuku style had nothing in common with the book by Vladimir Nabokov, the shared title confused almost everyone who encountered it.

I considered myself sex-positive, but in a very private way. My preferences were all pretty tame. They definitely didn't match the general public's kinky assumptions about girls in fancy pink dresses. Strangers often talked down to me —like I was a child—and then asked extremely suggestive questions in the same breath. No one seemed to realize just how creepy that was. Or what it said about how they viewed young women.

I couldn't shove the loaded syllables back in my mouth, so I pushed on with a better explanation instead.

"It's a feminist statement rejecting the male gaze. Sweet style is influenced by pop art and rave aesthetics. Hence, the youthful themes. For your information—not that you actually care—but I wear my clothes because they're interesting and beautiful. I'm not a bubbleheaded escapist, I don't want to be a kid again, I'm not trying to attract pedophiles, and it has absolutely nothing to do with sex." I shot him an accusatory glare. "Do *you* think it's sexy?"

"What? No!" The truth rang clear when he backed away and nearly tripped into my tub. "But I get it now."

"You read one of my magazines last night. They're full of fashion street snaps and brand advertisements. What part of that screams fetish to you?"

"Yeah, I get it!" he repeated, bolting both doors. "Bad assumption. My Japanese is rusty. You're right. Thanks for educating me."

"I wouldn't have to if you didn't jump to such awful conclusions about people based on how they dress!"

He remained silent until the steam behind my violent outburst fizzled.

"Lolita. Am I getting that right? I see what you're saying. I guess your stuff doesn't look like kid's clothes. They mostly wear gross sweatpants and t-shirts. Still—you've got to admit —whoever thought it up picked out a really, *really* bad name."

I sighed.

The long version of the origin story revolved around *wasei-eigo*, the borrowing and repurposing of words from other cultures. But I didn't want to confuse him, so I crossed my fingers and offered the short one, hoping he'd drop the subject.

"I'm aware. Odds are it stuck because it sounded cute."

He approached the door with caution. "That sucks for you. Can I come out now? Or are you still planning to bash my skull in?"

The opportunity to extort him dangled within my grasp.

"Only if you let me keep my outfit on." I doubled down when Brannon groaned. "We can even compromise. I'll switch my pink bow out for a white one. How's that?"

"Holly," he growled.

We both knew the threat in his voice was meaningless.

I leaned out of his line of sight and propped myself against the doorframe to pull splinters from my fist. "Enjoy your time in the bathroom, then." I teased. "You might want to clean up your mess while you're in there. You're a slob, by the way. I guess we'll have to look for the mutant later."

Defeat radiated from him. "You win. Okay? It's not like you've got anything better. Any other demands before you let me go?"

The sound of his phone ringing in his pocket cut me off before I asked if we could stop by the salon to see Chi Ho. This time he really did stick his tongue out at me when I rolled my eyes at Miley Cyrus's mangled electronic voice.

"Hello?" He spat into the receiver, redirecting his frustration. "What's wrong?"

I heard Nuñez's surprise on the other end of the line as he assured Brannon everyone in the lab was fine. He was calling because he was running late to meet us at the impound lot to rescue their vehicle.

"Shit. What time is it? They're open already?"

I snuck from my post to retrieve the bathroom key from a bowl on my nightstand and returned as their conversation wrapped up.

"Get on the bus," Brannon commanded. "We'll be there as soon as possible. Don't go in without me. I'm hurrying."

He hung up and called out to me again.

"Holly!" He pounded on the doorframe. "It's time to go. As fun as this has been, you've got to let me out. Now!"

"Only if you let me go see Chi Ho while you two deal with the car!" I unlocked and pulled the door open.

Carried by the swing of his arm, he came stumbling out and almost face-planted onto the floor. I skipped into the bedroom to avoid going down with him. When he caught himself, straightened, and squared his shoulders, I knew it'd be a massive pain negotiating the second condition of his release.

"Out of the question. We don't have time for you to visit your little friend."

I flung myself in front of him, blocking his path. "We totally do. You really think we'll get jumped before breakfast? If that other mutant's as hungry as I am, then I'm telling you there's no way. Besides, he doesn't want anything to do with me. And the people looking for him still don't know I exist. We can split up for a bit. I'll be safe."

"No." His eyes narrowed. "Move."

He ducked past my blockade, but I tailed him and begged harder as he grabbed his gun.

"Pretty please," I pleaded while he tried to ignore me. "It's not like you're going to need my help where you're going. You've got Nuñez! And he's way more capable than I am. I'd just get in your way. Where is it, anyway? Downtown? That's so close to Chinatown that you guys can come get me when you're done."

I made a pitiful face in a last-ditch effort to convince him I deserved some alone time. I'd stoop to any level in order to spend a few minutes with Chi Ho and decompress in her larger-than-life presence. Seeing the world through the blunt, reassuring lens of her advice always grounded me.

And I really needed her to fix my broken manicure. I couldn't do it by myself.

Brannon yanked the coffee table out of the way of the front door and holstered his weapon. He secured the tactical belt around his waist and looked at me as I amped up the desperation in my gaze. The staunch conviction I should go with him—held by a tremble at the corners of his mouth—lost its former strength when he saw me pouting. He bent to pick up his jacket. Its red stains didn't stand out as much after drying, but the crunchy fabric no longer swayed when he moved.

He tilted his head from side to side, weighing the pros and cons of giving in to me once more. "How far is it, exactly? I don't doubt it might be kind of hard to explain to the lot attendants why federal agents are carting Biker Barbie around town with them."

As we exited my apartment, I gave him a look to indicate —with no room for misinterpretation—that he might want to reconsider calling me names in the future.

"What? She's America's favorite doll. I didn't mean it in a bad way."

He rocked back and forth after a few long strides down the hallway, his body brimming with synthetic energy as he waited for me to catch up.

I stuck my arm through the hole to lock my deadbolt. "Does that mean I can go?"

We took the steps two at a time until we reached the lobby. The night watchman gifted us another polite nod.

I got my answer when we stopped on the sidewalk.

"I guess so. Odds are, you're right. You can sense the mutant before he has the chance to get close. I'm sure you'll be fine by yourself for an hour, but just because I'm letting you go doesn't mean I'm happy about it. You can think of it as an apology. For earlier."

I didn't believe him.

Brannon didn't seem like the type of person who tried to make amends for personal missteps. Not without the insistence of a large knife pressed against a kidney.

"No way. You're saying yes?"

He rubbed the back of his head. "I was wrong. About your clothes. I made you mad. I didn't mean to. And I'm sorry. Okay? Go see your friend so we can call it even." He stuck his good hand out. "Give me your phone."

"What?" I passed it to him. "Why? Shouldn't I keep it in case I need to call you?"

"That's going to be pretty difficult," he said, "if you don't have my number."

A cool wind whipped through us as he mashed the four buttons available to him to turn it on. He failed and grew grumpier and more adorable by the second until I snatched it back.

I had to put some distance between us.

"Why don't you know how to use a smartphone?" I asked. "What are you, some kind of alien-old man hybrid?"

The color of Brannon's cheeks deepened. "My parents are kind of, well—eccentric. I was homeschooled, so I never needed one. And the C.I.A. uses burners."

"Whatever you say, grandpa."

"Do I really look that old?" His face soured. "I turned twenty-three in August."

"Really?"

If someone asked me to guess how much older he was than me, I'd have said more than five years. He wasn't some ancient and unknowable creature. We probably shared more similarities than I guessed. Still, I didn't want to tell him what I thought of the fine, handsome lines around his eyes that danced with his rare smile—so I played my hand closer to the chest.

I studied him. "You look like crap."

"Whatever." He brushed my ego-bruising comment away. "Shut up, and tell me how to work this thing."

I made a new contact, showed him how to punch in his number, and tried to hide my disappointment when he didn't notice I'd cleverly listed his name as *00-Stupid*.

He hit save and returned my phone. "You'll have to text me the address so I have it. I won't remember if I only hear it once. That's what you kids do these days instead of calling, right? Just don't send me any of those dumb smiley faces."

Satisfied, he headed for the corner to hail a cab. One or two usually circled the park in search of joggers too rich and too tired to walk home, but none hovered that morning. Perhaps word had spread that my affluent neighbor's favorite outdoor area and the adjacent deli were no longer safe. They'd stay away until the memory of my unfortunate murders faded. A lone taxi spotted him and hustled over.

Brannon opened the door and looked back at me, unsure as to why I hadn't followed him like I always did. "We're going the same way, aren't we? You're not coming?"

"I'll just slow you down!" I shouted over my gurgling hunger pangs. "I'm going to walk. I'll be careful."

My declaration didn't inspire much confidence.

When he hesitated to enter the vehicle, its owner—a man

nearly identical to the one who drove us back from the bar—honked to inform his passenger that time was money.

"Don't worry about me," I said. Mercifully, he'd already closed the door three quarters of the way before I uttered my next request. "Say hi to your boyfriend for me!"

I instantly recoiled from my insensitivity. I'd blurted it out without thinking. Brannon quirked a confused brow at me as the car pulled away. I was only trying to solidify our common ground. I didn't mean to spill his secret to no one but the air. Maybe—with time—he'd accept that I knew and understood him. And maybe—with time—I'd learn to untangle the knot in my gut that formed whenever I thought of him and Nuñez together.

I turned south and convinced myself I was just hungry. That had to be it.

So, I took the long way to Visions of Serenity in order to grab a snack and eat my dumb, irrational, inconvenient, and impossible feelings along the way.

11

VILLAINS
UNKNOWN

I didn't usually wake up starving—but I had that day. Ferocious need clawed its way up my throat. I wanted to howl, desperate to find a pre-breakfast appetizer to satiate a growing state of hunger-induced rage with potentially catastrophic consequences. If I didn't stop for food, I'd devour all of Nai Nai's dumplings before she or Chi Ho got a single one.

And maybe I'd eat them next.

The bakery a few blocks from my apartment beckoned. A Halloween-themed cheese Danish waited for me in the window display. It was the sole survivor of the morning rush.

My pocket buzzed as I paid with cash. I hoped hiding my paper trail would impress Brannon if the subject came up. A goofy grin spread around the flaky skull held in my mouth, but my smile crumbled with my pastry when I saw Chi Ho's name instead of his fake one.

Her short messages came one after the other.

Sorry, phone was on silent.

Are you on your way?

Is the hottie with you?

I quickened my pace to show her in person. The drugstore we designated as the halfway point came into view when I remembered to text Brannon Visions of Serenity's address.

He didn't respond, but I didn't worry. I hadn't heard any gunshots, screams, or sirens during our short time apart—and I'd been carefully sifting through the noise of the city, just in case I did. He was probably busy, or ignoring me.

I crafted a second message, one exponentially more annoying than the first.

Radio silence, eh? You miss me that much already? :) :)

His phone looked too old to get regular emojis, so I had to type them out.

I dispatched it with a giggle. I'd sworn I wouldn't divulge any details about N.E.R.D. or our top-secret mission—and for the most part, I meant it—but I wanted to gossip with Chi Ho about the uneventful night I'd spent with the Stone Age jerk.

The smell of fresh fortune cookies and garlic sauces of various potencies drew me into a sprint. I rounded the corner into Chinatown. The shiny triangular roofs of its sardine-packed buildings called to me like the waiting arms of old friends. I flew by a handful of shoppers browsing overfilled carts beneath strings of colorful lanterns.

Before I knew it, I was hurtling down the empty slope to Visions of Serenity's dated storefront. Gravity propelled my speeding form like a missile on a path of destruction.

I dug my toes into the cracked cement, which did nothing but rip up huge chunks and send them flying. My thundering feet carved new potholes everywhere they landed. The soles of my indestructible rubber boots screeched like spinning tires. I groaned. Why didn't I own any cheap shoes from Taobao?

I had to think fast. I shrieked as I imagined the store's glass door and painted windows exploding if I bailed into them, eviscerating Chi Ho, her grandmother, and her cousins as they got ready to open shop.

I braced for impact and swerved into the recycling dumpster in front of the building next door. The steel wall caved like wet sand. I crumpled to the ground as the sound of the salon's over-the-door bell tinkled. Chi Ho hurried over in bedazzled slippers and hefted me out of the gutter that smelled like diesel and stale peanut oil.

"Are you okay? You really ate it hard."

I brushed myself off and she laughed—since I wasn't hurt.

When we went inside, she kicked her dirty footwear off next to a scarecrow holding a bowl of business cards. She didn't even glance at the crater I'd left behind, or notice the shredded sidewalk leading back toward my apartment.

But that was Chi Ho. Observant, as always.

I wiped dirt off my dress. Thankfully, most of it didn't stick. "I'm fine. I just suck at running."

"I know. I remember gym class." She plucked a wilted onion stalk from my hair and tossed it in the trash. "You should stick to what you're good at. That's why I told that detective he has to do all the hard work for your investigation. Physical activity isn't your thing. How's that going, by the way? I need to know."

I hated it when Brannon pressed me with questions and a time limit to answer like an unwilling participant on an obnoxious game show, but never minded when Chi Ho did the same. He didn't care what I had to say. She couldn't wait to hear it.

"Where is he, anyway? I thought you were going to bring him. Is he parking the car? I swear these tourists need to learn how to take public transit. It's so hard to find a spot around here. You look pale. Have you been eating enough?"

I almost touched my face with filthy hands. Without foundation, my new blue undertone probably made me look sick.

Nai Nai parted the beaded curtain at the back of the room, the one shielding the small hallway and stairs that led to the apartment above. Chi Ho and I barely cleared the five foot dash on the door's ruler tape—and she had me by an inch— yet we towered over her. The tiny matriarch didn't say much, but I rarely saw her without a smile.

Until Chi Ho turned sixteen and manufactured an air of responsibility, her grandmother came to babysit her and her brothers once a year when their parents took off on a child-free vacation. Her crooked smirk forever gave me the creeps. Or maybe it was the way she watched me. Not like Chi Ho's mom and dad did— like I'd corrupt their daughter if they so much as blinked—but with electric curiosity.

Like a storm chaser waiting for lightning to strike.

Her peach dress swept the floor as she approached. She glided through the empty salon with a large bowl of dumplings in her outstretched arms, past manicure tables decorated with stacked gourds and a row of massage chairs. Her wise gray eyes crinkled when she arrived in the waiting area and set the dish on the coffee table. She balanced a mug of her favorite herbal tea on its closed lid, a bright navy concoction that smelled like pine and rotting licorice.

Her knowing grin reached its toothy zenith.

Hearty tendrils of steam clouded my judgment. I couldn't stay mad at her for delivering the false prophecy that ulti- mately transformed me. Hypnotized, I didn't resist or flinch when she reached for me with both hands and pulled me down to kiss the top of my forehead.

She let go with a raspy chuckle and sat in the chair nearest the door.

"See?" Chi Ho hugged Nai Nai and nudged her at me. "I told you she feels bad. She sure did make your birthday exciting, though. I still can't believe you followed her advice. Let me go get some more bowls so we can eat. Then you've got to tell me everything!"

She zipped across the floor and vanished before I said a word. With my best friend nearby, my world flipped from all wrong to alright.

My muscles let go of the lurking tension I'd squirreled away for a day and a half. I wanted to dunk my face in my edible apology, but I'd wait until Chi Ho returned. To be safe, I backed away. My elbow landed on top of a pile of papers that slipped out from under me and fell to the floor like the dead leaves swirling outside.

When I went to pick them up, the sound of Nai Nai's happy wheezing grew louder.

Paralysis gripped me. My heart hammered in my chest as I stared at the army of black and white heads at my feet. Missing Persons posters carpeted Visions of Serenity's entryway. The once-human faces of the mutants—the one I'd killed and the one I sought—beamed at me with frightening clarity.

The two UC Berkeley students were athletes, though their bios said they played different sports. Both disappeared from the campus about forty minutes north of the city on Wednesday afternoon. I frowned as my eyes rocked between their frozen smiles. Their sudden appearance in the least likely of places sparked a whole new set of questions.

Who the hell were they?

Why would two upstanding citizens, as they were described in bold twelve-point font, live double lives as wicked spies? Could they participate in sports and run covert missions for the organization that broke into N.E.R.D.'s laboratory at the same time? Doubt weighed me down like lead.

What kind of heartless fiends took them? Didn't it make

more sense to experiment on their people rather than random innocents? If not, why kidnap these boys—loved by the same family and friends offering huge rewards for information regarding their whereabouts—rather than loner test subjects who had no one?

My gut clenched.

Someone like me.

Chi Ho returned with a wobbling tray stacked with porcelain bowls and matching soup spoons. She'd grabbed five sets by mistake, without me mentioning Brannon would be arriving with Nuñez in tow.

"Hugo Bowers." I read his name, avoiding John Lake's damning gaze.

I'd slaughtered a real person. He wasn't a monster. Not even close.

Those who kidnapped and changed him were ultimately responsible for his death. Not me. If it weren't for them, he wouldn't have been stumbling through the park in the first place. He wouldn't have scared me. I wouldn't have attacked him.

They killed John Lake.

But you stabbed me.

I jumped back as his imaginary voice made my flesh prickle. I'd unravel if I dwelled on him. I picked up a poster and zeroed in on the name of the other mutant with the swollen head I'd encountered the night before.

Chi Ho appeared by my side. "What? Oh, yeah. Some lady dropped those off this morning for us to put up and hand out to clients. You think she left enough of them? It's obvious she doesn't care about the environment."

"Hugo," I repeated.

I knew I'd heard his name before. It hadn't struck me in

the moment, but that's what the bartender shouted as I tore through his domain. John called his partner that during their walk through the park.

I didn't know what to do.

During my time with Brannon, I'd come to think of myself as capable of handling *almost* anything. But this new development launched me hopelessly out of my element. I snapped a picture with my phone for him to assess.

"Earth to Holly." Chi Ho chucked the place settings down on the table by Nai Nai and churned the air in front of me with her hands. "What is it?" She looked at the poster and locked on Hugo's kind face. "He's not really that cute, and he might be dead, anyway. No use falling for a corpse."

NEED TO TALK. I typed. My thumbs flew over the digital buttons on my screen. *HUGO IS THE MUTANT.*

"He's not dead." I exhaled as I waited for Brannon's reply. "Trust me."

Chi Ho's brain stalled while she processed my accidental confession. "What do you mean? Which one? Do you know these guys?"

I moaned as though I'd punched myself in the face with my powerful fists.

Sparkling dollar signs flashed in Chi Ho's deep brown eyes. She already knew too much.

And I'd take any excuse to tell her my harrowing tale.

Her squeal cut me off at the pass. "We're going to be rich! Or, wait. You're already rich. That's okay. You can give me the money. This time I've earned it. Finder's fee!"

She jiggled me as the phone in my hand finally buzzed. Before I tapped on the message from the man whose advice I desperately needed, Nai Nai chimed in.

"He says stay put." She patted the couch next to her. "You should sit. Eat dumplings. Long days ahead."

Chi Ho let me go and hastened to her grandmother's side, musing loudly about how we'd use her new fortune. The color drained from my face when I read Brannon's text.

Shit. Be right there. Don't go anywhere.

Nai Nai's new trick impressed and terrified me even more than the one she'd performed on my birthday.

I joined them in the waiting area. Armed with my new knowledge—that superhumans were real and I was the newest member of their ranks—I sat next to the laughing woman. I still didn't know if she was truly psychic, or just a trickster with eagle eyes. I thought I'd have time to find out later.

It didn't seem like my most pressing issue.

When Chi Ho filled our bowls, I lost myself in a melody of slurping juice from piping hot dumplings. I savored the opportunity to spend a few calm minutes enjoying a nice meal with them both.

My last one—as I haplessly guessed—before all hell broke loose.

12

STFU MIKE

It took about fifteen minutes for Brannon and Nuñez to arrive at Visions of Serenity. While I waited, it fell on me to tell Chi Ho her uncomplicated scheme to get cash fast wouldn't work. I decided not to spill the truth, and spun the dumbest story ever in its place.

I'd witnessed the two boys scuffling in the park—a fight that left one dead before the other ran. For decency's sake, I left some parts out. Like the vivid description of the bloody shower I'd taken in John Lake's guts. That wasn't polite to recount as we ate, and it didn't quite fit with my new version of events. I also managed to keep my powers to myself, even though harboring such an enormous secret gave me cramps.

Nai Nai watched us eat without touching her bowl. She giggled as I dodged the questions Chi Ho fired between bites.

I defended myself with fake details. Eventually these satisfied her curiosity about my ongoing involvement with the investigation. After I convinced her to abandon her dream of swimming in a kiddie pool full of cash, only one matter remained. Chi Ho wanted to know why we couldn't call the number on the poster advertising money for Hugo Bowers' safe return.

"I don't get it. Why aren't his parents involved? Is it legal bullshit? Why keep everything all hush-hush rather than just tell them their son is a murderer? Then they probably wouldn't miss him so much."

I concocted another half-baked lie on the spot. "It's just that, uh—" She raised an eyebrow and I panicked. "It's drugs."

"Drugs?"

"Totally," I said. "But not like weed. The hard, life-ruining stuff. The families are suspected drug lords, and the fight was probably over territory. They sent their kids to do their dirty work for them. Hugo ran because he wants out. If we catch him, he can help Brannon and his—uh—people—take down the rest of the ring. It's complicated."

She ate my fib up. "That's wild. It's like Shakespeare, but sad. I feel really bad for him now. Hugo, I mean. Not Brannon. This is his job."

Nai Nai curled the corners of her sunken eyes, catching my lies in every wrinkle. I ignored my mounting suspicion she somehow knew everything as I nodded in solemn agreement with Chi Ho.

The sound of footsteps approaching outside Visions of Serenity drew my attention. I caught the tail end of Brannon and Nuñez's conversation before I saw them.

And suppressed a groan when I figured out they were talking about me.

"Come on," said Nuñez. "How do you not know what Lolita fashion is? You've been all over the world, and you never once went to Japan? I thought you were there with your mentor from Interpol. It's like Punk or Goth for them. There's a huge community in America. They do parties and charity raffles and stuff. They've got their own online forums and everything."

They paused near the side of the salon. Brannon looked haggard and glum.

"I wasn't there for very long," he muttered. "My memory for kana sucks. I always get the characters mixed up."

Brannon sped to justify his ignorance.

"It's not like I was getting paid to sit around and watch girls. Give me a break. You only recognized it when you saw her because you spend way too much time on the internet."

Nuñez smiled. "That's what I pay myself for."

He took a step to continue inside, wearing yesterday's wrinkled clothes and dark circles like deflated tires. Lack of sleep made him look even rougher than usual. Brannon stopped him with both hands held up.

"I don't want her to think I'm some kind of pervert," he whispered. Our gazes met before his skittered away. "Please don't tell her I feel bad about what happened! I already look like an idiot."

"No promises," Nuñez teased.

Chi Ho jumped when the string of bells over the door chimed, but Nai Nai didn't move. Her polite nod skipped right past the older and shorter of the two and landed on the tired giant instead. The corners of her mouth crept up to her ears as her eyes darted between him and her granddaughter.

"Holly," said Brannon, surveying the opulent room and its occupants.

We were alone—an unusual detail I should've noticed the instant I arrived. It seemed too early to run errands, and I wondered if Nai Nai told the rest of the family to stay in the back or the apartment upstairs. Maybe she wanted to give us some privacy, though her motivations as to why remained unclear.

Chi Ho choked on broth as she tried to say hello to the strangers in front of her.

"Sup, Hols," said Nuñez.

The new nickname hugged my shoulders like a blanket fresh from the dryer, but by the time I dug myself out from under it he'd already turned to stare at Chi Ho. Her gorgeousness mesmerized most people right away. Acting like she was dying only made her more interesting.

"Is your friend okay?"

His innocent question triggered her volcanic temper, stoking an eruption the likes of which I'd never seen before. She hacked the rest of the liquid from her throat and flew out of her seat.

"Who're you?" she demanded.

Nuñez retreated from her like an animal trainer trying to escape the bite of an unpredictable lion.

Chi Ho backed him across the lobby and invaded his personal space. She tried to shove her face in his, but even with the added height of tiptoes her head didn't clear his chest. He bumped against the desk with nowhere to go.

She pressed her index finger against his breastbone, squinting to kill. "I know about Detective Brannon. He's helping Holly, but I don't know anything about you. And I can practically smell it. You have secrets."

Nai Nai clapped. Her barking laughter filled the room when Chi Ho jabbed him again, but Brannon's entire demeanor changed after her bizarre accusation. He shot me an unreadable look.

"Help. Please." said Nuñez. "Somebody."

"That's enough!" When I called to her, my bodyguard gave her detainee a nanosecond to breathe. "Diego Nuñez is our tech analyst. He's not a weirdo. You can calm down."

"If you say so." She returned to the seat next to me, but kept her eyes locked on him. "I remain unconvinced."

In a show of good faith, she handed both newcomers a bowl and pointed to breakfast. Nuñez reached hesitantly for the boat of dumplings, looking like he hoped he'd pull his arm back with his hand still attached.

Brannon watched him, shoulders tense, before he took his own meager scoop. He shoveled spoonfuls into his mouth at record speed.

"Did you have a good visit?" He glanced at the posters littering the floor. "You ready to go back to work?"

I stared at my broken nails, positive he'd force me to leave before Chi Ho could fix them.

She jumped to answer for me. "Very good, sir. Holly explained why contacting the number on the flyer is a bad idea. I'll make sure those posters end up in the trash. Good luck finding Hugo. I hope he helps you put those bastards in jail. Keeping hard drugs off the streets is important work."

Interpreting the confused head tilt Brannon gave her as detective-speak for *good work citizen*, she turned and cupped her hands against my ear. She wanted to let me know what she thought about him—and wasn't subtle about it.

At all.

"He's so sexy!" she squealed in a whisper that threatened to shatter my sensitive eardrum. "And he's not as old as he sounded on the phone. You should totally hook up when you're done working together. Have you seen the way he *looks* at you?"

Chi Ho's concerns about how well I was being taken care of vanished in Brannon's presence. But that red hot intensity she sensed behind every word he spoke to me didn't mean what she thought. I pissed him off, and not much beyond that.

She started in again as Nai Nai got up and brought two more chairs near the table. Nuñez ate and kept his eyes in his bowl while Chi Ho rattled off more made-up facts about the rise in narcotics distribution.

Brannon feigned understanding. He glanced at me a few times as she rambled on, either baffled or impressed I'd mislead her so well. I shrugged, adding a deliberate blink that said drugs were the best excuse I could conjure for a convoluted murder investigation.

I nudged the poster sitting on the table in his direction.

The smaller one, I mouthed, *on the right*.

He finished the food in his lap, stuffed the page in his pocket, and stood.

"Thanks for all your help, Miss—?" He had to take his informant's name for an official report that didn't exist.

"Lee Chi Ho, no Miss," she said. "But you can just call me Chi Ho. I think Lee makes me sound like an old white guy."

I knew that wasn't the only reason, but I didn't correct her.

Nai Nai shook her head. "Her mom decided. Wanted her to be tough, like a boy. But she's strong enough for ten men."

"What she said." Chi Ho smiled at her. "For pronouns, I go by she/her or they/them. Up to you."

Brannon adopted the same phony, arrestingly charismatic tone of voice he'd once used on me. "We'll be in touch soon, I'm sure. I promised to keep your friend safe, and I meant it. When we find our fugitive, you can have her back."

I didn't know if he believed what he said, but his speech made Chi Ho grin. The soup in my stomach somersaulted. In all likelihood, it'd be impossible to server my ties with N.E.R.D. even after we found Hugo. If Doctor Laura could reverse the effects of her serum, I'd return to my normal life with a normal body. If she ran out of the first round of samples with no cure in sight, she'd have to take more. At least I'd probably be allowed to come and go as I pleased, tested on an outpatient basis rather than held prisoner in her stinky aquatic laboratory.

"Let's go." Brannon tapped his foot, leaning toward the front door.

Nuñez drank his last drops of soup and turned to Chi Ho. He offered her a cautious olive branch to squash the bad vibes between them.

"Thanks for breakfast. It was awesome."

She sniffed at her grandmother, and he blushed before mumbling thanks to the right person.

Nai Nai let loose another chuckle as she reached for his face. She caressed the space around Nuñez's eyes with a tender hum, smoothing his brows with her thumbs. Her soft touch puzzled him, but he humored her to be polite. She glanced at Chi Ho when she let him go.

He looked, too—and away again a heartbeat before she noticed—as he got up to follow Brannon. The fanfare of Visions of Serenity's low-tech doorbell played them out as Chi Ho wrapped both arms around me.

She squeezed. "Take care of yourself. Stay aware, and do everything Detective Brannon says, okay?"

"Okay," I promised with a feather-light pat.

She released me with a devilish wink. "Especially if it involves handcuffs."

I tried not to trip over the coffee table as I scrambled up before she got a good look at my face.

Nervous word vomit spewed out of me. "Eww, ha ha. That's gross. You're gross. You know I'm not into that. He doesn't have them, anyway. At least, not right now! They're —uh—in the car. I've got to go. Bye!"

I waved at Nai Nai as I went through the door. Chi Ho remembered her last well-wish and shouted it at my back.

"Oh, and have fun at your tea party tomorrow! I hope you still get to go!"

How did I forget about the Halloween celebration bound to be the biggest event of the year? I loved the idea of attending, in theory, but social gatherings with other Lolitas always revved my anxiety. They were beautiful, gabby, and asked personal questions to get to know me that I wasn't emotionally prepared to answer.

Reservations aside, I didn't want to cancel due to N.E.R.D.-related circumstances. I'd never give up an opportunity to show off my newest coordinate, even if parading around like a rich peacock antagonized the same girls whose outgoing natures I admired. From afar.

I jogged to catch up with my coworkers as Brannon pulled ahead of Nuñez. A harsh static charge zipped between them and took the place of playful banter.

Was it my fault? Did Nuñez overhear Chi Ho telling me to pursue Brannon? Was he angry at me? I had to deflect.

"Why do you think he's so mad? Did you find anything on the traffic tapes?"

"Nope," he said. "Whoever took our stuff is good. No posts caught my eye on any apps, and I didn't find a single suspicious or abandoned vehicle the right size. Did see a kid in a hoodie hauling ass through a couple of intersections, though. Night joggers are freaky. Really dedicated. You know what I'm saying?"

I twitched, ready for him to strike at any moment and call me out for plotting with his new nemesis to steal his boyfriend. When he opened his mouth again, I had my best defense hovering behind pursed lips. I'd reassure him I wasn't interested in any kind of romance with Brannon. I wished them nothing but countless years of happiness.

To my surprise, the thought he aired was totally unrelated.

"Was not expecting that—" He glanced back at the salon. "Your friend Chi Ho. I never knew someone that pretty could be so scary. I mean, she's kind of intense. And that's kind of awesome. But why'd she come after me like that? Did I say something weird? Do I look intimidating? Or gross? Or mean? Do I smell? I know I haven't showered in a day. Or two. But I didn't think it was that bad…"

My anxiety ramped down. He wasn't thinking about me at all.

"Don't worry about it. She's always been overprotective of me. Ever since we were little. I don't know why." I lied again. "It's not like I can't handle myself."

"Oh yeah," he said, "Mike told me about the way you chased down the mutant. No hesitation, like Rambo. He was impressed."

My heart stalled like an old tractor. I couldn't believe Brannon said something nice about me. "Wait. Really?"

"Yup." Nuñez smiled like he knew something I didn't. "You just took off after him. That's pretty cool."

We rounded the corner and Old Red came into view.

"Well." I paused. "I didn't catch him."

No one ever complimented me on anything other than my unique clothing. His praise stuck to me like one of Doctor Laura's gold stars, but I didn't know how to show it without looking stupid. I wasn't a super secret agent like him, or the grump in front of us who stiffly shoved his keys into the driver's side door. I might be—one day—if I couldn't be cured. The thought of undertaking such a huge responsibility made me queasy.

"You two coming," called Brannon, "or what?"

Agitated, Nuñez yelled back. "Si, capitán!"

I'd always thought dropping into a different language was a TV cliché. The affectation wasn't natural. From him, it sounded like a warning.

He switched back to English. "I swear, he needs to learn to lighten up. He can be a real tool when he's in military mode."

"I've never heard you speak Spanish before." I was still stuck on his abrupt transition.

"I don't, much. It's hard on me. I'm just being extra to piss him off."

Brannon's pointed gaze bounced against the rearview mirror. It grated against me like sandpaper. I pictured myself in the back as the tension built between them in the front of the car. With me there third-wheeling, it'd be impossible for them to make up. If I wanted to physically split the awkwardness, I had to place myself in the passenger's seat.

I peeled away from Nuñez on our patch of sidewalk. "Shotgun!"

"That might be kind of hard!" he shouted as I ran toward the car. "Since you broke the door. Remember?"

As I approached, I saw the gnarled barrier bolted askew to Old Red's main body. I slowed—concentrating on where and how hard my feet fell—and circled around the bumper.

"Doesn't matter. I'll do it this way."

I motioned for Brannon to open his door and pushed inside when he did. Climbing over him to reach the empty seat seemed logical—until the cumbersome reality of maneuvering kicked in. I twisted to avoid crushing his legs or kneeing him in the crotch as he thrashed beneath me, trying to eject me from his personal bubble.

"What are you do—Get off of me!"

His hands found my haunches and shoved me off-balance. The sensation of his palms against my fuzzy butt distracted me from sticking a careful landing. Hidden metal crunched between the seat cushion and the floor as I rearranged my limbs. Brannon tried to make heads or tails of my incomprehensible desire to sit with him as the third member of our party came crashing in.

Nuñez, with tears in his eyes, mimicked the gleeful shrieks of a sadistic child wielding a rubber mallet against a hoard of plastic gophers. "That's genius!" he laughed. "Oh my God, Holly. You're too good. "

"Very funny, I get it." Brannon started the car and pulled the wheel away from the curb. "Cut it out. Now's not the time."

"You should have seen the look on your face." Nuñez acted out an electrocuted shiver before he congratulated me. "Way to go. Looks like you're way better at messing with him than I'll ever be."

When we high-fived, he hit the palm I held steady for him. I didn't want to swing my arm toward his with more potentially bone-shattering force.

Brannon kept his eyes focused on the road, his jaw clenched as we went south toward Hunters Point and the laboratory. Even Nuñez heard his teeth grinding. He placed his hand on his shoulder and broke the thick silence.

"Hey, what's your deal? You've been acting really weird ever since we got to the nail place. It's okay. You can tell me."

"Holly." Brannon addressed me instead of him. "Did you

hear a pop? Next to you? We should stop to check that the door's secure."

"I didn't hear—" I started to argue the truth before his dark, sidelong glance changed my mind. "Well, wait. Maybe I did."

"You think something's wrong?" asked Nuñez.

We pulled into the parking lot of an empty warehouse.

A nervous tingle started in my toes and worked its way up. "I guess?"

Brannon shut the car off in an area obscured from pedestrians and the road by a rusty shipping crate. Our pit stop's severe outdoor atmosphere couldn't hold a candle to the storm brewing in the car. The most clear and present danger came from the man next to me as he let out a sad sigh, unbuckled his seatbelt, and shifted around.

"Dude," said Nuñez, "what's going on? I'm not joking. You're really starting to scare me."

I stifled a cry when Brannon slid his good hand underneath the hem of his jacket.

He placed it on the hilt of his weapon. Fear flashed in his eyes.

"Diego." He used Nuñez's first name to show him how serious he really was. "Absolutely no bullshit. I need you to be straight with me. Right now. Are you working for anyone else? More specifically, the people who broke into the lab?"

Nuñez stiffened, blindsided. "What? No way. How could you think that?"

"You're going to have to do better," he said. "I need an answer."

"My word isn't enough? How long have we known each other? And I've been with Doc, like, forever. Why would I sell her out? And to who?"

I held my breath as I watched Brannon palm his concealed firearm.

"I didn't want it to come to this." he said. "You have to believe me. But I'm done taking chances. I worked it over in my brain all night and early this morning, trying to come up with a better explanation. I don't think the break-in could've happened without an inside man. Those people had to know where to get in, and exactly what to take. I didn't want to point the finger, but if even Chi Ho could pick up something off about you—and seconds after meeting—well, that adds to the long list of reasons to follow my gut."

"You're willing to throw away our entire relationship?" Nuñez bared his teeth. "Everything you know about me? And all because a person we just met made some baseless assumptions?"

"That was the last straw." His heated words raged like wildfire, but the last letter caught in his throat. "After I saw that poster, the one with the missing students. Hugo Bowers and John Lake. To convince two jocks to sign up for experimental testing, it'd have to come from someone young. Relatable. Nonthreatening. Someone like you."

"We've got names. Why aren't we concentrating on that? I can run them through the system and find out who they are!"

"Don't try to throw me off," said Brannon. "I've had a lot of time on my hands over the past year. Enough to read into everyone's background at N.E.R.D., and your story is the only one that doesn't check out. The C.I.A. has no record of you. I let it slide when we got closer, hoping it was a harmless error like Kyle's missing address, but—"

Nuñez's transparent hurt gave way to confusion. "Wait, wait. Hold up for one second."

"You're intelligent. A computer genius. Skilled with

knives and guns. It's clear you're trained, but I don't know by who."

Confusion became incredulous fury. "Mike, are you even listening to yourself? We spend practically all of our time together. How could I keep such a huge secret from you? We share *everything*. Dude, there's a pretty good chance I'm wearing *your* underwear right now. I don't even know what I grabbed out of the clean hamper. It was dark. I got dressed in a hurry!"

"You think I like confronting you like this?" Brannon couldn't hide the tearful glint in his eyes. "You're my best friend."

"I'm not a double agent," Nuñez declared. "And I wouldn't betray you."

He leaned forward to blast his own theory into play.

"Hell, you've got more reasons than anyone to screw us over. I know how bored you are with nothing to do in the lab. Basically all you ever do is complain about it. I bet you'd love to work with some brand new agency. Yeah! Then you'd get to feel useful and act like a big goddamn hero while throwing us off their scent. How do we know you're not the traitor?"

My world came crashing down when Brannon's emotional control finally cracked. He pulled his gun from its holster.

"Damn it!" he roared, aiming it between Nuñez's horrified brown eyes. "I don't have time for this. The clock is ticking."

The intensity of their exchange rendered me speechless. They'd forgotten I existed, and my invisibility made it even more jarring when I threw myself into the middle of their vicious argument. The look of absolute heartbreak that washed over Nuñez's face proved his innocence. I had to save him.

"Boys!" I hollered at the top of my lungs. "You two, stop it. Right now!"

I pounced to wrestle the loaded gun away from Brannon.

"Give me that!"

Startled by my attack, his grip slackened around the handle. Nuñez grabbed the barrel and shoved it away from his head as I pinned his adversary's chest against his seat. Brannon gasped, immobilized by my arm as I pressed the air from his lungs. I ripped the weapon from him, rolled down the window, and tossed it away. I watched the shiny black speck sail toward the horizon, unaware the man I held was starting to go limp and turn blue.

"Holly!" Nuñez's hand bolted from the pocket with the outline of his knife. He pushed me off and winced when a single shot popped when the pistol hit the ground somewhere in the distance. "Let go. You're really hurting him!"

Yelping, I released Brannon who coughed as a heavy lump congealed in my throat. Misery choked me.

Sure, I didn't really like anything about him, except his spectacular cooking. We didn't get along. His company barely rated mediocre. It shouldn't have inspired the need within me that it did to be near him as often as possible. Still, I couldn't bear it if my heroic rescue persuaded him to hate me forever.

It just wasn't fair.

"Are you out of your mind?" he fumed. "You could have killed me!"

"Like you were going to kill Nuñez?" I fired back. "Pot. Kettle. Hi. How's it going?"

"I wasn't going to shoot—"

His protest fizzled when a pained look from Nuñez caused the seriousness of his actions to sink in. He didn't seem as shaken as he should have, but his voice was low and strained.

"It sure looked like it," he said. "Dude. That is so not right."

"I needed to know the truth," said Brannon, massaging his bruised sternum. "We can't keep spinning our wheels while our adversaries get away. Or regroup to hit us harder a second time."

His stubbornness made me livid. How could he act like such a child with so much at stake? They loved each other. That'd never been clearer. I wasn't invested in their relationship, but I didn't want them to break up over a huge misunderstanding.

Especially not one I felt tangentially responsible for.

"Don't you think," I started a speech sure to end their fight, "that Nuñez would've pulled a gun on you too if he was working for someone else? I'm sure supervillains arm their spies. Come on. It's blatantly obvious you two care about each other. He'd never double-cross you. I think you really need to take a deep breath, slow down, and talk. Couples counseling is now in session. Who wants to go first?"

It worked. They momentarily abandoned their grudges to stare at me.

"Wait." Brannon spoke after a long pause. "What? You mean us?"

That wasn't the reaction I was looking for.

"Yes, you. Who else would I be talking to?"

"So. Okay. Hold on," said Nuñez, sifting through what I'd given them. "Let me get this straight. You think we're— together? Like, romantically? And thought now was a good time to bring that up?"

They blinked at me. Brannon's lethal persona disappeared and left unguarded sincerity in its wake.

"Wow. You really think someone as cool as D would want to date me? I kind of suck."

The strength of their bond—even if what they shared wasn't what I'd thought—tempered the misery fogging Old Red like mustard gas.

My cheeks went supernova.

I'd accidentally let Brannon know I thought of him as a real person. One capable of commitment. And affection. And possibly *sex*. It took every ounce of willpower I had not to sprint down the nearest dock and dive headfirst into the Pacific. I still got bi vibes from Nuñez. I couldn't imagine Brannon with anybody else if he did like men. Truthfully, I had no clue.

Either way, I looked like a fool.

And I vowed then and there to never speculate about anyone's orientation or relationship status ever again.

"I just—it's—you both, you," I stammered. "You live together. You work well as a team. You wear each other's clothes. You're so physical, always pushing and stuff! And you tease each other, you know, in that I'm-flirting-with-you-by-saying-mean-things-but-not-really, kind of way."

Brannon's sharpness returned. "Like how we're always busting each other's balls? I definitely see what you're saying. It makes perfect sense, and I can see it. But the thing is— we're *guys*."

"Yeah," said Nuñez. "We just do that. It only means something like, fifty percent of the time. Maybe more for me."

"Oh." Embarrassment hijacked the pathway from my brain to my lungs and made it hard to breathe. "I guess so."

The two almost laughed, but the sound blew out with as much cheer as a thin stream of air whistling from a pricked balloon. They weren't happy.

Brannon turned the engine over and crept back out onto the road. He opened and closed his mouth like a beached trout, glancing at Nuñez in the rearview mirror. When he found the right words, I recovered enough to warn him with a sideways look to keep his tone civil.

"So, you're not a double agent," he said, "and neither am I. I know Laura would never compromise her life's work. And Kyle—well—he's a smart kid, but he's not exactly an evil mastermind. He would've vanished into the night with whoever broke in if they were working together. They wouldn't have roughed him up and left him there."

Before chasing his line of questioning to its ultimate end, Brannon reexamined its worth. He didn't want to risk destroying what remained of his friendship with Nuñez.

"So, we still don't know anything about Hugo, or who made him. But—while we're on the subject of unsolved mysteries—it'd be great if you could explain why you're not listed anywhere." He fidgeted when no reply came, running his hand through his hair. "Here it is. The perfect opportunity to level with me."

Nuñez gazed out the window.

Brannon grabbed my leg and squeezed with a plea in his exhausted eyes. His odds of peacefully extracting the information he sought were better with two against one. I decided to help, even though I was still firmly planted on the other N.E.R.D.'s side.

"I think you should hear him out. It can't hurt. At this point."

Nuñez weighed his slim options and sighed. His dismissive puff let Brannon continue.

"I just want to know why you don't show up in any personnel databases. You can be honest with me. I promise, I won't judge. You know my sad story, and I should've asked for yours a long time ago. I hope you can forgive me for not doing that sooner."

I looked at him as he drifted off again, lost in thought. Maybe one day I'd discover the source of the memory that transported him back to a tragic moment captured like a snapshot. What I knew for sure, as Nuñez took a breath, was that I'd soon learn more about the most secretive and versatile member of our team.

"I'm glad you're both sitting comfortably," he said.

I positioned myself to give him the undivided attention he deserved.

"It's kind of a long story, so bear with me. We might be here for awhile."

13

PARAPSYCHOLOGY
AND PIZZA

Nuñez, as it turned out, wasn't a C.I.A. agent. He wasn't a plant from an internal service assigned to observe Doctor Laura's progress. He wasn't a hired killer who decided to stick around N.E.R.D.'s basement playing video games rather than completing a contract on Brannon's predecessor. He was —until captured and hired by the U.S. government—a growing drug syndicate's best man and worst nightmare.

I didn't want to believe it. A twist in my gut told me I couldn't if I wanted to be a good person. Nuñez wasn't the villain from the synopsis of a bad cop drama. He had a sticker of a cat pooping rainbows on his laptop and ate every meal like a starving Muppet. Instead of sorting him into a box, or using snap judgments like a barrier between myself and reality, I made my brain shut up.

I listened.

His parents married after graduating Cal State Pomona. He was born shortly after. In first grade, his mom's mental health spiraled—and so did his dad's ability to help her.

"He left for good," Nuñez said. "Mom could barely take care of herself. Her pops—Grandpa—came from Tijuana to get me before they took her to the hospital. No one stateside had the time or money for another kid. He had lots of both. And Mexico's not that far from SoCal. I could visit a ton."

He shrugged with lips held tight, letting the pain of childhood memories slide off his shoulders.

"It was supposed to be temporary. But I haven't seen her since. Or anyone, really."

I couldn't get over how similar our stories were. Same loss. Different endings. I struggled to keep up as he talked in fast-forward.

Grandpa owned a computer repair shop. Tinkering together on weekends imparted a love of technology to his grandson that taught him resourcefulness and self-sufficiency. Their lives remained uneventful until a local kingpin caught wind of the duo able to fix all kinds of electronics. That's when their successful business fell under criminal control a few months before Nuñez turned twelve.

We'd already parked Old Red in the lot of the empty reptile store when he reached the next part. His expression changed, and so did his voice. It became slower, steadier, and deceptively nonchalant. Brannon didn't notice the practiced switch. But I did. I'd rehearsed a thousand versions of the same routine in my old bedroom's mirror, curtains shut to avoid catching a glimpse of the cornfield reflected outside my window. It was poetry for liars—spoken word to convince everyone else that you're A-okay.

"They took me out of school, and I started working." He paused. "Let's just say—that's where I learned how to use a knife. And pretty much any kind of gun. I didn't sell. When I wasn't fixing things or embezzling money, I was an errand boy. And—trust me."

The act stopped. His eyes became hollow.

"You don't want to know what that means."

On top of his other duties, he drove shipments across the border. A real U.S. passport let him cross back and forth with ease. His likeable demeanor and youthful face meant he never got searched. Nuñez skirted over the rest of his early years until authorities apprehended him at eighteen. After he single-handedly orchestrated one of the largest drug busts of the decade.

"I couldn't keep going," he said. "Not after Grandpa died. That's when I didn't have anything to lose. Not anymore. What were they going to do if I got caught? Kill me? I didn't care. A part of me wanted to die."

Brannon grimaced when he guessed why. "Because you would've rather been dead than working for them."

Nuñez didn't say anything, but he nodded.

"How'd you do it?" I asked.

"I'd been teaching myself hacking for years. All I had to do was pick the day, the next time I was supposed to escort another big convoy to Beverly Hills. The guy who ran everything used to be a talent manager. He knew every contact in town. We packed the trucks with mountains of coke for more rich assholes. That's when I snuck away to flood the D.E.A. servers with the warehouse's security footage. I encrypted it so they couldn't turn it off on their end, and included details in the code about where we were going to be at what time. Then I prayed I'd make it for the next twenty-four hours—or as long as it took for them to come pick me up. I was kind of winging it…"

"And it worked?"

The hint of a smile appeared on him for the first time since being held at gunpoint. "Yup. And they took everyone down. During my interrogation, I told them I could turn the live stream off. They needed me. I was the only one who could cancel their subscription to the Cocaine All-The-Time Channel."

"I'm impressed," said Brannon, "but that still doesn't explain how you got here."

Nuñez prickled. "Be patient. I'm almost there. Can you do that?"

The mood between the two hadn't improved since our heated detour, no doubt because Brannon hadn't apologized. Nuñez only addressed his attacker when he absolutely had to.

"I struck a deal," he told me, "in exchange for no jail time. Besides cleaning their network, I'd tell them whatever they wanted to know. I gave them my boss, big members—where they lived, who their friends were. I spared no detail. Those bastards had it coming. I didn't get to see it, but I bet those middle-aged white guys were surprised when they ran the names and found out how many drug lords look just like them."

I was in awe of his bravery. "That's incredible. Weren't you scared?"

"Thanks," he said. "And yeah, scared shitless, but the feds promised to put me in witness protection—or something like it. That made me feel a little bit better. Someone high up must've heard about the stunt I pulled with their computers. They knew I was good with tech, so I got sent to N.E.R.D. where I'd be useful. Laura and Amanda assumed I was C.I.A. when I got here—some boy-genius like Kyle— and I never bothered to correct them. It didn't seem worth it."

"That's it?" asked Brannon. He yelled at me instead of listening to Nuñez. "What the hell was that, then? Back at the nail joint. Your friend went right for the throat. What kind of person goes after a complete stranger that way? Can we even trust her not to go blabbing to everyone what she thinks she knows about Hugo?"

"She's not nuts!" I leapt to Chi Ho's defense. "But she might be psychic."

I wasn't sure if he believed me.

"Well, Nai Nai thinks she is," I said. "That's her grandma. The old lady we had breakfast with. Apparently, it's a family thing. She says they can both see the future. Maybe sense auras. I don't know—all that stuff. It might not be true."

The startling accuracy of their predictions over the last two days hung with me. My revelation inspired some hesitant curiosity in Nuñez, but Brannon frowned like he wanted a better reason.

"Chi Ho probably jumped on Nuñez because he took her off-guard. She wanted to figure out who he was. If you haven't noticed by now, she's kind of hyper-vigilant when it comes to my safety."

"Big understatement," said her victim.

I apologized. "I'll admit that her timing wasn't great on this occasion. Especially since *he* was already suspicious of you."

I pointed at Brannon—who did nothing but sulk—before asking the question I'd had since Nuñez's tale began.

"Anyway, if you're still here, then those people are still after you. Am I right?"

His answer whistled out. "Nah. I doubt it. That was so long ago. Grudges like that are forever, don't get me wrong. But you're free, you know, once they forget about you. Until they remember again."

"Then why stay with N.E.R.D.?" asked Brannon.

"Dude, would you give me some space!" Nuñez snapped. He took a steadying breath. "Honestly? I hoped the system forgot about me. It might sound strange, but I really like it here. For four years it's been nice and quiet. I've been able to live my own life. There's nobody around forcing me to do awful things I don't want to. No one to threaten me the second they don't get the answers they want. That is, before today."

"Can we move past that, already?" Brannon threw his hands up. "I didn't have all the information. I was just trying to protect Laura and Kyle."

"We should go inside," Nuñez said to me as he exited the vehicle. "Do you have a copy of that flyer with the mutants' faces on it? Maybe with some digging we can find out where they were last seen. While they were still human."

The driver's side door flew open and slammed shut.

"At least wait for me!"

Brannon ran into the storefront as I carefully climbed out of the car. I steeled myself against the frightening impact of the building's monstrous scenery and hurried to arrive at the elevator, led by the frazzled sound of his voice.

"Let's be realistic." He tried to corner his quarry inside the metal box. "You'll have to talk to me eventually."

"Do you want to press the button?" Nuñez asked me, looming in the corner.

Another groan from Brannon obliterated his commitment to giving him the silent treatment.

"Did you really mean what you said?" He spat at him, spooking both of us. "Back there in the car?"

"What do you mean?" asked Brannon. "I don't get it."

We arrived at the bottom of the shaft. The door rumbled sideways into the wall and Nuñez crossed the lobby with a rocket-propelled stride. He stopped in front of the sealed door.

"That I'm your best friend. Because if I really was, then you wouldn't have done that."

"I—well—" Brannon started sweating beneath his hot glare. "Yeah, you are. I guess—if I'm being honest—you're my only friend."

He slid past him to input the code to disable the backup security system, and used the intercom to announce our presence to Doctor Laura and Kyle. With the bewildered eyes of a puppy shoved off new furniture, he asked the world's stupidest question.

"Am I your best friend?"

The opportunity to apologize sat gift-wrapped for him, but Brannon didn't know how to take it.

Nuñez sighed and opened the door. "You were until you held that gun in my face."

Doctor Laura overheard what he said and honed in on Brannon with fierce suspicion. Rather than sitting with the machine gun, she stood next to the reorganized work table with some kind of magic potion in hand. An old rock song played on the radio by her elbow.

"Gun? What gun? *Your* gun? What happened? What did you do?"

She put down the beaker and stomped over to condemn him before any of us answered. A pile of playing cards and granola bar wrappers near the abandoned barricade whooshed and scattered, spreading a small mess on the floor that was cleaned overnight.

"Let me tell you later." I gently took her arm and led her away. "Everyone's fine. We didn't run into any danger. It was all a misunderstanding, but I'm pretty sure they need time to figure it out on their own."

That didn't satisfy her completely, but it gave Brannon a chance to set aside his personal problems to relaunch our mission to locate the other mutant.

He withdrew the poster from his pocket and handed it to Doctor Laura. "We've got a name. Hugo Bowers. The kid on the right. He's the one Holly saw."

She scowled at the new puzzle piece. "UC Berkeley. That doesn't make sense. How did he get mixed up in all this?"

"Whoever took our serum took him," Brannon replied. "That's my best guess. And John Lake. Why those two? Maybe they wanted athletic subjects to pad the success of their tests. I'm not sure, but there is one thing we know now. He's not an evil monster or a trained soldier. Holly was right. He's scared and he's running away from the people who kidnapped and tortured him. The easiest way to reel him in will be to convince him we're on his side."

I figured that might be difficult, since he was terrified of me.

"How do you suggest we find him?" I asked. "Do we drive around the city all day hoping I'll pick up the scent? I'm not a bloodhound."

"Right, I forgot." He took aim with vitriol, harboring resentment inspired by my misconduct in the car. "You're an attack dog. Just let me talk to Laura."

His justified anger stabbed me in the chest. I sucked in a breath to patch the wound together.

Rather than stay where I wasn't wanted, I went to stand by Nuñez. We leaned against a fish tank and watched Brannon two-step away from Doctor Laura as she interrogated him about our eventful morning.

"So—" I tapped one of his crossed arms. "This might be a bad time to ask, but—uh—for clarity's sake, you and Brannon, you don't, you've never liked each other? Like that?"

He relaxed a little and scanned my purpling face. "You

don't have to be so formal. You can call him Mike like the rest of us."

I'd never get used to that, but I didn't say as much.

"And no. I like people. He only likes girls, once he gets to know them."

Nuñez was pan. And Brannon fell somewhere on the ace spectrum? That must have been what Doctor Laura meant. My erratic heartbeat's brakes malfunctioned. I was going to crash.

We had a chance, even if I absolutely did *not* want one.

Maybe.

Someday.

"You're bi, right?" he asked. "I saw your phone case."

I just blurted out another ridiculous question.

"But what about his tattoo? Not trying to stereotype—I know that's wrong and I shouldn't. I'll stop. But it's so—feminine. It doesn't match, and I guessed—"

Nuñez didn't let me flounder. "He got it for a friend that died. On the mission that flailed before he got sent here. He drew it himself."

I couldn't wrap my head around what that revealed about Brannon before his booming voice invaded our quiet corner. He shouted over Doctor Laura, changing the subject back to the lost mutant boy.

"I know I said earlier that I wanted you to sever their tele-pathic connection, but now I want you to do the opposite."

"Amplify it?" Doctor Laura halted. "That's impossible. We would need to remove all outside stimuli from Holly's scope of view. Even then, the path might only work one way. She probably wouldn't be able to have a full conversation with him."

"We've got to find a way to do it," he insisted. "We need

to talk to Hugo again. Longer this time. It's risky if he's fallen back into custody since last night, especially if he starts acting weird while they're watching. It's still our best chance to get the answers we need. We have to hope he's out there on his own. Then maybe we can draw him to us."

A muffled flush from the unisex bathroom next to the rec room announced Kyle's arrival. He crossed to my other side as Brannon and Doctor Laura kept arguing.

When her bodyguard didn't—or wouldn't—acknowledge her points, she abandoned calm and yelled at him in the plainest terms. Without an isolation chamber, a lidded hot tub full of salt water, his request was impossible to fulfill. The pieces of luxury equipment cost a fortune.

That was why she didn't have one.

"What's going on?" Kyle whispered, wiping the remains of a nap from his eyes. "Why are they fighting? What'd I miss?"

The back of his head looked better with a crusty scab than the bandage he'd worn the day before.

"Lots," I said as we watched them. "The mutant has a name. Hugo Bowers. Kidnapped college student."

He stifled a hiccup. "What? How do you know?"

The way his voice trembled made me worry he'd suffered some brain damage from his injury after all.

"Found a flyer in my friend's nail salon. Names and faces. He's not a spy. Brannon wants to send a psychic message with my powers to find out who took him. That's what they're fighting about."

He reiterated the words of his mentor. "The connection won't work unless he's close, but that's probably for the best. You don't want to talk to that scary mutant anyway, right? That's asking way too much of you."

I didn't need him to protect me, but knowing I had someone looking out for my general well-being warmed my heart.

Even if it was just Kyle.

"It's a good thing, really," he repeated, relieved, "that it's impossible."

An idea struck Nuñez like a semi-truck. Excitement parted the storm clouds around his head as he joined our conversation.

"No, it's not."

"What?" Kyle and I asked as one.

"The Ganzfeld Experiment!" He cried out, hands cupped around his mouth.

Brannon and Doctor Laura stopped screaming at each other and looked at him.

Curiosity replaced the exasperation in her eyes. "What are you saying? I'm not sure I'm familiar…"

"Me neither," said Brannon. "What's that?"

To help us all, Nuñez broke his vow of silence again. "I saw it on TV, on some ghost hunting show. It's this paranormal psychology thing. That chamber, what did you say, Doc? It's for sensory deprivation?"

"That's right," said Doctor Laura, "but I've never heard of this. You're going to have to explain to me how it works."

"Okay, this sounds bizarre, I know—but hear me out. You tape ping pong balls over someone's eyes and stick them in a quiet room with headphones playing white noise. Then you flash red lights at them. It makes regular people hallucinate terrifying shit. For psychics, it's supposed to turn their abilities up really hard. I can show you what I mean so you can see for yourself. I'm thinking it might totally work. Right?"

"Great idea." Brannon latched onto his lifeline. "We've

got everything we need right here. Fire up a computer and let's figure out how to do it."

Nuñez's lips thinned. He begrudgingly acknowledged the order and walked over to the terminal in the far right corner of the room.

We crowded around as he scoured the internet for a detailed set of instructions. After a few failed searches, the information we sought popped up on a website with a hideous red and yellow header. Its sidebar advertised ancient artifact sales and vampire dating sites. When I read what the procedure entailed, I let go of the knot tying my shoulders together. It didn't seem too lengthy or invasive.

Doctor Laura chewed the flashing words skeptically. "I don't know. This doesn't sound very scientific."

"I agree," Kyle said, feigning authority. "It's probably dangerous, too. Looks like it'll induce seizures. Think of Holly."

"Will it hurt?" I looked to the smartest N.E.R.D. in the room for her input. "I mean, if it works at all. Will it fry my brain? Because I'm willing to do it as long as it's kind of safe. Maybe I can get a short message out to Hugo. Even if he can't talk back."

"We should try," said Brannon. "Think about it, Laura. How long will it take? A half-hour? Maybe an hour, max? It's a shot in the dark, but it's one worth taking."

With only her intern to back her up, she gave in.

"Alright, but you're all out of your minds. Holly, Kyle's right in thinking there's a good chance it'll cause nothing but convulsions. But those won't kill you. I guess. We can set up in one of the empty patient rooms. Let's get started. Mike, it looks like you get your Hail Mary after all."

She sighed and scooted away with Kyle to find a piece of

paper and something to write with, smoothing his wild cowlick as they went.

Nuñez took a step back from the bats tangoing across the top of the computer screen. "I'm still hungry. What about you, Hols? Want to go with me to get a snack?"

I walked with him to the kitchen. Brannon hurried after us.

"How can you two think of food right now? We've got more important things to discuss."

"I don't think anyone invited you." I sneered. "You should go help Kyle and Doctor Laura."

I'd felt horrible about almost suffocating him an hour ago, but that guilt waned with each passing second he didn't use to apologize to Nuñez. Saying sorry wouldn't absolve him of attempted murder, but it seemed like the best starting point. He'd said it to me after assuming I wore my clothes for disgusting reasons. Why couldn't he extend the same courtesy to his best friend for a mistake a billion times worse?

"Can you eat and talk?" He wouldn't back off.

Nuñez opened the refrigerator. He glared at Brannon and deliberately pushed every tub of colorful, aromatic leftovers to the side in favor of the frosty pizza box behind them.

"Okay," I said, taking a bite of the shriveled slice he gave me. "Getting in contact was your bright idea. Why don't you tell me what to say to him?"

Brannon sputtered. I'd called him out before he got his act together.

"Clock is ticking." I pulled my hand down from my mouth to spray crumbs at him. "Come on. You're the one who's in a hurry."

He wiped his lapel and advanced, undeterred. "And you're the one whose brain we're about to blow wide open! I figured we should collaborate. If you're too busy stuffing your face, I'll be happy to tell you what to do."

Listening to us bicker resurrected Nuñez's bad mood. He picked up the pizza box and slid toward the door.

"Okay, that's it. You're not my parents. I don't have to listen to this. If you're going to keep fighting, I'll go eat in the living room."

I reached out to stop him. "Sorry. You're right. Let's get this over with. Brannon, just give me the bullet points."

He paused to think again. This time, Nuñez and I waited with a bit more patience than before. Uncomfortable silence reigned as contemplation rendered him speechless until we finished our food.

"Tell him," he said when his plan jelled at last, "that we're on his side. That we can protect him from the people who took him."

I'd have to convince Hugo I wasn't going to turn him to pulp before I conveyed either of those things.

"Got it," I said, "but that can't be all. That doesn't help us find him."

The wrinkles in Brannon's forehead deepened.

"No," he said, "and it doesn't sound like he'll be able to tell us where he is."

"What do we do?"

He rubbed his temples. "Set a time and place to meet. To pick him up and bring him in. Then we hope he shows."

"Where?" Nuñez asked. "Here's too risky if someone's following. We've only got so many guns, and somehow I'm betting the bad guys have more. Holly and Kyle's apartment building is in a pretty rich neighborhood. People might get freaked out and call the cops if they see a weird giant loitering in the lobby. I can't think of anywhere else."

Genius gripped me. Hugo's towering body and unique face made him a mythical being.

I recalled the invitation I'd received by e-mail a few weeks prior. Most Lolitas used messaging systems tied to social media, but because I'd deleted mine before I moved, I got updates the old-fashioned way. The cursive text wasn't elaborate, but it told me what I needed to know about my community's storybook-themed Halloween party. I could label my misshapen plus-one a makeup artist transformed into a troll for the occasion. He'd fit right in.

Our enemies wouldn't conduct a firefight to take back their lost mutant so publicly. They valued their low profile far too much to start mowing down guests in frilly skirts. The roaring fire within me startled Brannon and Nuñez. They braced themselves as I squealed.

"Tomorrow's tea party. It's perfect!"

Nuñez's surprise kept him on board. "Where's that?"

"What the hell?" Brannon wanted to shoot me down. "Holly, that's—"

But he was wrong. I was right.

And I was going to let him know it.

"I know, I know. Shut up! Sit down and hear me out. Or I'm letting Nuñez punch you while Kyle's not here. He's way stronger, and I'm sure he wants to."

My deputy slid within pummeling distance and waited for me to say the word. Trapped with no exit, his charge took a seat on one of the rickety dining chairs.

"Go ahead," said Nuñez. "I think he's listening."

I thanked him with a nod. "Good, because Brannon, I don't care if you like it or not. This is the best idea I've got. Unless someone else has a better one, it's what we're going with."

Without interruption, I let them know why my whimsical notion made perfect sense. I'd arrive at the party at its appointed start time. Hugo—if willing and able to obey my instructions—needed to show up fifteen minutes later to slip inside with a sizeable group of meandering guests. After that, I'd pull him away from the crowd and whisk him off to a private place. Then I'd give a quick speech about N.E.R.D.'s kind intentions to persuade him to return with us to the lab.

I finished with a flourish while waiting for the round of applause I genuinely believed I deserved, despite my plan sacrificing speed for safety. We wouldn't reach him until tomorrow, but that didn't negate the importance of meeting somewhere with a dense population. A place where he'd blend in and villains unknown couldn't easily follow.

Brannon held his hand up for permission to comment. After my signal, Nuñez prompted him with a jab.

"You want to go alone? Really? I don't think that's such a good idea. If we're going to make this work, I'm going with you."

My enthusiasm deflated. His stupid, distractingly handsome face would stand out in the worst way. While wives, girlfriends, and non-binary significant others abounded, few all-American men ever accompanied their significant others to holiday parties. Those who did preferred to sit in an antisocial huddle playing handheld video games. They didn't mingle—as I was sure he would to disguise conducting surveillance.

Competition fueled Lolitas like logs on a spitting campfire. They all loved the chase—forever searching for a more extravagant dress, a better secondhand deal, a bigger headpiece, or a more interesting living accessory. Standing side-by-side with Brannon as the G.I. Joe to my Barbie glued a target on my back. I didn't want anyone to envy me, or start speculating about the details of the personal life I worked so hard to hide.

I grasped at nothing. "I don't think that's—"

"I want to go too," said Nuñez.

He qualified what he meant when he observed my anxious dread.

"I don't have to go in. If I can hack into the hotel's security feed, I can watch the main entrance for Hugo. And all the others. Just to make sure no one tries to sneak up on us. Is there a café or something across the street for me to hang out at? That way I'll be close in case you need me."

"The hotel is by a big intersection," I said.

I couldn't come up with a reason for him and Brannon to switch assignments despite how much I wanted there to be one.

"I'm pretty sure there's a restaurant on one of those corners."

"Awesome. I'll set my laptop up there." He looked past me to where Doctor Laura and Kyle stood in the doorway. "Are you guys done, Doc? Can we start the experiment?"

"I think so," she said. "Whenever you're ready, Holly."

"Did you hear the whole plan?" I asked, wondering whether or not I should fill them in.

Doctor Laura expressed tentative enthusiasm as Kyle swayed beside her, shifting his weight from foot to foot. I smiled at him even though he had his eyes on the floor. He didn't need to worry about me. I was a big girl who could take care of herself.

Or so I hoped.

We filed out of the kitchen and into the hall. Before we went any further, Doctor Laura led us all on a detour that ended in front of the board with gold stars. My name now started a new row squished in at the bottom.

Brannon winced when she took the rest of his points and gave them all to Nuñez.

"Let that be a lesson," she said, squinting at him.

Kyle and Nuñez walked out with her, but we stayed behind—staring at the ranking that made us equals. Brannon's arm brushed against mine as he turned to leave.

"Come on." He waited for me by the door. "We've got a mutant to catch."

14

THIS ASTRAL PLANE SUCKS

We relocated to the hall where Doctor Laura scanned me the day before. She led us to another clear pod, empty save for the equipment required to conduct our experiment of dubious merit. A desk lamp covered with a red cellophane candy wrapper sat opposite a swivel chair. Its hellish glow altered the expressions of those around me from familiar to freaky. It was just a trick of the light, but my uneven breaths tightened when concerned stares morphed into dark grins in the shadows.

Kyle placed a clunky pair of wireless headphones over my ears. Nuñez approached with a halved ping pong ball and a roll of duct tape. I wasn't sure if my hair regenerated like my skin, so I warned him to watch my eyebrows.

"I'm going to put these on now," he said, his voice more muffled than I'd anticipated. "I'll be careful with the tape. If I'm hurting you, squeeze my arm. Carefully!"

Kyle chewing his lip like bubblegum was the last thing I saw. The overhead speaker crackled when Doctor Laura came on.

"I want you to count to thirty. That should give the boys enough time to clear the room. When you feel like you're ready to begin, hold your hand in the air above your head. That's when we'll start strobing the lamp."

The sound of a scuffle followed as Brannon took over to deliver his own instructions before I dove headfirst into the ether.

"Remember the points." He concealed his worry for my safety better than everyone else—assuming he felt any at all. "Time and place. Those are crucial. Tell him where to meet us."

I guessed the thud and the groan I heard next happened after Doctor Laura thwacked him. He made sure to offer a few comforting words before he signed off.

"Don't worry. We'll be right here watching if anything happens. You'll be fine. Concentrate on finding Hugo. Get that message out."

White noise filled my ears. I hesitated for a moment before I lifted my fingers toward my face. The instant I gave a little wave, the pinkish aura bathing my pupils started flashing.

Soon, sitting in the crimson-shadowed nothingness felt like being in a cheap haunted house. All sounds other than static disappeared from the small room. The air blowing from the vent smelled stale. Even the itch of sticky vinyl against my thighs vanished as the boring seconds wore on.

My mind wandered and I pictured the other N.E.R.D.s sitting outside the door. I didn't have to see Brannon to know he was scowling. I imagined him pacing as he tried to stare the blinking experiment into submission. Suddenly, this image appeared between my eyelashes and the insides of the smooth white domes pressed against them, plain and bright as day.

"You guys." I watched him react to me. "Something's happening. I think it's work—"

I never got to finish my sentence—though I'm sure they figured out what I meant by the way I started shaking when the universe blew an invisible hole in my skull.

I left my body and spiraled up from the mortal plane.

Harsh winds whistling through endless rows of corn in the Midwest drew me first. I crashed back down. A kaleidoscope of whirring combines drenched in blood descended upon me. I willed myself through instant tears to fly anywhere else, wiping my clamped-shut eyes as I tried to think happy thoughts. An instant later, the life-saving bass of a Japanese rock ballad by Malice Mizer made me open them again. Rolling sound waves flattened the dangerous machinery and surrounding fields. Beauty replaced despair.

Lolitas of all shapes and sizes from across the globe popped up like fertilized weeds. Their environments bled into one another to create a living watercolor as they went about their business. Some got dressed while others strolled along with friends and shopped, ate, or perused the gilded halls of huge museums. It all looked like so much fun. I wanted to join them.

But I couldn't.

A wistful breath escaped my lips with an ethereal burst of glitter when I remembered Hugo and the task at hand. I focused on the mutant again. Gorgeous girls and lush scenery melted until their colors swirled together at my feet. The dull, overcast wash of San Francisco's skyline replaced their vibrant outfits.

Soaring north through the gray, I peered at the buildings below drifting in a sea of autumn's dying glory. A rainbow sprung from N.E.R.D.'s parking lot as I swept past.

Opalescent tendrils—one for each of us—arced out to shine on our homes. The first three ended at two separate buildings a few blocks away. Doctor Laura's bright gold beam echoed the warmth in her soft touch. It illuminated rusty bricks so they sparkled, but nearby a different scene unfolded.

Thunder and lightning accompanied the wrestling match of a fiery red ribbon and a calm green one. Brannon and Nuñez clashed and spun around each other. The complimentary Christmas colors sparked and spit electricity, darting up in angry pillars from their second story apartment like smoking wizards engaged in an epic battle.

The last rays—shimmering blue and pink—ended at the building Kyle and I shared. We really were like twins, both consumed by our hobbies. The depth of his obsession with science rivaled mine with fashion. So much so it'd almost gotten him killed. But the boy next door lived to defend me.

It didn't matter that no one ever listened to him.

The Golden Gate Bridge rose in the distance, its red towers emerging from the choppy harbor like the long arms of a giant squid. Sentimentality belonged back in the real world, waiting for me to accept or reject after I delivered Hugo's invitation.

Perhaps I'd give everyone a hug upon waking to express how much I appreciated them. Except for Brannon. He hadn't earned his yet. And he wasn't going to anytime soon if he kept on being such an asshole.

I redoubled my efforts to tune into Hugo's frequency.

Finally, I found him at the edge of the Presidio, a national park with pines and sparse trees flanking the rocky shoreline. He lounged across a boulder in the shape of a bench, holding a homemade barbell over his chest. Dozens of milk gallons filled with yellow liquid swayed on vines tied to the end of his tree branch. He pulled it down and hefted it up again, exhaling as he counted.

"Eighty-nine."

Whether it was necessary or not, I felt bad about dropping in on him unannounced. He definitely couldn't see me, and I feared the sudden intrusion of my voice might make him drop the bar and hurt himself. I didn't want to kill him, too. That'd rip my soul in half. I waited for him to lower it before I spoke.

"Psst," I said as I swooped down. "Hey. Hugo."

"Ah!" he bellowed, his trance broken. "Bad lady!"

The apparatus he flung at me sailed through my astral body and landed with a slosh a few feet beyond where I stood. He barreled to his feet and spun in circles, shouting for me to show myself.

"Go away. I'm happy. This is my home now." He didn't look as sure as he sounded. "You can't get me!"

I took a step forward and tried to be supportive. "That's great, Hugo. My name is Holly. I know we got off on the wrong foot before, but I'm not here to hurt you. I promise."

His defensive stance didn't change. I had to convince him I was telling the truth.

"I'm not here at all, actually." I elaborated to calm him. "It's all in your brain."

He stopped spinning and scratched his bald patch. "My brain?"

"Like last night. Except this time I'm far, far away. It's just you in the park. You're totally safe."

"Safe?" He did another sweep with his bright blue eyes to confirm.

"That's right. I just want to talk."

"No." Hugo's hand whooshed in front of his face, shooing the buzz of my disembodied voice away. "I don't like you."

We weren't getting anywhere. I needed to build his trust—

or at least enough of it to get him to do what I planned on asking. I turned my thoughts inward.

What would I want, in his shoes? I'm lost. Confused. Definitely scared. Okay, Holly. He's like a little kid. You've got to think that way. What do they like?

A light bulb materialized above my head as the answer came to me.

Mirth. Games.

Dolls.

"But you liked my outfit, right?" I asked. "When we met. My big, fluffy dress. I know I didn't want to play with you. You probably weren't trying to hurt me. I was mean, and I'm sorry. For everything that happened. But what if I told you there's more of us? A whole tea party full of pretty dolls."

I had Hugo's attention.

"Dollies? Like Madame Alexander? Where?"

The former jock knew the expensive toy brand?

I shook off my surprise. "That's why I'm here, to invite you. We're all getting together tomorrow. There will be yummy drinks, and cookies, and sandwiches. It starts a little after noon. Can you remember that? I want you to walk to the road on the edge of the park and find a nice person in a yellow car to give you directions. Okay? Try to stay hidden the whole way."

I gave him the address, and let him repeat it back to me as many times as it took to make sure he wouldn't forget. Hugo grinned and started bopping around like a bobblehead riding down Lombard Street.

"Noon," he agreed. "Yes. I will come!"

His excitement transferred to me as he danced in place chanting *tea party* and *dollies*. I interrupted him to lay out a few more rules, planting my feet in the soil to kick off.

Which way led to Hunters Point? Did it make a difference? I still hadn't quite figured out how to break myself of
my dream state. Would I fade away from existence if I stayed
under too long, leaving my body a withered husk? I started
tapping my heels together like Dorothy, hoping the thought of
home could take me there.

"I can't wait to see you," I hurried to say, "but you have to
be on your best behavior. Ask the girls nicely before you
touch anything they're wearing. Don't grab. And absolutely
no roughhousing."

This code of conduct barely made it to him before unseen
hands gripped me under the shoulders and yanked. The fall
landscape around me dissolved as I flew backward through
stars and swirling galaxies of light.

My eyes popped open—freed from their blindfolds and
back in the lab—as my soul slammed into my body. Excruci-
ating pain wracked my limbs. I screamed without sound as my
vocal cords seized. Over the course of my metaphysical road
trip, I'd made my way from sitting upright to lying on the cold
concrete floor. Every muscle in my body contracted in a terrifying rhythm.

Brannon kneeled over me and kept the others back as he
held my shoulders.

"Holly," he cried. "Holly!"

If I'd had the foresight to heed Kyle's words about how
treacherous Ganzfeld's wild ride really was, I would've
prepared a better farewell. Like get your damn hands off me,
or something just as memorable. I shed a tear through blurred
vision while the Grim Reaper drew the curtain on my brief,
unexceptional life. Even though I wasn't sad for myself, every
tiny piece of my evaporating essence ached.

All because I'd lost my chance to screw with Brannon one last time.

15

(LESS AWKWARD)
SLEEPOVER PT. 2

When I regained consciousness I didn't open my eyes right away, but I could tell I was somewhere totally unfamiliar. The scent of sweat and dried blood—with maybe a hint of sweet florals—filled my nostrils as I pressed my face against the warm, living wall beneath my cheek. I wasn't in pain or burning hot, so maybe I wasn't in Hell. But when I listened for choruses of seraphim, I couldn't find any, so I probably wasn't in Heaven. Snuggling into the endless arms wrapped around me, I went limp and hoped I'd hear the steady breaths of my mother and father nearby.

Perhaps the afterlife was nothing more than the loving embrace of the cosmos—an eternal reward for a job done well enough.

I rose and fell with the chest of the guardian cradling my crumpled body. Its thick fingers stroked the top of my crown, catching softly on my messy ponytail. Apparently, the outfit I died in went with me to the other side.

Had I known that morning's clothes were destined to stay with me, I would've ignored Brannon and chosen something more special. I thought of him back on Earth with a pang of regret. With so much happening, he didn't need our last encounter to haunt him for days, weeks, or maybe even years to come. An extra helping of guilt when it came to the matter of my death seemed unfair. It wasn't his fault.

Not *entirely*.

Curiosity about my new dimension compelled me to take a look around. Past an elbow sheathed in black, I saw the wall framing my bathroom and bedroom doors. I was in my apartment? I'd always pictured the great beyond as much roomier. Maybe I wasn't dead after all. A pinch of heartbreak eclipsed my relief when I realized my parents remained as far away from me as ever.

Stiff, fuzzy, and a little sad, I tilted my head up at Brannon as we sat together on my sofa. He didn't shove me off when our eyes met, but his fingers stopped moving through my hair.

"Where's everyone else?" I asked.

"I told Kyle he could go next door for awhile. To shower and clean up. The poor kid deserves a break."

I listened to the clanking pipes delivering hot water to my neighbor as they worked overtime. "But what about Doctor Laura? Nuñez?"

"Still at the lab," he sighed. "I offered for them to come with us, but you know Laura. She's more determined than ever to find your cure. After today. When reason didn't work, I tried apologizing to D, but he's still pissed at me. He'd rather guard the door."

"I understand," I said.

My human armchair tensed.

"I mean, you did aim a gun at him. I'd be mad, too."

Brannon shook his head. "I did what I had to do. If I stew in regret about my decision, it undermines my leadership. I need everyone to trust me, especially now. It doesn't matter how I feel. My hunch was logical. It had to be tested, and I had to have you there with me to do it. For backup. I was wrong, but what if I hadn't been? I never wanted to hurt him, and I only pulled my gun because I needed it. You know how dangerous he is. I never would've guessed why."

The last rays of the magenta sunset floating through my kitchen window caught the wet film over his tired eyes. I yanked my drifting hand back down before it caressed his cheek. He let me take the full weight of his arms.

"I didn't want to accuse him," he confessed. "I'd actually decided not to—earlier this morning—but then your friend scared me. There were too many variables. Too many clues pointing to his guilt. I'm exhausted. I hardly slept. I wasn't thinking straight. All I wanted was to protect Laura and Kyle."

Brannon looked so vulnerable. So helpless. He laid himself bare, and waited for me to clothe him with the comfort of a single word or a sympathetic nod. His open heart dwarfed the size of his ego. To avoid falling in and getting stuck forever, I changed the subject and tried not to squirm in his lap.

"Uh, by the way—why are you holding me?"

When he still didn't let go, I risked a glance at his face.

"You passed out," he said, "after the Ganzfeld experiment. Kyle was right. It overloaded your system."

"I'll tell you all about it if you let me in on how we got here. This is kind of an awkward position."

He didn't return my forced chuckle. "There was nothing more to do once Laura made sure you hadn't suffered any permanent injuries. Coming back here made the most sense. They should be safe in the lab for another night. You needed to rest while we got ready for tomorrow. In case you got the message out. I wasn't sure you'd wake up in time."

"Get ready? You were still going to go without me?"

"Our Plan B," said Brannon, "was to put Kyle in a dress and have him attend in your place. He's small enough to fit, and probably wouldn't look that bad with a wig and some makeup. Or one of those big floppy hats in your closet."

He meant a bonnet, but I didn't correct him.

"Now, he can be an extra pair of eyes. In his regular clothes. Did you get in contact with Hugo? Successfully?"

I shifted against his chest. "Nope. You've got to answer me first before I keep going. This is kind of weird. It's not like you're usually so touchy-feely—"

"You think your unconscious body crossed town and took three flights of stairs by itself?"

He'd carried me home—*duh*. That took care of the how, but I still wanted to know why he kept me close even after we arrived at my apartment.

"That doesn't explain why you didn't put me down once we got back."

My pulse raced as he exhaled. I hoped he couldn't feel it.

"Truth? Because I could go ahead and tell you this was the best way to keep track of your breathing, then leave it at that. If that's what you want."

I trembled. "S-sure."

Had Brannon lost his mind while I was out cold? I'd never seen him so soft, so candid. What was he going to do next, kiss me? I leaned back.

That'd never happen.

"It was my fault," he said. "I pushed you too hard. Even when I knew strapping you into that machine was taking a big risk. It's been such a long two days. When we got up here—I guess—I was just too tired to let you go."

He waited for me to say something, his heart beating a bit faster than before.

When I turned his confession over and over again like a middle-aged grill expert tossing a well-done hamburger, only one conclusion landed.

"Is that your way of saying that you care about me?"

A loud knock on the door swallowed his answer and made us both jump.

Kyle reappeared, cloaked in the relief a warm shower offered. He smelled fresh and wore a new pair of gray track pants and an orange Science Olympiad sweatshirt.

Brannon bolted upright. He dumped me from his lap with no warning.

"Ouch!" I cried as I scraped my knees.

The floor shuddered, but nothing fell or broke.

"You asshole!"

He pointed at me. "She's awake. See?"

"Uh—" said Kyle, whose limited life experience told him he'd walked in on a very strange scene. "Great. That's really good. Now I won't have to wear a dress. Hey Holly, do you feel better?"

"Sort of." I picked myself up, eyes drawn to the bundle of wrinkled cloth under his arm. "What's all that?"

"Oh, these are for him." He turned my deadbolt and crossed to the couch as he shook the pile out. "I figured you'd want something different after spending so much time in the same clothes. No offense, but what you've got on is pretty gross and torn up. At least these are clean. Even if they might be a little small."

Brannon held up a white t-shirt and a pair of blue pants embroidered with stars and rocket ships. He stretched their elastic waistband and looked back and forth from his own dusty slacks to the childish trousers.

"Are you serious?"

"Yeah," said Kyle. "If they fit. Go ahead. You can try them on."

Brannon glanced in my direction. "I don't know."

The option of shedding his suit grew more appealing by the second. With another push, he'd do it. Then I could make fun of him as he stomped around in Kyle's tiny pajamas.

"Come on," I said. "It's our last sleepover. If all goes according to plan tomorrow. We might as well do it right. Ugly jammies and all."

"You got through to the mutant!" said Kyle.

"I did. Hugo's got the name, the place, and the time. He seemed pretty excited."

Brannon didn't mirror the other N.E.R.D.'s relief. "That's good news. Where was he? Could you see? Was anyone with him?"

"No. He's been hiding in a park by the bay. It's pretty remote. I doubt his kidnappers will be able to find him again before noon tomorrow. If they haven't snatched him by now, I'm positive he can make it another half-day."

"And he'll be there?" he asked. "For sure?"

"Totally. It wasn't too hard to convince him to come out of hiding for free food and cute girls to play with."

Kyle shot me a bewildered look as he struggled to calculate the sum of a whole new set of variables.

"Play with?" His nose curled as though he smelled something foul. "What kind of Halloween party is this?"

He hadn't received the same primer on Lolita fashion I'd given Brannon that morning.

"It's not like that!" I said. "Hugo thinks we're dolls. He

saw me wearing Puppet Circus on Wednesday night. We're not. Dolls, I mean. The people who dress like me. But that was a pretty easy sell. He's not stupid, but he processes differently. It takes him time to think things through, like a kid. Probably because of the serum."

Kyle was more confused than ever. "What's a Puppet Circus?"

When Brannon answered for me I almost fainted again.

"It's the name of a dress, I think."

How did he know that?

"They have names. The prints." His eyes darted away from mine. "D told me earlier, you know, before—"

He stopped there. Kyle didn't need to know the details of their ongoing fight. I took his spindly arm. Brannon deserved some time alone to figure out how to patch things up with his best friend. We were just distractions.

"You should get changed." I told him, herding my new protégée toward my closet. "Leave your jacket and shirt out. I'll sew them up before bed. Right now, we have to plan our coordinates for tomorrow."

"What's a coordinate?" asked Kyle. "Like an outfit? But you're awake. Why do I still have to dress up?"

I grinned when he fumbled at my forceful nudge—ecstatic I'd tripped him without crushing bones or ripping flesh. I was getting better at handling my strength.

"If you're going, then you have to look the part. Brannon only gets off easy because he's too big to wear anything but a suit. Don't worry, though. I'm thinking pants for you. I tried Boystyle once before I figured out it wasn't for me. That set should be lying around here somewhere, and we're going to find it."

Kyle's stomach growled before we reached my bedroom

door. He snuck a glance at his phone, shoved it back in his pocket, and pulled his wallet out.

"I'm hungry," he said, tossing it to Brannon. "Let's get pizza. We might as well, if we're really going to do this sleep-over thing. I could go home, I guess. But it's kind of quiet over there. And lonely all by myself. I'd rather stay here. I've got lots of cash, so order whatever you guys want."

"Anything?" he asked.

"Within reason. None of those weird toppings you always get. Whole sardines aren't even edible."

That remark shot Kyle straight to the top of my list of favorite people.

"Thank you." I beamed at him. "Brannon, there's a bunch of menus in my kitchen drawers. I'm not picky, but keep it simple."

We disappeared around the corner. The pitter-patter of solid footsteps followed us, and then the sound of rustling papers. Kyle hovered on the threshold of my wardrobe, gobs-macked by the cornucopia of pink, blue, white, and black lace.

Most Lolita garments accommodated a plethora of body types thanks to generous shirring. Having a living mannequin to experiment on—however hesitant—made me dizzy with excitement. I'd spent hours daydreaming about matching outfits, but Chi Ho hated all the pomp and circumstance. She was a grunge demigirl at heart, gorgeous even in muddy boots and piling band tees.

Witches, fairies, high fashion dragons, and princesses galore promised their attendance at the fairy tale-themed party. I'd planned on wearing a Sleeping Beauty-inspired ensemble, but abandoned that idea as I dug through hangers and decorative boxes to find my Wonder Trip Regimental salopette. The striped overalls by Angelic Pretty got buried at the back of my closet as soon as I unboxed them, an experimental purchase that solidified how much I loathed pants.

The piece that inspired our new *Alice in Wonderland* coordinates wrapped around Kyle's short, skinny legs with room to spare. He eyed the pink fabric—head cocked to the side— as I proclaimed we'd go as the White Rabbit and Cheshire Cat.

In a ballroom filled with elaborate veils, halos, and bows, our animal ears would stick out and let Brannon keep track of our positions. I set a pink beret with cat ears on Kyle's head and caught his infectious smile when he returned from the full-length mirror. We finalized his outfit by adding a white cotton blouse, a pearl necklace with a charm shaped like a cookie, white socks emblazoned with gold teapots, and chunky pink platform shoes.

I chose to build my look around my pink Wonder Story jumperskirt—a dress printed with books, bunnies, and teacups. The rest of my items were white, save a pair of matching boots with fuzzy cuffs. A sheer blouse with pastel details, opaque tights with a row of pink bows, a furry cape edged in delicate lace, and a homemade bunny hat completed my set.

Kyle got an overview of the party's structure and social hierarchy as we steamed our pieces in the bathroom. Boys rarely wore the fashion well due to its elaborate nature, so he'd get tons of attention. The Lolitas I knew loved to talk. They'd do his share of the work as long as he listened. He wasn't required to know anything besides the basics, like the difference between a one-piece dress (OP) and a jumperskirt (JSK).

And the grand sin of not having covered shoulders, a petticoat, and legwear with formal outfits.

The rules for day-to-day wear were a bit more lax.

"If the fawning gets to be too much," I said, "politely excuse yourself for more tea. You can come get me if it's really bad. Oh, and watch out for the glompers. They're rare these days, but I don't want you getting hurt."

He raised an eyebrow as he banished the last wrinkle from the bottom of his pumpkin-shaped pants. "What are those?"

I leaned forward and to tell him a truly horrific tale.

"There are some people that love all things Japanese to an unhealthy degree. We call them weeaboos. Glomping is what they love to do most."

"Why? What's that?" he asked. "What are they going to do to me?"

"A glomp can occur at any time." I had him right where I wanted him. "As soon as a wild weeb spots a target they wish to hug. Whether they know them or not, it doesn't matter. No one is safe from their sweaty embrace. Without warning—with no time to get away—they'll tackle you, the object of their affection, with a startling cry of *Nyaa*!"

I pounced at him, making catlike motions, and Kyle shrieked. He switched off the bubbling steam machine at his feet and punched me in the shoulder while I giggled.

"That was mean!"

He tried to keep a straight face, but his resolve broke when Brannon rounded the corner to check on us. His crop top t-shirt and high water pants made him look like a catalogue model forced into the wrong set of clothes.

"You dorks having fun?"

We burst with laughter. Brannon coughed and adopted a fake frown that became real when he tried to talk over us.

"Okay, okay." He turned burgundy when every gesture pulled his shirt up more. No matter how he stood, it wouldn't settle. "Ha ha, I look funny. I get it. At least I'm not sitting in a dirty bathroom playing dress up like you two!"

I wheezed. "That's precious. You should wear that all the time. It really makes you look younger."

"Screw you!"

His steely gaze dared Kyle to say a word, but before he could pluck up the courage, a knock on the door sent us all scampering into the living room. The sight of the overstuffed black duffle sitting on my island drew me away from the course they stayed.

Curious, I went to unzip the piece of luggage that'd produced the boring plainclothes Brannon forced me to wear during our first trip home. This time it overflowed with equipment for our sting—walkie-talkies with headphones and microphones, rope, binoculars, knives of various sizes, and two guns like the one I'd tossed from Old Red sat inside. Lumps of thick bulletproof material covered even more supplies.

I doubted we'd need any of them to subdue Hugo. He'd remained reasonable and kind despite his botched transformation. But it was nice to know Brannon was prepared for anything in case our mysterious enemies did show up. As I shut the bag, the glint of two metal bracelets caught my eye from one corner.

The sound of a scuffle pulled me back to my guests. Brannon held Kyle out of the way, determined to reassert himself in a position of authority by answering the thuds coming faster and faster. I didn't blame him. On the off-chance that danger waited in the hallway rather than dinner, I wanted him to stand as our first line of defense. After some more pushing, he won and turned the lock.

A teenager with long black hair, matching peach fuzz, and bloodshot eyes stared at us. As he took in my unusual décor and the mismatched appearances of our small group, a lazy smile spread across his serene, stoned face. His uniform had the same logo as the box of leftovers Nuñez and I demolished earlier.

"You guys look like you're ready to party," he said.

Brannon struggled to get to Kyle's wallet. He tugged at his fly while he turned his pocket inside out, trying to hide the bulging outline of his junk. His face was as red as the delivery bag by the time he handed over two twenties and shut the door.

"You're not worried it might be poisoned?" I joked as we rushed to my kitchen.

"Nope," said Brannon. "If our enemies knew about you and where you lived, we'd be dead by now. Sending a spy to every takeout restaurant in the city—just waiting for us to order—that's a huge waste of resources."

He didn't know I wasn't serious, which somehow made his reply that much nicer.

Kyle took my bar stool, but Brannon stood and left his open for me.

He shoved a piece with pepperoni in his mouth and started talking. "Thanks, rich kid. For getting us food."

"You guys are always making fun of me for having money," said Kyle. "You and D. But you know it's not that easy for me, right?"

Brannon rolled his eyes. "You live *here* as an unpaid intern. I'll bet your monthly rent is close to what we pay in four or five."

"So does Holly," he whined, "and you're not picking on her."

"Her parents are dead," Brannon said.

He didn't notice when I recoiled. Only Nuñez knew my secret. He probably hadn't meant any harm, but while I wasn't around he'd relayed the personal information I wasn't comfortable sharing.

"Holly inherited everything she's got. It's not like she had a choice in the matter. She doesn't try to pretend she's like everyone else."

Kyle didn't understand. "How does that change things?"

"It's about transparency. I know you're a trust fund baby. We all do. There's no use trying to hide it. You've got to own who you are, or people will be able to use it against you for the rest of your life. Your father works somewhere in D.C., you got your PhD super early, moved out here, and now you live off his money. That's okay."

Mentioning his dad provoked him.

"Well, for your information," he said, "he's cutting me off. If I don't make something of myself by my eighteenth birthday. Which is really soon, by the way. And—"

He stopped, but Brannon pressed for more.

"How would you show him any of your work? Everything at N.E.R.D. is top secret. Though, he probably has the right clearance if he helped get you in. But wouldn't it have been easier? To go work at a cancer research facility, or some other place where you could actually put your name on what you've done?"

Kyle knew he'd already let too much slip. He absently kicked the side of my island.

"Doctor Baba. She's amazing. She was my hero all throughout school. I read every single one of her papers on molecular biology. Every journal article she ever wrote. I had to work with her." He prepared himself for an unpleasant reaction. "I've been doing my own experiments. On cell rejuvenation. Things like that. But only in my spare time. When she doesn't need me. I was going to show him that."

His color returned when Brannon placed his broken hand on his shoulder.

"Is that what you were doing?" he asked. "Down in the lab when the break-in happened?"

"I know it was dumb. And dangerous. Working all by myself. But I want to make my Dad proud of me. That's all I've ever wanted. You can understand that, right?"

Brannon gave him a sympathetic pat. Kyle took his first deep breath in minutes.

"Have either of you ever done something stupid? Or selfish? But for a good reason?"

I thought of the fairytale coordinates hanging in my bathroom. Back in the lab, I could've told Brannon that returning to the karaoke bar might've been our best option. The bartender knew Hugo's name. I knew that wasn't the case now, but there was a chance he could've given us enough information to tail him the old-fashioned way.

But I wanted to go to the tea party.

To cast suspicion away from myself, I shed light on Brannon's recent indiscretion.

"He tried to shoot Nuñez earlier," I tattled. "That's why they were fighting."

Kyle gasped. "What? No way. Why?"

Brannon gave me by far the nastiest look in his arsenal, but I didn't flinch. I sent him a nicer one to offer a few words of wisdom.

He'll find out eventually. Give him your side of the story. While you still can.

"I didn't do it," he mumbled. "It was earlier. After we picked up Holly from Chinatown. I had an idea—about a traitor within N.E.R.D.—and I had to find out if it was him. Maybe I was a little too forceful. That's all. Satisfied?"

Kyle went whiter than a ghost, overwhelmed by the mere mention of a double agent. He counted with his fingers, curling them one by one until he arrived at the last remaining suspect that wasn't him.

Doctor Laura.

His voice broke. "Do you still think that?"

"No." Brannon reassured him. "You're all cleared. I'm sure we'll figure out the truth soon enough."

He'd found a way to move forward without divulging Nuñez's past. I was impressed.

Kyle wrung his sweaty—or greasy—hands. "But while you acted, you thought the ends justified the means. And that was enough to make it right? Right?"

Terse seconds ticked past, choking the air with a thick layer of gloom.

"Yes," he said finally. "I did. Even though I'm beginning to think I was wrong."

Someone needed to bring our sad sharing circle to a close, or Brannon would spend all night moping about his falling-out with Nuñez while Kyle contemplated his uncertain financial future.

I appointed myself master of ceremonies and shut the top of the empty pizza box. "I think that was the worst game of *Never Have I Ever*, ever. We didn't even follow the rules. So I, for one, vote no more talking."

"But we've got to go over the plan." Brannon didn't have the energy to put up much of a fight. "For tomorrow."

"Let's do it in the morning. We'll all be up early. It's going to take us hours to get ready. There'll be plenty of time to run through the mission breakdown as often as you want. I'm going to go put on my ugly nightgown while you two get our bunks ready. Then we should watch a movie before bed. Go look for my *Kamikaze Girls* DVD on the bookshelf. Think of it as an informational video on Lolita fashion if you have to. You've both got a lot to learn."

When no one objected, I left to pull my heavy flannel off the top of the bathroom pile. The hoard of dirty clothes expanded with each new sunrise. They'd overtake the entire space if I didn't suck it up and deal with them.

Usakumya looked at me with gratitude and relief, glad I'd chosen him to salvage above all others. I draped the dry bunny bag on my jumperskirt's hanger. His powder blue hue put the finishing touch on my party ensemble. I just had to mend the broken strap dangling by his side. He'd stuck by me at the start of our unfathomable adventure. I needed him with me to end it.

I made space in my closet for the clothes Kyle and I left above the tub. I'd bring my old friend with me to the living room, even if I knew Brannon would mock me if it looked like I was trying to sleep with a stuffed animal. Once redressed, I put the rabbit under my armpit and moved onto the laundry.

The outfit I just took off was mostly clean, so I deposited it in my hamper. Brannon's black t-shirt didn't cost enough to keep—but I picked it up anyway. That left my stained coat, shoes, petticoat, socks, headbow, and my beloved Puppet

Circus. No soap or dry cleaning chemicals existed to rid its rich velvet of bloody blue stains.

I shed a tear, and said goodbye.

Each piece deserved a proper burial—a profound farewell like the flames of a Viking pyre or the mighty booms of a twenty-one gun salute—but I didn't have the resources. Or the time. I collected the fallen soldiers in the crumpled shopping bag next to the toilet and retrieved my sewing kit before making my way into the kitchen.

Brannon didn't join my somber parade, but he watched as I poured my clothes in the trash can under the sink.

He and Kyle sat on my heirloom blankets spread out in the living room. Their beds ran perpendicular to the couch so both N.E.R.D.s could face the television. The coffee table took up its former post by the front door.

I sat on the couch and stationed my favorite purse by the folded shirt and jacket on the armrest. My roommates took turns using the bathroom while I worked to hand-stitch each item by lamplight.

When Brannon returned, he stopped beside me. I watched from the corner of my eye as he studied the practiced movements of my fingertips before lying down. He wedged his solitary pillow against the foot of the sofa.

A sharp tug tweaked the space between my ribs. Our hands rested worlds apart. I couldn't spin around and change my sleeping direction without a good reason, and I didn't have one. Not one I'd say out loud. I finished and dropped his patched clothes on his head.

But we've already spent so much time touching today.

I frowned as Kyle navigated the movie's grainy menu to find its English subtitles.

Why do I want more? Isn't that enough?

I sighed. It'd have to be. Most likely forevermore.

With everyone comfortable, our movie night commenced. I got up and grabbed the remote to press play, prepared to chastise each viewer if they spoke other than to ask questions over the course of the next two hours.

I'd already learned so much from them about the importance of teamwork—amongst other things. In some small way, allowing them this glimpse of myself felt like giving back. I hoped I could teach them something in what little guaranteed time we had left together.

Even if it was just about fashion.

16

ETIQUETTE
LESSONS

At ten-thirty sharp, we set off to meet Nuñez at the diner kitty-corner to the hotel.

We decided to walk since I refused to marinate in cab stench right before the tea party. Doctor Laura—Kyle told me as we exited our building—promised to hold Old Red's keys hostage until she felt any of us could be trusted with her car again.

That meant we'd be hoofing it for the foreseeable future.

The sunny, temperate day unfolding didn't belong at the end of October. A breeze tickled us, but it wasn't strong enough to undo the tight ringlets I'd pressed into my hair.

Considering the date, Brannon stood out more than we did, yet he insisted upon walking ahead. He wanted nothing to do with the gumball creatures trailing behind him. No one could tell we belonged together. Kyle got his attention every now and then with a comment about the weather or the softness of my socks. Whenever I tried to join them, he ignored me.

He wouldn't even look my way.

Each time I asked why, he shrugged off my accusations of avoidance like a slippery mattress salesman dodging questions about warranties. I gave up when he got lost with Kyle in an argument over which character they liked best from last night's movie. Brannon always acted weird, but more in a general sense than toward anyone specific. His reason for shunning me became my new obsession.

He'd made it clear that he didn't like how I dressed, and I didn't care. Few people did. But I couldn't figure out why the semblance of curiosity he expressed for the other N.E.R.D.'s outfit didn't extend to mine.

Did skirts and dresses repulse him rather than the color pink? Did my bunny ears look tacky and hideous? Did I have a piece of tomato or oregano stuck in my teeth after scarfing down leftover pizza for breakfast?

When we arrived at the restaurant, we found Nuñez on a bench outside wearing a tight pair of black jeans, suede hiking boots, a brown messenger bag, and a burgundy flannel that smelled faintly of weed. Clean and wearing clothes that fit, he merged with his hip surroundings like another red brick in a wall.

Brannon's lips tightened when he saw his transformation.

Nuñez smiled and tossed his damp bangs out of his eyes. "Wow, you guys look great! Turn around for me."

He pushed my backpack, spinning me like a proud parent. Mid-rotation, Usakumya's stomach started buzzing. He pulled back quizzically. I immediately knew who was calling.

"It's my phone!"

Getting ready with Kyle kept me so busy that I'd forgotten to text Chi Ho to say good morning. That marked the first day I'd missed since we bought our starter cell phones together in middle school.

I shifted out of my shoulder straps, trying to maneuver without ruining my hair. I needed help. Fast. Before the ringing stopped and switched to voicemail.

"Can you get that?" I lifted Usakumya and pointed to his zippered compartment. "Answer for me really quick. Then put it on speaker."

Nuñez rummaged inside him.

If I held the screen to my face, I'd smudge the warm-toned makeup blended to make me look more human and less plastic. I waved at my artificially rosy cheeks as he paled at the name on my caller ID and hit the blinking button.

"Hey." He held the phone a safe distance away, like Chi Ho might reach through the receiver and whack him at any moment. "Hold on a sec."

She groaned. "Ugh, you again? Where's Holly?"

I held out my hand to relieve him—but Nuñez didn't budge. Instead, his mouth curled into a snarl as he dug his feet into the sidewalk while he pulled her against his ear. The wind whistling between us blew his timid façade away.

"Okay, enough!" he prickled. "What's your problem with me, anyway?"

I pictured Chi Ho's startled face on the other end. No one talked to her like that. Not without a death wish.

"I don't have a problem," she said, more flustered than I'd ever heard her. "Let me say hi to Holly."

He hit speaker and thrust the device in my direction long enough for me to say hello, but nothing else before he yanked it back.

"What's up? We're kind of busy."

"Yeah?" Her next question dripped with sarcasm. "What're you doing there?"

Nuñez bit back an annoyed growl, but the magnetic antipathy that drew them together made sparring with Chi Ho irresistible. The rest of humanity vanished whenever they collided. Before Brannon took a step forward to feed him a lie, the truth tumbled out.

"We're getting ready for the tea party. I'm setting up surveillance. We're supposed to meet Hugo."

Her tone changed when she put the pieces together. "Like a sting?"

Nuñez fumed when Brannon struck like a snake lunging for a bird on a branch and grabbed the phone from him.

"Hi, Chi Ho." He tried to sound as professional and authoritative as possible. "It's been really nice talking, but we're going to hang up. We'll call you later."

"Wait!" she shouted. The screech of feedback knocked his finger away from the screen. "I want to help. It sounds like I'm on speaker again, right? Holly, those bad feelings I had Thursday morning are back. I wanted to make sure you're okay. I was going to come down there to check, but Nai Nai's got me stuck at the salon. She says it'll be a really wild day. She made me drink that awful blue tea she loves so much to give me more energy. Augh! It tastes like pinecones and feet. Anyway, I don't know. I keep getting these flashes of chaos in Union Square. I'm probably bugging, but I'm gonna keep an eye on the news. Can I let you guys know if I see anything weird? Please?"

I snatched the phone from Brannon as the *no* formed on his lips.

"Sure." I shot him a glare that said I'd break more bones if he dared contradict me. "If that'll make you feel better, but don't worry! Everything is completely normal here. At least, right now it is. I'm in charge of looking for Hugo, so I won't be able to talk. You can call Nuñez if something's really important."

I watched his eyes light up at the prospect, but couldn't tell whether he was pissed off, excited—or maybe both.

"Fine," Chi Ho huffed, "but I better hear from you later!"

"You will." I added another affirmation. "I promise."

With that, we said our goodbyes. I hung up and handed the phone to Nuñez so he could send her his number and a string of rude emojis. He locked the screen and I gave him my passcode, after I swallowed the rising dread Chi Ho's new hunch inspired.

Kyle had been quiet during the whole exchange. He coughed to remind us he was still there. Brannon stared at me, caught himself doing it, and promptly went right back to pretending I didn't exist.

"Thanks for humoring her." I turned from him to face Nuñez. "It'll make our lives easier in the long run. Trust me."

"It's no problem." He tamped down an odd half-smile as he whipped his head away from me, changing the subject to Kyle. "You clean up pretty good, kid."

"Thanks." He beamed. "Holly's awesome. I never thought I'd be able to pull this stuff off, but I guess it's kind of fun. I actually think I look handsome. For once."

Warmth radiated through my chest. Maybe he'd want to come with me to future events.

"Better than usual, for sure," Nuñez teased. "You're lucky she dressed you. I was going to put you in this. Thought it was in the lab, but I found it in the back of my closet. It's probably leftover from last Halloween."

He dug inside his trendy satchel to find a thinning red hairpiece with tangled fibers. It got tossed into the nearest trashcan when he saw me cringe.

"That's what I thought." He called to the outsider on our periphery. "See? I told you that wig was a stupid idea."

Brannon grumbled. "Whatever. Let's go inside and set up. We've got way too much to go over, and not a lot of time to do it in. Come on."

Once inside, we hunkered down to memorize the orders he gave again and again. He wanted us to know them as well as the backs of our hands. The rhinestones on my jagged nails caught the orange light of the neon sign in the window. I hadn't remembered how much TLC they needed until then. As we huddled in our corner, I picked at the edges of each broken appliance.

Nuñez sat with his back to the wall behind him, pulled his laptop out, and plunked it onto the table's chrome top. Cords that swayed like tangled vines fell over the side, connected to another clump of whirring gizmos and gadgets in the bag at his feet. I tried not to gag when he nabbed a nearby order of abandoned fries and started eating.

He'd stay put and communicate with Brannon via a nearly invisible earpiece and microphone worn by both. It was his job to look for Hugo out the window to his right, in case I got caught up socializing and failed to sense the mutant before his arrival. He'd also monitor the hotel's security cameras for strange activity as Brannon and Kyle made rounds at the party, doing the same from within.

I sighed—ready to bite the bullet and rip the plastic off my fingers—but Nuñez distracted me from the painful task. He leaned across the table and handed me a folded map of the city.

"Okay, Hols. I need you to slip this into the kiosk with all the other booklets in the lobby. I've never seen a hotel that didn't have one. There's a transmitter inside that should give me access to their system, but it's got to be within fifty feet of a computer. If you think the stand might be too far away from the front desk, tuck it somewhere out of sight. Without this, I can't watch you guys remotely."

I opened the top page to get a closer look at the home-made mass of chips and wires inside.

"Why me?" I pulled Usakumya from my back, but replaced his straps on my shoulders once I figured out my package wouldn't fit in his belly.

Brannon heard me, but he gave my answer to Nuñez and Kyle. "I'm going to be busy getting this thing in without arousing suspicion."

He placed his heavy bag on the table and unzipped it. The only other person equipped to handle a firearm reached for one of the matching handguns. Nuñez surveyed the room to make sure no one saw him shove it into his waistband—and not a second too soon.

Because I was about to cause a scene.

"You know," I said, bumping into Brannon. "You're going to have to look at me eventually."

He glanced at the old couple sitting a few feet away. They mumbled to themselves, unable to imagine what someone as cute as me must've done to upset him. Bolstered by their support, I pushed his shoulder and forced him to face me.

"What?" he barked. His eyes lingered on mine before they leapt out the window.

The way he said it sounded angry, even though it didn't strike me that way. His uncertain, awkward expression didn't mean anything. It wasn't meant to convey, in a quiet yet personal manner, that he thought I looked nice but wouldn't say it.

That'd be useless to hope for.

Kyle's wheezy presence during our second night together kept me safe. Alone, I'd have tripped into more tender conversations with Brannon like a hunter falling into a loaded bear trap. I didn't hate him as much as I did three days ago, but that only made things worse. Each time he caught me, I had to dig my way out, my will to remain indifferent toward him bloodied and bruised. I wished he'd change his endlessly fascinating behavior.

He did the exact opposite when he took a step closer and let his arm brush against mine.

"We have to concentrate," he said, "on lugging this gear past security without getting stopped for a bag check. I've got my badge, if it comes to that, but I'd rather not show some guard everything we've got stashed in here. If he wants to throw his weight around, one phone call will sink us."

I came up with a solution. "Just say you're a photographer, if anyone asks. You look the part. A young guy carrying a big black case. Use your scary, official voice and stare them down. That'll work, right? It seems like it usually does."

Nuñez and Kyle agreed.

"I still don't know why you're bringing that in. I'm sure I can convince Hugo to come with us. There's no need for you to use force. Of any kind."

"I'm not worried about him," he said, "but we're going to need everything if the organization that captured him in the first place isn't far behind."

He paused as though what he wanted to say next—particularly when it came to me—didn't come easy. His dark and serious gaze fell on Nuñez first.

"I've got to know that you'll all have my back. In a fight. If it comes to that."

Kyle jumped in. "I'm sure we'll be fine. We'll go in. We'll eat. I'll talk to new people. After that, everything should be easy."

"He's right," said Nuñez, "we're getting ahead of ourselves. Let's regroup and look on the bright side until things go south. Which I'm definitely not saying they will. Fingers crossed. I'm pretty sure we all know what we're doing by now."

Kyle and I confirmed, but Brannon's edge remained.

"When that goes smoothly, we'll sneak out early and Doc can drive us back to the lab."

Brannon finally noticed we were one N.E.R.D. short. "Why isn't she here? Where is she? You didn't leave her down there by herself, did you?"

"You know how she is." Nuñez shrugged. "Said she was finishing a few tests. She'll come pick us up when I call. After I walked home, I took the bus uptown. It'll be a tight fit, but I guess Holly and Kyle can probably both sit on Hugo's lap. Besides, you already said it's more likely for the people hunting him to show up here. If they even do at all. Don't worry too much. She's armed."

A small group of Lolitas glided past on the sidewalk wearing billowy chiffon gowns and carrying scepters to match their headdresses. Porcelain fairies spinning inside sparkling globes topped each elaborate staff. We watched them stop on the corner. Brannon didn't have time to argue about Doctor Laura's safety—or why his orders to stay away from their apartment went unheeded.

He closed and shouldered his duffle. "What time is it?"

Nuñez glanced at the green numbers on the bottom of his mobile battle station. "About ten minutes until noon. You guys better get going. Put your headphone in so I can test it really quick."

A sharp buzz assaulted his ears when the system came on. Nuñez tapped the barely noticeable microphone on his plaid lapel. They reversed the procedure to make sure messages could be sent and received both ways.

"We're all set," said Brannon. "Guess we'll see you on the other side."

We had to say goodbye. Nuñez shuffled over to hug me first and Kyle second, but stopped short of the third member of our party. Neither of them seemed sure what to do.

With a sigh—and a warning look at me—Brannon dove in and grabbed him.

He squeezed tight, held on tighter, and pulled away after a few clumsy pats, looking like he didn't want to. "So, that's that, then. I—are we—okay?"

Nuñez shook his head.

"Not yet, but we'll get there."

Brannon smiled, relieved their broken bond could be mended. He went for the door with Kyle close behind. I lingered beside Nuñez and his gross, empty plate.

"I've heard the food here is pretty good. You should get something fresh while you wait."

He looked toward the hotel, gazing through it. "Nah, I'll hold off. I don't really want to eat right now. Just in case."

I heard his stomach churning and wondered why he hesitated, until a grim glimmer in his eyes mirrored the expression he wore after vomiting in the deli.

Violence didn't seem to make him sick, but blood did—when he wasn't expecting to see any. The implications of his hunger strike seized my heart. I still didn't know everything about his past life. Or the memories that clung to him like thorns.

Outside the window, his gaze refocused on the Three Blind Mice. Each of them wore handmade ears, veils, and a different colorway of a jumperskirt with a print inspired by

The Nutcracker. They were watching Brannon and Kyle throw their whole bodies into another *Kamikaze Girls* debate. What an utter waste of time.

Someone had to use it the right way.

"D." I held my fingers against Nuñez's sleeve until he looked at me. "I'm sorry for what happened to you. Whatever it was, exactly."

"Same," he sighed.

The sound bridged the gap between us. It filled the diner until there was no air left. I couldn't breathe, because the pain I saw reflected in his weary eyes told me he wasn't just talking about himself.

Nuñez bent down and put his hands on my shoulders.

"Look, we both know what it's like to get fucked by fate. The world isn't like your pretty dresses. Bad things happen to people. Every day. Everywhere. Sometimes they're Black, Asian, you name it. Occasionally they're white. Sometimes they're you. And I know it's not easy, or nice, and it'll never make most people comfortable unless they're already racist douchebags—but they can look like me, too. That's how it is. That's real."

"It shouldn't be."

I had to clear my throat to say it. When he saw me blink faster, Nuñez gave my arms a squeeze.

"This is why I didn't want to tell anyone at N.E.R.D., because they have no idea what it's like to stare down the barrel of the biggest shit cannon life's got. You're different. You got hit. Now you know why we have to guard who we are. And to be honest, Hols, I've been stabbed, shot, drowned, beat up, set on fire—pretty much every other horrible play in the game—and the only thing on Earth that scares the living crap out of me is you. But I promise I won't treat you any

differently, if you can still pretend I'm the same dork you met
Thursday morning."

I swallowed hard, and then hugged him again. I could do
it. I'd even fight to the death if it meant he didn't have to.
Brannon waved me on through the window the moment I
let go.

I gave him the finger.

"You are the same dork," I said, handing Nuñez a napkin
on my way toward the front. "You've got secondhand ketchup
on your nose."

His soft laughter followed me out the door as I dabbed my
eyes with my knuckles.

When I caught up with the boys, they were quiet. Kyle
was ahead of Brannon, projecting nervous energy by biting
his lips and fidgeting like ants crawled up his legs. He probably didn't have the opportunity to interact with strangers
very often. Neither of them did, for all I knew.

The shadow of my ever-present anxiety darkened and
closed in. I had to change gears. Shake the fog from my head.
Resist the urge to run and hide forever. Five minutes, maybe
less, remained for me to teach them enough etiquette to ensure
they didn't offend anyone.

"Remember," I reminded them in a voice that creaked,
"Lolitas are *real* people. We're not cartoons or amateur actors.
The party is fairytale themed, but it's Halloween. You're not
playing squires or princes. You're my guests. Okay? And your
behavior reflects on me."

"You need to relax," said Brannon.

A new group of girls swam past us, chatting and waving
like happy mermaids splashing in a waterfall. The one in front
wore a seashell crown atop gorgeous red waves and a mint
dress embellished with pearls. My cutesy style looked retro in

comparison, but together we all formed a gorgeous rainbow. Seeing groups of Lolitas—like beautiful French pastries lined in neat rows in a bakery window—made me giddy whenever we gathered.

Kyle stared, enraptured.

"I'll be good," he promised. "I can talk about prints. And the movie. And what brands people like."

"I'm sure you'll do well. Thanks, Kyle."

I didn't doubt he'd behave. He'd crammed his brain full of plenty of fun facts about my favorite fashion.

My pleas were meant more for the caveman whose disdain for anything girly forged my biggest concern.

"Brannon," I said. "I'm going to go ahead and tell you the same thing I told Hugo. Best manners, or else. Wait for answers when you ask questions. Chew with your mouth closed. Don't go up and touch anyone's clothes without asking!"

"I know how to act," he whispered as he opened the lobby's heavy door and held it for everyone filtering through. "I've gone undercover before, you know. I can pretend to enjoy a party. If I have to."

I waltzed through walking layer cakes and deposited my high-tech parcel in a bookcase near the reception desk.

A concierge directed our forerunners to a ballroom on the mezzanine story, standing at attention while dressed as an English Beefeater. The hotel offered a royal experience. His gimmicky apparel added to the lush atmosphere guests loved, but the way Brannon and Kyle gawked at him—probably unsure if he was an employee or a helpful attendee—brought me to my second point.

"This world is new to both of you. It's easy, I know, to think of and treat us like sideshow freaks."

Brannon's forehead wrinkled. "I wouldn't do that. I'm not a total—"

Kyle cut him off to stutter his own good intentions. I had to talk over them both.

"It's okay. I'm not trying to make you guys feel bad, but I don't want you to accidentally make fools of yourselves. See, for me, since I don't wear any other styles, lots of attention is normal. I can ignore it—for the most part. For the majority of people you'll meet today, Lolita fashion is a hobby, not a lifestyle."

"Really?" asked Kyle as another group wearing all black entered and drew his eyes away from me.

"Yes!"

"Go easy on him," said Brannon. "He's excited." He gave the nearest doorman a corny smile and pointed to his bag. "I'm the cameraman. If you were wondering! Someone has to make these girls look good. It's not like they can do it themselves!"

His lie slid by the unobservant guard as I twitched. Brannon was a lost cause. I prayed his handsomeness would distract from how much of a dick he could be—intentionally or not.

"Kyle—" I addressed the partner I wasn't ready to give up on. "If I'm being honest, they probably dress like you most days of the year."

His face fell. Since his initiation into my airy realm of Rococo, he'd had the opportunity to believe in magic as well as science. He listened as we went up a carpeted flight of stairs.

Precious seconds ticked past.

I still wasn't satisfied.

"They might take offense. That's all I'm saying. Don't

invade their personal space. Not too much. If you start acting nosy rather than knowledgeable, don't blame me if the outcome isn't great. Please don't embarrass me!"

The sounds of celebration drifted out to meet us on the landing, past open doors wearing a frame of leaves, tulle bows, and carved pumpkins. It was up to them—I knew although I didn't like it—to obey the rules.

The community members I'd met were all welcoming and kind, but I couldn't shake the nagging fear it'd only take a single faux pas to alienate myself. Every time I tried to socialize, war raged within me as my desire for acceptance fought the need to remain safe from the scrutiny of their friendship. With Brannon and Kyle with me, it'd be even more difficult to manage my image.

I took a deep breath. I'd done everything in my power. I could no longer protect myself—or either N.E.R.D.—from curiosity, both well-meaning and not. Nuñez was right. I was one of the most dangerous people in the solar system. But the girls in the room still terrified me. No matter how hard I tried, I couldn't ignore the feeling we were walking into a trap.

A den filled with ravenous wolves in queen's clothing.

17

7 MINUTES
IN HELL

The lavish hall bustled with activity.

We navigated a maze of tables topped with spider web linens and centerpieces made of purple orchids, realistic bats, antique storybooks, cauldrons, orange tea sets, and beaded masks on sticks. A crystal chandelier hung in the middle of the room, illuminating the charming tableau with the help of a long bay of windows to our left.

I scanned the coordinates of the girls milling about and let out a satisfied sigh. Kyle and I weren't best dressed—or most creative—but our matching outfits added a nice splash of pastel pink to the assorted candy-colored mix.

Tooth fairies, toy ballerinas, wicked step-mothers, goblins, pixies, and fair maidens flitted about. Everyone hobnobbed with feverish glee, except the group wearing plain brown dresses and dour expressions who sat in self-imposed exile by the buffet.

There were lots of attendees I didn't recognize, but I'd only been to two events since moving to San Francisco. It didn't help that most people never wore the same wig twice in a row, or let their natural hair out to breathe for big cele-brations.

Faces blended together in my memory. If I tried to find

anyone I thought I knew to say hello, I'd get their names wrong for sure. Lucky for me, my fuzzy ears and bright pink dress stuck out. The event's blonde host spotted me from the other side of the room. She waved and parted the crowd to make her way over.

"Please," I begged Brannon and Kyle, "be delicate."

I hid my nerves and pasted on a smile as the older girl in the light blue Baby the Stars Shine Bright jumperskirt approached. The princess lookalike glided to a halt and wrapped her arms around me—but I didn't know where to put mine. When she pulled away with a warm grin, I felt my legs buckle like softened butter.

She remembered me, but did she really like me? I didn't feel worthy of her embrace. Our community leader embodied elegance and grace, and I had more in common with a potato.

"Holly," she cooed. "It's so good to see you. When was the last time? Labor Day?"

While I wasn't looking, her co-host snuck up to greet me.

"So good," echoed the brunette dressed entirely in Baby's sister brand, Alice and the Pirates.

I couldn't remember her name, either.

"I'm glad you could make it."

My jaw dropped. Inspired by the Red Queen, she wore a one-piece printed with roses to compliment the thick mane of dark brown hair piled on her head like a crown. She was tall, mature, toned, striking, and totally out of my league.

I'd always wanted a girlfriend who loved Lolita fashion like I did, but I never tried to get one. The prospect of sharing my wardrobe in the name of love made me just as uncomfortable as sharing my secrets.

My knees trembled harder when she hugged me. As the

Queen stepped back, the Princess welcomed Brannon and Kyle.

"Hi. It's nice to have you here. Holly, who are your friends?"

"You look so cute!" The Queen squealed at the boy by my side.

He thrust his palm foreword. "Hi, I'm Kyle."

She gave it one polite pump before she saw Brannon and got sucked into his gorgeous orbit along with the Princess. They bit their lips as their eyes combed every inch of his muscular frame.

I coughed to hide the growl that popped out as the hair on my arms stood up. We'd failed to prepare an explanation for the presence of my polar opposite plus-ones. A fake role for Kyle came to me as I shoved him in front of the other N.E.R.D., hoping to redirect their focus.

"This is my brother!" I lied. "He's always wanted to try Boystyle. I let him borrow some of my clothes."

My plausible answer sailed right past them. If I back-tracked and called him a visitor from Mars, they'd nod again with clueless smiles that said they'd be happy to show him where to stick his alien probes. Besotted with Brannon, they peered past my human shield and dared each other with a sidelong glance to ask the most important question on their minds.

"So," said the Princess, "is this your boyfriend?"

Before I opened my mouth, the man to my left swooped in and took her plump hand in his.

"Michael Brannon." He kissed the base of her fingers. "And definitely not."

Spellbound, they giggled when he repeated the gesture for

the benefit of the Queen. He charmed them without sticking his entire foot in his mouth.

But I wasn't happy about it.

I wasn't proud.

Right then, I would've given anything to be the Incredible Hulk instead of me—barely adequate Holly. I wanted to turn green and smash furniture. The girls offered their names, but I couldn't hear them over the blood rushing through my ears.

I'd probably puke if Brannon ever pressed his lips against any part of me. Why did his phony flirting make me so cranky? He couldn't even look at me, much less touch me on purpose. The sound of his merry laughter joined theirs as I scowled.

We all wore the same clothes he hated, so why treat them like gold and me like dirt? Did it come down to our looks? Our ages? I knew they were both closer to thirty than twenty. Did they appear elegant and poised in their ruffles and lace while I didn't? Was I a misshapen troll? A flashy beacon of ugliness?

No way.

I knew I looked as good as they did.

He's just an asshole.

Kyle, who was preoccupied with checking his phone, didn't notice the imaginary steam wafting out from under my furry hat. Loose nails popped off when I tightened my fists. Tiny blue droplets splattered my skirt. I cursed and uncurled my fingers. He heard me and put his cell away, wincing as I gathered the pieces from the ground before peeling off the rest.

Brannon reappeared and drew me in by my waist.

"Hey," he said. "I'm moving to get a better vantage point. I'll be near the back of the room. I need you to stay focused on Hugo. Find me when he gets here. Or I'll come get you, if D sees him first."

I pushed him away. "No touching! Do whatever you want."

He backed up with hands raised to where his new tour guides waited, eager to whisk him away.

"Alright, my beautiful ladies," he said, "why don't you show me where the bar is? I'd love to get you both a drink, even if it is just tea."

Brannon glanced over his shoulder. I glared at him. When he disappeared into the bustling crowd, I turned to Kyle.

"Are your hands okay?" He knew I wasn't hurt, and asking didn't disguise that he was too mesmerized by the sights, sounds, and smells of the party to care.

I marched us to a table and sat at an unclaimed place setting. With the help of a free water bottle, I scrubbed the stains on my dress before they dried. While he waited for me, Kyle seized his opportunity to discover more about the different kinds of outfits he saw. Explaining the differences between Sweet, Classic, and Gothic Lolita didn't take much brainpower. A good thing, since all my attention belonged to the task of eavesdropping on our absent squad leader from across the room.

I wore Sweet.

Brannon told an off-color joke and his growing audience giggled.

Pastels and cutesy motifs once ruled supreme, but elaborate solids and jewel tones took their place as trends evolved. Classic Lolitas donned luxurious fabrics with delicate details, hard bonnets with feathers, and pressed skirts with smart pintucks. They looked like heroines from Dickens novels.

I ground my teeth when another star-struck girl stroked my least favorite person's injured arm.

Gothic devotees who stuck to white, black, and royal blue loved heavy metal and all themes macabre.

Violent rage bubbled within me. I didn't tell Kyle, but if I didn't cool down I'd soon dip my toes into Guro: The sub-style spattered with blood that, in this case, would be real.

He whipped his head toward the door when a new group entered. "And what about them? Over there."

The greasy hoard transfixed him by announcing their arrival in broken Japanese. They each wore a different version of the same off-brand black and white maid dress and filthy converse shoes. The one in front sported a headband made of neon green and pink dreadlocks. It lit up with every step she took. Some misguided souls used meet-ups as live-action role-playing events, and it looked like she'd come dressed as the Empress of Anime.

The flashing tubes enthralled him. "Those are neat. I've got to know how they work. I'll be right back."

He scampered across the room to the wrinkled sides of the Ita Lolitas whose name meant *oof*. They were the glompers in scratchy lace I'd mentioned in my tale of terror.

The Empress squealed, picked him up, and spun him around. Kyle's grin spread to my unwilling face as I watched him poke her tacky headgear. Meeting someone new and enthusiastic about his presence—even someone with questionable fashion sense—sent him sailing over the moon.

The hushed voices of two girls wearing yellow ice cream themed jumperskirts and melting cone-shaped hats tore my gaze away from him. They paused near where I sat.

"That hot guy is with her?" asked the first. "He's so friendly, and she's, well—is it too mean to say stuck up?"

"Maybe. I don't know much about her." The second took a sip from her teacup. "She kind of appeared out of nowhere, and she doesn't talk to anyone. But you're right. He's so nice. You really think they're dating?"

Brannon's presence torpedoed my mystique and ruined my chances of enjoying a plate of macarons and a cup of cider in peace. That's all I wanted, if I ever made it to the buffet.

I held my breath and tried not to let on that I could hear their conversation.

"Do you remember what she wore to the aquarium meet?" continued the first. "That rare special set? I wonder if he's the reason she has such an expensive wardrobe. He looks successful, and there's no way she's old enough to have a high-paying job. Maybe he buys her dresses?"

As soon as I saw Doctor Laura again, I'd ask her to build me a time machine. I wanted to go back to the beginning of June and kick myself for making such a splashy first impression.

"She's so lucky. I mean, I love saving to earn my pieces, don't get me wrong, but I wish I had a rich, cute boyfriend to spoil me every now and then."

Cups clinked on their saucers as they strolled away, no doubt to spread what they thought they knew about me to anyone who'd listen.

Uncontrollable fury shot past the anxious gunk in my throat as I sprang to my feet. The girls meant well with their educated guesses, but any rumors about me—good or bad—paved the road for others to chip through my impenetrable exterior. I couldn't risk letting that happen. I didn't want to form deep connections with anyone.

Or experience the inevitable heartbreak that came with them.

Brannon, regardless of whether he spoke or stayed silent, drew too much attention. He couldn't stay.

Get rid of him! Usakumya screamed over my shoulder. *Mission be damned!*

I tore into him for my phone. I had to find out how long I'd have to remove my target from the party before Hugo arrived. The clock, sitting above a dozen texts from Chi Ho I didn't even skim, read a quarter after twelve.

Do it now!

I flew past swishing skirts toward the banquet tables at the end of the hall. Brannon faced out and addressed an enormous semi-circle of enamored disciples. They hung on his every word, worshiping him like their sexy new Pope.

He regaled them with some stupid story. "And then—"

My entrance put his punch line on hold. I wormed my way to the front, broke their ranks, and grabbed the collar of his jacket. The microphone of his high-tech walkie-talkie shattered beneath my fingers. I'd reimburse Nuñez later for the cost of equipment destroyed on my crusade.

"Holly, what are you—"

"Ladies," I said, squashing his protests. "I'm sorry. Do you mind if I borrow *Michael* for just a second?"

The sound of his first name on my lips sent him scrambling. It immobilized him as I dragged him through the crowd. His brain didn't reboot to ask questions and hurl useless commands until we reached the empty landing.

"Holly," he said, struggling.

The duffle bag on his shoulder threw him off-balance.

"Let me go!"

I tightened my hold on him. Brannon gave up fighting physically when he realized he'd have to rip the front of his formal wear to end our tug of war.

But that didn't stop him from yelling.

To prevent concerned girls from coming to his aid, I hurried to find somewhere private for us to talk. We stumbled down a short hallway with an unmarked door that opened into a cramped supply closet.

I tossed Brannon into the dark. A loud crash and a grunt followed before I found the light switch. A single bulb revealed him sprawled in front of a wire shelf, digging his way out from under a pile of soap and toilet paper. I planted my feet to confront him.

"What the hell?" He massaged his sore arm. "What was that back there?"

All the courage I'd plucked up to tear him away from the party dissolved when I saw the pinprick of pain hiding behind his narrowed eyes.

I stuttered. "I—I, y—you. You're messing everything up!"

"What do you mean? I'm doing exactly what you told me. Everything's going according to plan. I haven't spotted any trouble, but we need to get back. Can you tell me what your problem is?"

Another avalanche of bath products knocked him down.

No good answer existed.

I'd stand there flopping like a fish gasping on land as he shoved me aside to return to his gregarious, reputation-wrecking post. I wasn't willing to use more superhuman force to keep him locked away. Not after our close call in Old Red.

I shied away from his penetrating stare as a fat frog sat on my voice box. I knew deep down what upset me, and it wasn't the thought of accidentally making friends—or enemies—as the result of harmless gossip. The battlements around my heart exploded as the real reason surfaced from the depths of my subconscious with nuclear consequences. I wasn't mad.

I was hurt.

Brannon knew how to be human. I'd seen it in the way he loved Nuñez and cared for Laura and Kyle like family, but he'd delighted in treating me like crap for three straight days.

He wasn't my friend. I didn't even like him. His constant coolness—interspersed with gentle moments straight out of a Hallmark movie—gave me whiplash. I just wanted him to be *nice* to me. Nothing less, and maybe more.

But I couldn't tell him how I felt, so I tried to divert my inexplicable anguish by training my eyes on the floor. When I did, I found my life raft.

I knelt by the duffle bag he'd dropped and ripped it open.

"What is all this crap, anyway?" I asked, jettisoning its contents around the room. "Guns, knives, rope, whatever. I don't like you carrying all this dangerous stuff around those innocent girls."

"Stop that!" he shouted. "Is that what's bothering you? I already told you. If things go bad—"

My words sizzled like acid as I chucked a Kevlar jacket at the space above his head. "We're *fine*! Like you said, it's going great. There are no evil boogeymen lurking in the hotel. Nuñez would've seen them by now."

"Not necessarily," said Brannon, "there's still the possibility of—"

"We don't need any of this. When Hugo shows up, all I have to do is talk to him. Then we'll leave. It's that easy. You make everything so difficult!"

He didn't understand. "Me? I'm not the one derailing our mission in a stinking closet. Look at what you're doing right now. I was just being prepared!"

"Shut up!" I snapped. "Why do you always have to be Mr. Macho Man, anyway? You think you're always right. Even when you make dumb mistakes. Like holding a gun in your best friend's face, or putting me in some homemade horror machine."

"I —" he said. "That's not fair."

"You're always bossing me around like I'm some kid who doesn't know anything. And I'm not!" Tears came without warning. "Why do you hate me so much?"

"What? I don't hate you. Holly, I think you're—"

"I do practically everything around here." I sucked back sniffles and retreated from the hands that shot up to steady my face. "*I* kept you from shooting Nuñez. *I* figured out how to lure Hugo with our psychic link. Now *I'm* going to go bring him in all by myself. Because that's the job *you* gave me. And worst of all—!"

That's when I spotted the pair of silver circles twinkling at the bottom of his bag. Brannon didn't get a word in before I started again.

I knew what I had to do.

"You never have a kind word to say about any of it. No, *Oh good job, Holly* or, *Gee, thanks for helping me, Holly* or even a *Wow, Holly! You actually look kind of pretty going to your big party*—especially under such stressful circumstances. You've never even said happy birthday! And you want to know why? Because you, Special Agent Michael Brannon, are a big, stupid jerk! And I'm not going to take it anymore."

I snatched the hidden handcuffs, locked one bracelet around his unwrapped wrist, and shackled the other to the metal shelf behind him.

The white saucers of his eyes dwarfed their matcha tea-colored middles. "What are you doing?"

"You're staying here." I pocketed the keys and stood,

shaking carpet lint off my skirt. "Until I come back to get you."

Brannon fought against his super effective restraints, rattling the bars of the rack bottled to the floor. "You can't do this!"

"Too bad, because I just did. I'm sure your loyal fans will miss you, but they'll have to manage while you entertain yourself in here."

I turned to leave, but Brannon's low chuckle froze my hand on the knob.

"There's no way," he said. "I didn't think it was possible..."

My heart leapt so high it bruised my uvula. "You didn't think what was possible?"

Danger loomed. I had to run.

But I didn't.

"What are you talking about?"

"You sure love acting like I'm the worst person ever." Absolute certainty replaced his disbelief. "But you're such a big liar. You're jealous, aren't you? That I was talking to those other girls. Go ahead, admit it!"

I pinwheeled away from my feelings. "You wish! You're old. Kind of. And mean, too! I do *not* like you. Especially not like *that*."

Brannon wasn't listening.

He fixated on the side of my skirt hiding the keys and beckoned me closer. "Aww, Holly. It's okay. You don't have to feel bad. Come here. Let me give you a hug."

When I didn't buy his act, he abandoned the barely pass-able affectation and sneered.

"Come on! If I tell you you're a special princess, too, will you let me go then? Hunh? Pretty please?"

I didn't have time to volley a comeback before the draw of my strong sixth sense alerted me to the other mutant's arrival several stories up. I didn't know why he came from above, but I didn't care. The sooner I led him back to the lab, the sooner I'd permanently remove myself from Brannon's irresistible and maddening presence.

"Got to go," I said. "Hugo's on the roof. I'll be back. If you're good."

The desire to plant a wrathful kiss on his open lips—a longing I fought with every screaming cell in my altered body —sent me speeding from the room. Brannon cursed and shouted my name, but his cries went unheeded. While I tried not to think of his mouth on mine, I hurried to make my important rendezvous up and out in the crisp fall air.

18

THE ROOF

Instead of heading straight for the stairs, I made a quick detour back to the party. I wanted to find Kyle to tell him an abridged version of recent events. Sure, locking Brannon up was petty—but I didn't want to deal with him. Or the way my dignity fled whenever he stood near. Returning to apologize and free him undermined the success of our primary goal.

Hugo was waiting, and it didn't seem prudent to leave him alone for too long.

Gurgling laugher pulled me toward the buffet.

Kyle sat glued to the boisterous girls I'd left him with. His clique swarmed near him like toddlers vying to pet a fluffy kitten. The Empress took her place as his owner in my absence. She fed him a coffin-shaped petit four while he laid in her lap and made cute nibbling noises, having the time of his life.

He sat up and swallowed when I stopped in front of him. "What's up?"

"I need you for a minute. Can you follow me?"

He searched my face for clues. He'd obviously forgotten our true agenda. The attention he received from his new circle got him punch-drunk on good vibes.

I clasped his hand and led him toward the middle of the ballroom.

"Hugo's on the roof."

Kyle shook off his stupor. "Oh, well, that's great. I guess…"

His happiness faded. The mutant's arrival would force us to leave.

"Shouldn't we tell Mike? He'll probably want to know." Kyle scanned the room for him as he thumbed the phone in his pocket.

"He already does," I said, offering the truth before a lie. "But he—uh—stepped out to take a break. Don't worry about it. Everything's fine. I just wanted you to know I'll be gone for awhile."

"Did something happen?" A fearful twinge sobered him up. "Why'd he leave?"

"We had a—sort of disagreement. For now, he's in the supply closet down the hall. Taking stock of inventory. You know. In the bag."

I snarled when a guest in an oversized bonnet rejoiced at the news of our supposed breakup.

Kyle didn't take it as well as they did.

"That's not good. You know how he gets. A bunch of weapons plus a pissed off Mike is a really bad combination."

His tone made me less sure of my safety when it came to the matter of my captive's eventual release. I didn't think he'd hurt me—he couldn't, really—but I wondered what fate awaited Hugo if the two butted heads when they met.

Kyle rocked back and forth on his platform shoes.

"Don't worry." I waved away his concerns. "He's just cranky. What else is new, right? I've got to go get Hugo. For now, you can keep enjoying the party." I playfully hid my worry. "Go have fun with your new girlfriend."

"My girlfriend?" He snorted, taking me literally. "No way. I'm not interested in her like that. Or anybody, for that matter. Never have been. But those girls are interesting. I like talking to them."

He let our conversation die and focused on the carpet as he took a few steps in their direction. I was about to go when he stopped and turned back. Deep sadness lurked beneath the surface of his light, anemic eyes. The look disappeared in a flash, consumed by the glint of a porcelain cup reflecting off his glasses.

It was so brief. I didn't even think to ask what was wrong.

"Okay," I paused to let him jump in if he chose to. "I'll see you in a bit."

Kyle took a deep breath.

He let it out.

"Holly, can you promise me something? That you'll never get mad at me? At least, not how Mike might. No matter what happens. Okay? Can you do that?" Remorse filled his quiet mumble. "I really tried my best. To do everything right."

I couldn't tell what prompted his earnest, undeniable request. Maybe fear of failure when it came to following orders during the tea party. He'd abandoned his post to make friends, and didn't want to incur Brannon's wrath—or mine— by having too much fun. The stink I'd made on our way in about best behavior haunted him. Kyle didn't want to disappoint me.

That's what I guessed.

"Trust me," I said, "I know. I promise."

The sound of my oath lifted a great weight from his shoulders. I held both thumbs up for him to see. To get my point across, I channeled every P.E. teacher I'd ever known. I gave him my best you-can-do-it smile.

"You're doing great. Get back in there. Okay, champ? I'm sensing a big win for all of us today."

I didn't wait to see him react before galloping out into the hallway to find the stairwell with roof access. I went up and pushed through the steel door, glad to dismiss the pulling sensation that occurred whenever Hugo was near.

Fear tiptoed up on me like a wicked, silent assassin. I hoped he wasn't standing by a ledge. When my sensitive eyes adjusted to the glaring sunshine, I found him in the shade of the hotel's heating and cooling towers. Two large plumes of smoke—one north and one south—billowed in the distance. The overpowering stench of ammonia wafting from the closest one momentarily distracted me from the beauty of his handmade costume.

He wore the same tight pants I'd seen him in behind the bar and at the park, now covered with delicate garlands made of ivy. Woven strands of wildflowers hung like a wreath from his neck. A bushy crown of flaming red leaves framed his thin tufts of black hair. He'd transformed himself into a woodland fairy.

He looked up as the pressure between us dissipated.

It would've been smart to let him make the first move, like a chipmunk taking bits of food from a hiker, but I called to him with a question instead.

"What are you doing up here?"

When Hugo didn't run, I approached.

He reached out as I arrived next to him, but stopped his outstretched fingers an inch above my billowy sleeve. I smiled and nodded to let him know he could touch. He caressed my fluffy ears and straightened the pink bow decorating the base of my hat. Usakumya's blue strap drew him in.

"Same bunny?" He peeked behind my back. "Like before?"

"That's right. You can hold him, if you want."

I gave him to Hugo, who looked into his bright red eyes and pulled him to his chest. As long as he held my furry companion for comfort, our meeting would go just fine.

I started again. "I'm glad you like Usa. We can all talk together. Does that sound alright? You can tell us why you didn't use the main door."

Hugo's smile shriveled.

If he got agitated and left, I'd never hear the end of it from Brannon.

"It's okay." I rushed to accommodate him. "Take your time. I'm here to listen. No judgment."

Hugo gazed out over the hazy city skyline and exhaled. "Too many people. I tried to hide, like you said, but I couldn't. They were friendly. Mostly. But they all wanted pictures. With me."

The same thing happened to me over the summer on a daily basis. October made matters worse. Onlookers often asked for snapshots, desperate to capture the memory of the quirky Harajuku girl. Although it no longer fazed me, I sympathized with how uncomfortable the attention made him. I chose to dress the way I did, but Hugo got no say in how he looked. His transformation from regular jock to towering muscleman made it impossible for him to walk unbothered.

That took some getting used to.

"I was going to be late," he said. "So, I went up."

"Good idea. I'm really glad you made it. You look terrific."

I meant the compliment. Even half-naked—a sight with the potential to shock more modest guests—his whimsical outfit captured the opulent spirit of the occasion.

He beamed as he admired my dress again. "Thank you. You look beautiful."

His sincerity pierced my heart. I had to find a way to entice him downstairs.

Maybe he could teach Brannon some manners.

"Are you ready to go to the party?"

Hugo looked beyond me to the stairs leading to the rest of the dolls whose company I'd promised him.

His sparse brows furrowed as his lips churned up the right words. "I'm worried."

"Why?"

"Because," he sighed.

His stale breath hit my face like a warm gust of wind.

"What if they don't like me? I'm not so good, now. At talking."

Hugo only spent three days in the wild, but solitude gave him ample time to overthink interacting with strangers. Anxiety plagued him, too.

"But what about that guy at the bar?" I asked. "He knew your name. You've already made one friend as the new you."

"Yes. I guess. I don't know. After I ran from you—in the park—I kept going. I fell asleep in a doorway. When I woke up, the old man was standing over me. He told me to leave. I was going to go. Then I saw him struggling with the box I used. As a pillow. It was heavy. I picked it up. He gave me pants. And food. In return for work. He let me stay."

Hugo took a deep breath. Stringing so many sentences together in one go tired him out.

"See?" I encouraged him. "That sounds nice. You'll do

fine. Come down and meet the dolls. And my teammates. They're good people. Not intimidating at all."

This lie would become apparent the second Hugo met Brannon. Although the N.E.R.D. in charge was less than half his size, I had no doubt the bark of the smaller dog could convince the larger his bite was just as nasty.

"Well, one's kind of grumpy, but he's excited to meet you. I'll make sure he treats you well. The other is tiny. A little redheaded boy who's like, a hundred pounds soaking wet. He's definitely not a threat."

Hugo laughed.

At first, I thought he was humoring me. My description of Kyle hadn't been particularly funny. But he soon let me know otherwise.

"Like the boy who made me strong?" Hope radiated from him. "He was very small. With big hair. Like a cartoon."

I froze as he chuckled. "Wait. What?"

The blue blood pumping within me turned to ice.

No.

It couldn't be Kyle.

The facts wouldn't allow it. He was injured in the break-in, practically to the point of death. And his closeness with Doctor Laura made her more like his mother than his mentor. He'd never do anything to harm her.

I urged Hugo to go on. "You're talking about the bad people, right? The ones who kidnapped you? From school. One of them had red hair? Can you tell me what the others looked like? Do you remember?"

When he shook his head—as though I'd made a mistake—I winced and gave thanks I hadn't eaten anything since break-fast. I wanted to hurl.

"Only one boy," he said, "with a nice apartment. He came

for us in a cab. It was very easy. We signed a piece of paper. Then went to sleep. And then woke up. But he was gone. We went to look for him."

"How'd you get that far?" I asked. "Without anyone seeing you? It's not like you could walk right out the front do—"

The drowsy face of my building's night watchman crystallized in my mind's eye. Everyone knew the notoriously deep sleeper often snoozed on the job. This never bothered me, or the rest of the homeowner's association, since he prided himself on minding his own business. Having him behind the desk looked fancier than hidden cameras in the ceiling. He got paid to be an ornamental marker of status, not a real measure of safety.

Hugo caught my train of thought.

"Yes. We went through the park and found you. Then we fought. And you killed the one I was with."

"I'm sorry!" My heartfelt confession spilled out for him, and John—wherever he was in spirit. "It was an accident. I didn't mean to hurt him. Not like that. I was scared. I wanted to get away."

"Me, too," said Hugo. "He blew up, and I ran. But I got lost. The city is so big. I tried to go back to the building. So the little boy could take me home. But I couldn't. I didn't have directions. Not like the ones you gave me."

I understood every word he said, but not one of them made sense. If Kyle injected Hugo and John with mutagenic serum—as the insurmountable evidence suggested—his reasons remained unknown.

Was he working for a team of rival scientists? Experimenting on his own with no ulterior motives? I remembered the loud clatters and clanks I heard coming from his side of the wall. The noises that sounded like small explosions jelled in the context of a homegrown laboratory. What I knew didn't make it easier to mentally switch him from helpful geek to mad inventor or vile henchman. If he really was evil, he was the best actor in the history of the world.

"You're absolutely sure?" I wanted him to be wrong. "No one took you? You know, by force?"

"No," Hugo assured me. "I went. To get bigger. To play football better. To make my parents proud. There were big risks, but big rewards. Just like he promised. I wish I could remember his name."

He handed Usakumya to me, and I returned the bunny to his perch on my shoulders. My collected exterior concealed the screaming within.

Why would Kyle lie?

Hypotheses crashed around my skull like cannonballs fired in a cage. He had to have known we'd all find out about what happened after a brief conversation with Hugo. What did he have to gain from keeping his mistake a secret from the rest of the group?

I still hoped it'd been only that.

Kyle was terrified of Brannon, and of what he'd probably do if he found him conducting unauthorized tests on human subjects. Did that prompt his convoluted cover-up? I gnashed my teeth, done thinking and ready to act.

"You know what?" I played it cool to keep Hugo as calm as I wasn't. "By the sounds of it, we might have a friend in common. I think I know who made you. Does Kyle Lambert ring any bells?"

He clapped his hands. "I think so. Is that him?"

"It's a good bet." I faked cheerfulness as I herded him toward the door. "He's at the party right now. We should go get him. Then, maybe, he can explain everything that's happened. I know I'd love to hear it."

I wanted to wring the answers to my burning questions from his willowy neck. A chill spread from my core. I'd left him alone, and fault fell on me if he snuck away. I gave him the chance to run from justice, or worse—inform his cohorts of Hugo's location.

And Brannon's. And Nuñez's. And Doctor Laura's.

I quickened our pace as Hugo and I started our descent toward the unknown, determined to find Kyle.

That's when the ground beneath us started to shake.

19

FAMILY AND FRIENDS

A massive earthquake picked the worst possible time to occur. Walls cracked, misting us with plaster dust as we climbed down to the first floor. Hugo and I tried our hardest not to topple forward as the stairs swayed underfoot. Mother Nature was doing her best to keep Kyle from his date with destiny. A violent tremor threw us into the hall.

Guests clung to furniture on the landing. We pushed through the wave of bodies leaving the ballroom. The heartiest party-goers went about their business as though the building wasn't crumbling around them, waiting for the chaos to stop. They put on brave faces, but I saw their knuckles turn white as they gripped chairs and low-hanging sconces.

Glass beads from the swinging chandelier fell on pirate caps and witch hats. The buffet flung ghost cookies, cucumber sandwiches shaped like fingers, and the blood-red contents of full punch bowls in every direction.

I held onto Hugo. We had to stay together as we searched desperately for Kyle. Bows, veils, and one castle sculpted into a pale blue wig—but no cat ears—flooded past us on the screeching heads of their owners. Hotel employees yelled for evacuation.

"Where is he?" Hugo covered his ears. "Should we stay?"

The windows shattered and eviscerated our options. A hail of broken glass rained down as a bellboy pulled the fire alarm to get his point across. Those who remained wailed and fled with deep red gauges on their cheeks and arms.

"Keep an eye out for Kyle," I called to him. "We can't let him get away!"

Sirens in the distance approached faster and faster. The loop of their horns mixed with the metallic ringing overhead. Rumbling joined the mix. A stampede from higher floors filled the mezzanine. Hundreds of people surged toward the front door. Cracks rang out like gunshots as the expensive building's foundation shifted. Men and women screamed for their loved ones to make their whereabouts known in the human tide.

The multitude of sounds made it impossible for me to concentrate. No matter how hard I tried, I couldn't focus solely on the crowd. The boom of shockwaves deep underground vibrated against my overstimulated eardrums.

Despite the odds stacked against us, I wasn't willing to leave.

Not yet.

I cried out for Hugo to pick me up. He lifted me into the air so I could get a better look around. Behind us, the hall's gigantic light fixture broke free and crashed to the floor. A thousand exploding crystals played a melody of destruction.

The last Beefeater shouted at us as he ran out of the room, his beaver hat hanging by its chinstrap.

"You two have to go. Now. If this keeps up, the whole place is coming down!"

He didn't stay to find out if we obeyed.

Hugo put me down without warning. His frightened gaze followed the swarming occupants who exited. A team of emergency responders—ones dressed all in black—forced their way into the lobby. He turned to me with a meaningful look.

We're strong, but—

I finished the thought for him. *Probably not strong enough to survive a collapse.*

A terrible realization hit me like a sledgehammer.

Brannon was trapped.

I shoved Hugo toward the stairs. "Go. Get outside! Look for Kyle if you can. He's wearing a pink cat hat and overalls. Don't go too far!"

"Wait!" he shouted as I careened down the hallway.

The ballroom's doorframe dismantled itself where we'd stood. Solid beams crushed pumpkins and spewed their guts in every direction as Hugo dodged out of the way to avoid a direct hit.

He fled and I let him, even as I weighed the enormous risk of leaving him unguarded. If he got swept up in the bedlam and flushed out into the city, he'd have to fend for himself again. Even if he managed to elude those hunting him for a little while, I doubted I'd survive a second Ganzfeld experiment to find him before they did.

Terrible consequences accompanied my decision to let Kyle go, and every moment he spent out of sight magnified their lethal potential. If his coconspirators wanted Hugo, their desire to study him probably extended to me as well. I pictured my limp body rotting behind bars like a monkey in a forgotten zoo.

The fear that manifested didn't slow me down.

I tore the closet door off its hinges and flung it over my shoulder. A suffocating perfume of spilt chemicals emptied from the makeshift cell. I peered inside the dark space and fumbled in my pocket. The metal slab landed on soft padding that squelched while someone shouted. I looked up instead of behind me to check for bystanders I might've maimed, keys out, ready to free Brannon.

But he was gone.

How he'd escaped didn't matter. I needed to know where he went.

He didn't pass by during the pandemonium. I couldn't pick Kyle out of the masses, but I would've found Brannon the instant he wandered into my line of sight. That's how attuned I was to him, even though no supernatural tie existed between us.

He wouldn't leave without me, not to mention Kyle and Hugo. Brannon denied every one of his good intentions—and often made awful decisions to negate them—but that didn't change what he was: A hero to his core. He'd endeavor to save his teammates at all costs. Especially—I hoped as I ran back to the service stairwell—the one that'd locked him in a supply closet in a fit of jealous rage.

I threw myself into the twisted funhouse of shaking steps. Rails cracked beneath my hands as I pulled myself up. Scaffolding fell all around me, shredding my delicate layers and the skin beneath them as I ran past sharp pieces of rebar. The pain didn't stop me, and neither did the destruction of my clothes. Finally, I arrived on the last quivering shelf.

I didn't have a clue how we'd make it out, but the memory of Brannon's hand on mine as we fell asleep in my far-off living room consumed me. Together, we could do anything.

All of us.

I held onto that belief for dear life as I charged through the door to find him.

We nearly collided for a second time, but another lurch

threw us to the ground. Relief flooded my chest. Brannon rolled to my side as I clambered to my feet.

"It's Kyle," I screamed over the dissonant sounds of disaster, pulling him up. "He's the one!"

He cursed and shook his previously uninjured hand. His thumb sat at an odd angle with a huge red welt. However he'd dislocated it to slip out of his cuffs, he hadn't done a very good job jamming it back in.

"What?"

The gravity of what I said sunk us both, but I couldn't leave room for second guesses.

"Kyle!" I repeated, louder this time.

The chop of spinning blades in the air closed in from a few blocks away.

"He took the serum!" I cried. "He made John and Hugo. I don't know why, but it's him!"

Ribbons of smoke blossomed into huge mushroom clouds during my short absence. A stinging breeze that smelled of ocean water, burnt cinderblock, wood, lilac, and vanilla made my eyes water.

The earpiece of Brannon's broken headset crackled. It dangled by his collar and carried Nuñez's frenzied whispers over the mob trying to swallow them whole.

"Mike, I'm telling you. Something's wrong. These guys headed into the building, they're just not right. Where are you?"

Brannon couldn't hear him, and the location of our new adversary kept him too preoccupied to anticipate more danger approaching.

"Where is he?" He pulled me closer. "Where's Kyle?"

"I don't know!"

A helicopter slowed overhead, casting a jet black shadow like the outline of a looming beast.

I shouted over the cutting gusts manufactured by its knife-like propellers. "I let him go. I'm sorry. I had to come get you!"

Brannon forgave me with a genuine hug before his hands flew for his gun.

Warm.

Strong.

Desperate.

Reassuring.

I knew he had to, but I never wanted him to let me go.

The windstorm that beat at us lifted my skirt and petticoat. It ripped my fuzzy hat from my head and blew it away. Next to me, I heard faint voices from the speaker before its frequency went out on Nuñez's end after a sharp cry.

"Don't worry," said Brannon, too stuck on Kyle to worry about his best friend. "We'll find him. Get behind me!"

He angled his body in front of mine as the aircraft's sliding door unlatched. Bullet holes marked the machine an instrument of war rather than a search and rescue vehicle.

The ground shuddered to a halt when its long metal feet touched the roof. An eerie calm replaced the din of trembling buildings. The coincidence was far too great for me to assume the two were unrelated.

This new quietness made it easier to hear strange sounds coming from the broken stairwell. Steel whined as light foot-fall announced two new players traveling up the reassembled passageway. The tectonic plates shifting beneath the city gave way to rolling aftershocks.

Brannon projected a steady exterior, centered to strike, as a gnarled hand reached out to push the helicopter door open.

The clop of platform shoes on an uneven surface made me turn around.

Kyle—accompanied by a tall, thin woman with short raven hair and a fitted black jumpsuit—tripped onto the roof. The fact Hugo wasn't with them provided some small comfort.

Maybe he'd escaped.

The stranger squinted at us from over the top of the mechanical face mask covering her nose, mouth, and neck. Her black apparatus sat flush to pale skin. It appeared as though it couldn't be removed without great difficulty. A ribbed speaker, one illuminated by bouncing waves of red light, tapered from the middle point and sank into her inflamed trachea.

The traitor by her side leaked shock from every pore. He glanced past where Brannon and I stood as a deep chuckle the texture of gravel in an open wound scraped over our shoulders.

"That's enough, Katarina."

The woman who held Kyle by the strained straps of my salopette let her throat lights go out. The Earth stilled. She controlled our calamitous weather, but that revelation wasn't enough to distract me from the man she answered to.

He was about sixty and solid, with a thick mane of gray hair tinged with a distinct, unmistakably familiar shade of red. The navy three piece suit he wore—accessorized with a gold pin the shape of a twisted tree—looked much more expensive than the pieces I'd lent his trembling son.

"Well done, Kyle." He stepped down onto the roof. "I'm incredibly pleased with what you've managed to accomplish!"

Behind him, hidden inside the winged vehicle beneath a canopy of riffles, Doctor Laura gazed at us with mounting horror. We called to her as the sinister figure chuckled, but she couldn't respond. A long slash above her right eyebrow dripped down onto the gauze gag that made it impossible for her to speak. Slicing cables bound her hands and feet.

"You son of a bitch," yelled Brannon, "let her go!"

Shaking, he pulled his gun and fired two rounds at the monster standing before us. A dull hum from the mysterious woman at our backs shot up a wall of shimmering sound waves in front of her master. The bullets ricocheted back.

Brannon cried out and dropped his weapon when one struck him in his thigh. Blood poured from it as I screamed and hastened to his side.

The blue eyes of the villain looming over us narrowed. His lips twisted into a terrible smile as he spoke again, his voice as intense and arresting as the bite of a viper.

"Never mind him. There's nothing you can do. If I'm not mistaken, I believe it's time for a proper introduction, Miss Roads. My name is Calvin Lambert, and I must say it's a pleasure to finally meet you. We have so much to discuss."

20

NOT CUTE

Before I could reach for the abandoned firearm, the sound of another automatic weapon being loaded rang out. A helmeted goon hopped from the helicopter and circled to my right.

The older Lambert did nothing as he watched my hand retreat from its deadly objective. He wasn't the type of man who'd shiver at the sight of a small girl holding a gun. Calvin and his entourage remained safe as long as his powerful underling hovered nearby to shield them.

"That's not a good idea, my dear," he said. "I'd advise you to leave it be. Let us talk like civilized people. For now."

Brannon groaned. "Do what he says."

He tried to apply pressure to his wound, but it wasn't enough to stop the steady gush of blood soaking his pant leg and the floor.

I wished the bullet hit me instead. That would've given me the opportunity to evaluate the damage I'd take from a hail of gunfire if I launched an assault.

The evil gray-haired man triumphed. For the time being, we were at his mercy.

"Please," said Brannon.

His green eyes pleaded with me to do what he asked. Just this once.

"I'll be okay." His look hardened as it moved from me to Calvin. "What do you want? Leave her alone."

"To chat. With *Miss Roads*. As I said."

"I have nothing to say to you!" I shouted.

Undeterred, he continued as jovially as though I'd complimented the clean lines of his tailored jacket.

"Then you may listen to what I have to say. You're very important, Holly. May I call you that?" He didn't wait for my reply. "It's crucial that you know how much. If you could bear with me for a few moments, I will explain."

The choices he left me with stalled my free will. I held my ground as he grinned and took a deep breath to begin.

Brannon told me before that he didn't believe supervillains liked to give grand speeches. As soon as Calvin Lambert puffed his chest, I knew our enemy was cut from a different cloth.

His dark presence oozed like ink to blot out the bright sun as his one-man show commenced. "You see, I am the leader of a humble organization of likeminded individuals operating deep within the Department of Defense—hiding in plain sight amongst those we seek to dismantle. We call ourselves Titan, the same as those great beings who created the gods of Olympus to rule the heedless masses. And we want what's best for humanity."

"Somehow, I doubt that," Brannon muttered, his face growing white.

"You should save your strength, agent," said Calvin. "Your comments aren't needed."

"You're in charge right now. We get it," I said. "Just get to the point."

Our adversary frowned when he realized his careful words went unappreciated.

I glanced back at Kyle—who listened with rapturous awe. His mouth hung open even wider than before.

His father let out an agitated huff.

"Very well. If you insist upon a quick and tasteless eluci-dation, then so be it. You'll learn all you need to in due course. Suffice it to say that we are amassing an army across the globe. It is a monumental task, but one undertaken with love and the utmost care to ensure the longevity of the human race. Mortals with no special talents allotted by birth—or magnified by science—can no longer be allowed to govern themselves. They will continue on the path of destruction they've chosen, proliferating endless wars in a dance of deaths dealt in fear and retribution, until a mitigating body seizes power. Titan is that force for good. For years, we have endeavored to collect and enhance superhuman soldiers to help us realize our goal. We aim to restore peace on Earth."

"To sum it up," I said bitterly, "you want to take over the world."

Calvin's thin lips gave way to another sly smile. A bemused expression crawled across his wrinkled features, like a child trying to conceal the brilliant placement of a mean April Fool's Day joke.

"I suppose you might see it that way," he said. "Although that is putting it rather crassly."

A new voice joined us when a strangled question sprang from Kyle's dry throat.

"Dad, is this true? I always thought you just worked for the government!"

"Every word," he reassured him, "and now that you've proven yourself worthy of being brought into the fold, I have no more need for deceit."

His straightforward answer proved too brief and inexact to satisfy Kyle, who couldn't make sense of it all.

"I don't understand. Why not tell me earlier, instead of showing up like this? I expected you to come alone—you know—to help me explain what happened with Hugo and John. This is way too much to handle!"

"Slow down," said Calvin in a stern attempt to calm his floundering son. "I can hardly take you seriously in those ridiculous pantaloons."

Kyle's eyes started watering. I didn't feel sorry for him.

He betrayed us all, accident or not. The weight of the solemn promise I'd made him earlier tipped the scales away from my growing urge to lunge for and dismember him.

The way Brannon stared at Kyle—with his left hand inching toward his gun again—told me he felt the same call for blood.

The boy sniffled. "All I wanted was someone on my side. Someone with the authority to convince the others not to kill me or kick me out of N.E.R.D., even though I messed up. That's why I asked you to be here."

I leaned down and squeezed Brannon's shoulder hard enough to make him reconsider acting on the impulse mentioned.

"You really didn't know anything?" I asked, prepared to confront him with a few questions of my own. "About any of this?"

Kyle shook his head. He swallowed a cough to shed the confession he'd harbored in his bony chest for nearly four days. Calvin nodded at Katarina. Her sharp nudge made him continue.

"It's like I told you. I only ran the experiment because I

wanted to make Dad proud of me. For once in my whole life! And to show Doctor Baba our serum really works."

A string of muffled curses from the helicopter crumpled his face as he looked away from his mentor.

"I'll admit it, okay? I shot too high, but I really thought I was ready. I'd been testing on rats and things for months before I found two jocks on a forum about weightlifting. I asked them to volunteer. I didn't make anyone do anything."

I remembered what Hugo said. "You offered to make them stronger. That was irresistible."

"No one was supposed to get hurt. You've got to believe me. I told them all the risks involved. They even signed a waiver. But when Wednesday rolled around and I went to meet them at UC Berkeley—I was so nervous. I hadn't eaten anything all day. I strapped them in for the transfusion and left, just for a minute, thinking I'd have time to go to the deli before they woke up. All I wanted was a sandwich. It should have been fine!"

"But it wasn't," I said. "They escaped. I know that part."

Although we were no longer touching, I sensed Brannon had shifted. To make sure his condition hadn't worsened, I listened for changes in the rise and fall of his shaky breaths.

Kyle kept babbling. "I saw you fighting with them on my way home. When you stabbed John and he popped, I panicked. I wasn't sure if you'd finish Hugo off. Maybe he'd rage out and get you. Not that I wanted that to happen. That would've been terrible. The only thing I knew for certain was that I had to cover my tracks. To make sure none of it got back to me."

I exploded. "You selfish little prick!"

"I'm sorry!" said Kyle.

His apology meant nothing.

"I really, really am. I didn't know what to do! I just took off and ran back to the lab. I figured if I made it look like a break-in—like someone else took our stuff—then no one could blame me. If Hugo didn't blow up before stabilization set in, then I could call Dad and he could send a team to find him. That's what I thought. I was too afraid to tell Doctor Baba what happened. And I figured he'd shoot me if I did!"

He pointed at Brannon as Doctor Laura shouted more unsavory things at him from behind her gag.

"I had to make it look like I got hurt," he said after another dismal glance at her. "To make my story more believable. It all made sense at the time, but then I hit my head way too hard and I got stuck in the lab. That's when everything spiraled out of control. There was no way for me to ask for help. I was being watched. I couldn't get a message out until last night."

I hung onto my will not to murder again by the thinnest thread.

"What about me?" I asked. "When it comes to tying up loose ends, it sure seems like you forgot a pretty big one."

Kyle paused until I forced the issue.

"Just tell me!"

He glanced at his guardian and considered retreating behind her before he spoke. Her lithe, narrow form offered all the cover of a sapling.

He shook his head. "It was impossible. I never dreamed you'd be infected, too. I still don't know how it worked. Maybe it's destiny. Fate. Magic. Or maybe you just got lucky. Whatever happened, I wasn't expecting you to show back up at the lab. I didn't really think about you. Not until then. If you went to the police about what you saw—if you made it past Hugo—I knew they wouldn't pay attention. You know,

because of the way you dress. That was my only considera-
tion. If he didn't kill you. Which was more likely, and probably the cleanest outcome. At least for me."

He didn't say it like he wanted me dead, but his callous
remark set off the ticking time bomb of Brannon's temper. Up
until that point, he'd listen with silent purpose, using stealth to
disarm those around us while he shuffled to retrieve his lost
gun. He grabbed it with a furious cry and twirled, woozy, to
take his shot.

Kyle's bodyguard manifested another shiny blockade. Her
lightning fast reflexes beat Brannon's poorly telegraphed
attempt at retribution.

The rebound of his third bullet missed him, but it stung as
it grazed the top of my left shoulder.

"See what I mean?" Kyle cried, his suspicions confirmed.
"I told you so!"

Rather than stay by her charge's side, Katarina advanced.
The boom of Brannon's gun echoed through the warped
atmosphere of the rooftop as her mask alighted. She slung the
wall of sound forward and delivered a blow that stunned him.
This gave her the opportunity to rip the firearm from his trembling hand as he caught his breath.

"No more."

Her speaking voice wasn't human. The sound of its unsettling pitch—like sheet metal torn from the side of a barn
during a tornado—made the soldier aiming his riffle at me
flinch.

His misstep came at the best possible moment.

Before she pulled the trigger, I rushed forward without a
second thought. I shoved Brannon out of the way. The bullet
meant for him tore through the shredded panels of my jumper-

skirt and petticoat. My indestructible hip bone stopped it as I spun around to clock her.

Vengeful demons possessed my fists as they flew by themselves, pushing her away from the man beneath us. I didn't want to trample him as we fought. She threw up sonic barriers as I punched with all my might. They buckled beneath my blows until one made contact and glanced off the side of her sinister prosthetic.

Industrial grade plastic and titanium shattered. The flesh I exposed—hidden eternally from the bright light of day—appeared withered and rotten. Once struck, she unloaded the remaining rounds inside her weapon into my chest.

The fresh holes in my bodice and flesh didn't stop me.

Blood burst out and hung in the air, glowing like neon pieces of sky on the periphery of my vision before it splattered the floor.

She shrieked with uncontained volume—unleashing a sound even more terrible than the first words she'd uttered. The ground beneath us quivered again and knocked me to my knees.

I wanted to rip her apart, but Katarina redirected her last attack to hold me in place like a contortionist stuffed in a box. I tried to free myself as she doubled in half, heaving. Her strained breaths came in spurts like the cruel gasps of an iron lung.

A familiar grunt of intense pain pulled me away from her. I struggled to turn so I could see Brannon moan in agony as Calvin ground the sole of one shiny loafer into his bullet wound.

"Girls, that's enough," he called. "It's splendid to see, Holly, how well your new body functions. You've surpassed my wildest dreams, but I'm afraid all this unnecessary gunplay is drawing too much attention to our cause. Come. It's time to leave."

I grappled with my invisible restraints. "What are you talking about? I'll never go with you, you evil bastard."

Calvin motioned for his armed employee to join him and sighed as though I'd given him the answer he expected. A spark of glee twinkled behind the frown he wore for show.

"Believe me when I say I didn't want to behave so crudely, but now I suppose I must. I could threaten you, of course, but that won't get us anywhere. No, it's become quite clear that you value Agent Brannon's life far more than your own. Which is why you will come with me. Willingly, I might add. Without a fight."

He turned to the man with the biggest gun between us to punctuate his implications.

A wolfish grin spread across his face. "If you don't, I won't hesitate to dispose of him. Miss—"

"Holly, don't do it!" Brannon shouted. "You can't. You're more important than me. Just run and don't look—"

Another scream tore from him when Calvin stomped down on his broken hand.

"Holly!"

"I suppose we have a deal?" asked Titan's vicious leader.

Brannon begged me again to say no with a sorrowful gaze glazed with frustration and anger. But his tearful request— meant to appeal to my most basic instinct for self-preservation —went unheeded. My bloody baptism on Wednesday night changed me into something more than selfish. I wasn't the same.

I wasn't human.

Not anymore.

Katarina yanked me back to my feet and led me to the

helicopter, away from Brannon and the choice he couldn't fathom. The one that made him thrash and cry out in protest.

Calvin swept toward us with a satisfied grin as I slid in next to Doctor Laura. With no more tears left to cry, she scooted close to grab my hand. When she squeezed it, I finally recognized the inexplicable emotion that prevented me from acting in my own best interest.

I'd only known my new friends—my new family—for three days, but those hours knit us together in a tapestry the universe itself couldn't unravel. I loved them.

Hard and deep.

Plain and simple.

The whir of propellers blew my beret off Kyle's head as he climbed into the last row of seats, his father pointing the way. He didn't look me—or Doctor Laura—in the eyes.

Katarina, breathing with all the dulcet grace of a diesel engine, delivered me a malicious glance when she entered. Calvin slithered into the front next to the pilot—a boulder of a man dressed like the rest of his fearsome thugs.

A cold collar clicked into place around my neck. Someone behind me said the device would detonate if I attempted to remove it, or tried to injure my captors.

The lackey who kept the aim of his merciless weapon locked on his target returned last. He snaked his arm around a bar and leaned out the open door.

I unshouldered Usakumya's straps and held him as we watched Brannon crawl after us along the cracked cement. Even my fear of heights couldn't keep me from looking down. We lifted higher and higher into the air.

First five feet, ten, and then twenty.

Did they have Hugo in custody, too? Did they even want him with me on the hook? I didn't know what Titan planned to do with us in their push for world domination. The possibilities were too awful to focus on.

To sooth myself, I reached down to the bottom of the upended Pandora's box in my mind—the same one that'd unleashed a hoard of wretched emotions—to pull out a glimmer of hope.

What'd happened to Nuñez?

My question got its answer when the last N.E.R.D. standing burst through the stairwell door with his laptop bag hanging from his shoulder. His pocket knife, an extension of his tight fist, glinted in the sun.

The sight of him—covered from head to toe in bright red blood as I'd once been in blue—rendered me inconsolable.

Until I looked harder and realized that none of it was his.

He moved with frightening agility to his best friend's side and righted him. Brannon's eyes locked on mine as he used what little strength he kept in reserve to shout into the sky.

"Holly, don't panic. I'm coming for you!"

A silent exchange occurred between them before Nuñez pointed his gun at the helicopter. Brannon leaned against him for support, unable to do much else, as he fired at the craft whisking us away.

As if guided by the unseen hands of some supreme being, the bullet sailed through the air and smacked straight into the connecting joint of a spinning blade. When we lurched, I found myself rejoicing. I remembered my interaction in Old Red with the friends trying to help me.

If we crashed, I'd survive.

With a little luck, I'd pull Doctor Laura from the fiery wreckage. In my fantasy, we'd run far from Titan's clutches and regroup with the two men on the roof to mount an offensive against the forces of evil.

This wish, however, got ripped from me with my fuzzy companion when the last vestige of my old life ejected from the airborne vehicle as it tilted up and flew way.

"Bye-bye, Holly," said Usakumya in a singsong voice, falling to Earth in slow motion. "Good luck."

For the first time, I saw his lips move. I was hallucinating from stress. He waved to me as I did the same—though I wasn't ready or willing to say farewell.

Goodbye, Chi Ho. Goodbye, brand. Goodbye, Brannon, and what maybe could have been.

As the sickening refrain repeated itself in my head like a haunted chorus, I knew my future would be anything but kawaii.

ACKNOWELDGEMENTS

So many thanks to all the people who made *Magic Mutant Nightmare Girl* a reality. Everyone in my family deserves a shout out. My husband Alex for always believing in me and this book, our daughter Wendy for being the kind of whirl-wind that'd make Holly proud. All of my parents, Mom, Dad, Karen, Chris, Rose, I can't tell you how much I appreciate you being with me every step of the way! My sister Mary, who's always inspired and encouraged me to follow my dreams. My other sisters, brothers, aunts, uncles, cousins, nieces, Grand-mas, and everyone else in the family crew who asked "When's that book coming out?" with absolute joy and sincerity. Family friends, you're in this crew too and I'm forever grateful!

Thanks to all the amazing people I've met on this writing path. My first CPs Stacy and Mary for all their insights, my first beta reader Andrew Simmons, and Katherine Buffington and Adrian Belmes of Badlung Press for your notes that helped shape this story into what it is today. My friends and cheer-leading hype squad deserve the most praise, Cat Bakewell, Bethany Baptiste, Lyndall Clipstone, Stevie Kay, Alice Scott, Melissa See (who designed the text of my beautiful cover), Ashley Shuttleworth. Lucy Mason, you're the ray of light that convinces me I can do anything. Destiny Rae Smith, my soul sister, you kept me sane while raising a baby and revising this book, I'm so happy I found you. Leanne Schwartz and Kate Havas, my E.L.K. Lodge, I'll never forget putting the last otter on my pass pages with you by my side. Thanks to the YA debuts of 2020 and 2021 who helped me along the way, especially Laynie Bynum, Leslie Rush, Cat Scully, Kim Smejkal, Shveta Thakrar, I'll always treasure your kindness and your friendship! Thanks to everyone who's offered a blurb or a kind endorsement, online or in person. Special thanks to Julie of Struck by Stories and Anna of Reads Rainbow, my street team, and every blogger I've worked with. You're the backbone of the YA community and your work is so valuable!

Thank you to the entire SoCal J-fashion community for listening to me talk about this book for years and waiting patiently for it to arrive! My eternal love to everyone in the group chat when I wrote the first sentence: Marley and Aubrey Berish, my rocks and forever sounding boards, Maddie Caffarel, your creativity and talent leaves me constantly in awe, Rikki Rae Fischer, you have the kindest heart of anyone I've ever known. Thanks to every friend I've talked to during this wild ride, especially my lifelong partners in crime Tracy Gundy and Briana Tucker for always indulging my weirdest ideas.

Thanks to the artists I've worked with to bring my characters to life: Sienna Liao, Kaiser Ramos, Nolan Smith, Andry Tague, Em Rowene. And finally, the biggest thanks to my production teams, both first and last. Thank you Mandy Melanson and Emma Gitani for taking the first chance on this book, and for Elle Beaumont and the Midnight Tide team for giving it the perfect forever home. Biggest thanks to my cover artist Hotaru Sen for her gorgeous portrait of Holly, and to my designer Kristina Tran, your bows added the cutest finishing touch! If I've forgotten to mention anyone by name, know that my thanks will always live in my heart. I appreciate every magic mutant soul who made this journey possible.

ABOUT THE AUTHOR

Erin Grammar writes YA fantasy for teens who want to wield incredible power and look fabulous doing it. She graduated from Ohio University with a degree in Fine Arts, specializing in Playwriting. She's passionate about bringing stories to young readers that will inspire the next generation to reach for the stars and shoot past them. When she isn't writing, she's happy to search the SoCal hills for gemstones, thrift Hello Kitties to add to her massive collection, and play mom to one incredible daughter and two very demanding cats. Find her at eringrammar.com and on most social media @eringrammar.

GLOSSARY

THE SUBCULTURE

Harajuku fashion – Used to refer to a group of fashion styles, including Lolita fashion, popularized in the trendy Harajuku neighborhood of Tokyo, Japan, famous for bright colors, patterns, and unique shapes.

Lolita fashion – A Harajuku fashion style that emerged in the 1980s and 90s as an aggressively feminine act of rebellion against societal expectations, inspired by *mahou-shoujo* (magical girl) heroines of Japanese media, as well as Rococo and Victorian gowns. Now shared and worn worldwide with the enthusiastic support of the Japanese government's Kawaii Ambassador, a position dedicated to promoting empowering cuteness for everyone.

Boystyle, also known as Ouji fashion – Complimentary style to Lolita fashion that draws from traditional Victorian boy clothing, including short jackets, long socks, vests, capes, top hats, and other appropriate garments.

Lolita community – Comprised of local and worldwide groups gathering online and in person to share their love of

Lolita fashion by participating in discussion and coordinate advice forums, fashion shows, tea parties, and other social platforms and events.

EGL – Abbreviation for Elegant Gothic Lolita, a formal name for Lolita fashion.

Shimotsuma Monogatari*, also known as *Kamikaze Girls – A light novel and movie adaptation by novelist Novala Takemoto, a cornerstone of Lolita fashion media that follows selfish Baby the Stars Shine Bright fanatic Momoko as she navigates new friendships and transitioning to adulthood.

Kawaii – Japanese for *cute*, enthusiastically used to describe many Harajuku fashion styles and their flourishing subcultures.

Kowai – Japanese for *scary*.

THE CLOTHES

Brand – Term used to designate a lolita garment produced by one of the major Japanese designers, including Angelic Pretty, Baby the Stars Shine Bright, Innocent World, Metamorphose temps de fille, and Moi-même-Moitié.

Lolita coordinate – An outfit adhering to the guidelines of Lolita fashion composed of a main piece (JSK, OP, salopette, or skirt), headwear such as a headbow, rectangle headdress, or bonnet, socks or tights, shoes, and a petticoat that gives the style its poufy shape.

Headbow – A large bow, usually the Alice in Wonderland style that sits in the middle of the head, attached to a headband and worn with many coordinates sold in matching print sets with JSKs, OPs, and skirts.

Rectangle headdress – Common headwear for Lolita fashion consisting of a small strip of fabric adorned with lace and ribbons, worn across the top of the head and tied behind ears.

Bonnet – A rounded hat tied under the chin or behind the ears to frame the face, often adorned with ribbons, flowers, and feathers.

Jumperskirt (JSK) – A sleeveless knee length dress with straps, or a corseted bodice in place of straps, typically worn in combination with a blouse, bolero, cardigan, cutsew, or jacket to cover bare shoulders.

One Piece (OP) – A knee length dress with short or long sleeves that can be worn with or without the items added to coordinates utilizing JSKs.

Salopette – A casual, overall-like dress worn the same way as a JSK, often without a petticoat depending on length and shape. Salopette can also refer to an overall garment with shorts in place of a skirt.

Cutsew – A top made with jersey material, ornamented with ribbons, lace, or screen prints, the Lolita fashion equivalent of a t-shirt.

OTK socks – Over the knee socks that hit the wearer just above the knee.

UTK socks – Under the knee socks that hit the wearer just below the knee.

Petticoat – An underskirt with many layers of chiffon, tulle, or organza worn to give skirts a full, voluminous shape.

Bloomers – Long undergarments similar to shorts with elasticized waist and legs, can be worn in combination with a petticoat for ease of movement and modesty.

Parasol – An umbrella used to provide shade and UV protection on sunny days. Brand parasols often double as weatherproof umbrellas that can be used in the rain.

Usakumya – Brand mascot for Baby the Stars Shine Bright, a plush white bear with bright red eyes and a long-eared hat that disguises his true nature, making him appear as a rabbit. Holly's Usakumya is a backpack purse.

THE SUB-STYLES

Sweet Lolita – Sub-style of Lolita fashion focused on youthful, traditionally feminine themes such as cute animals, hearts, pastels, pastries, and princesses.

Gothic Lolita – Sub-style of Lolita fashion influenced by dark, macabre themes, Gothic romanticism, and metal music from Japanese Visual Kei bands, largely popularized by Malice Mizer guitarist Mana.

Classic Lolita – Sub-style of Lolita fashion that borrows most heavily from Victorian fashion, including soft earth tones, structured solids, delicate lace details, and bonnets.

Ita Lolita – Derogatory term designated to lolita coordinates and wearers that deviate from quality standards in garment construction or appearance, derived from the Japanese *itai* meaning *ouch*.

THE BRANDS

Angelic Pretty – Popular brand among Sweet Lolitas founded in 1979, a staple for whimsical motifs and purses in novelty shapes such as hearts, strawberries, and moons; Holly's favorite brand.

Baby the Stars Shine Bright – Established in the late 1980s, this brand provided the wardrobe for the film adaptation of *Kamikaze Girls* and is renowned for embroidered prints, a fairytale aesthetic shared with its sister brand, **Alice and the Pirates**.

Innocent World – Brand with a focus on Classic Lolita consistently praised for mature solids, neat construction, and dramatic prints inspired by European history.

Metamorphose temps de fille – Founded in 1997, this is a favorite of Sweet Lolitas that has since added more Classic and Gothic pieces to its collections, well-known for its use of velveteen.

Moi-même-Moitié – Gothic Lolita brand created by Malice Mizer guitarist Mana, features designs that incorporate crosses and other motifs found in traditional Gothic architecture.

MORE BOOKS YOU'LL LOVE

If you enjoyed this story, please consider leaving a review!

Then check out more books from Midnight Tide Publishing!

The Girl in the Clockwork Tower by Lou Wilham

A tale of espionage, lavender hair, and pineapples.

Welcome to Daiwynn where magic is dangerous, but hope is more dangerous still.

For Persinette—a lavender-haired, 24-year-old seer dreaming of adventure and freedom—the steam-powered kingdom of Daiwynn is home. As an Enchanted asset for MOTHER, she aids in Collecting Enchanted and sending them to MOTHER's labor camps.

But when her handler, Gothel, informs Persi that she will be going out into the field for a Collection, she decides it's time to take a stand. Now she must fight her fears and find a way to hide her attempts to aid the Enchanted or risk being sent to the camps herself.

Manu Kelii, Captain of the airship The Defiant Duchess, is 26-years-old and hasn't seen enough excitement—thank you very much. His charismatic smile and flamboyant sense of style earned him a place amongst the Uprising, but his fickle and irresponsible nature has seen to it that their leader doesn't trust him.

Desperate to prove himself, Manu will stop at nothing to aid their mission to overthrow MOTHER and the queen of Daiwynn. So, when the Uprising Leader deposits a small unit of agents on his ship, and tasks him with working side by side with MOTHER asset Persinette to hinder the Collection effort, he finds himself in over his head.

The stakes are high for this unlikely duo. They have only two options; stop MOTHER or thousands more will die—including themselves.

Available Now

Lyrics & Curses by Candace Robinson

Lark Espinoza could get lost in her music—and she's not so sure anyone in her family would even care to find her. Her trendy, party-loving twin sister and her mother-come-lately Beth, who's suddenly sworn off men and onto homemaking, don't understand her love of cassette tapes, her loathing of the pop scene, or her standoffish personality. For outcast Lark, nothing feels as much like a real home as working at Bubble's Oddities store and trying to attract the attention of the cute guy who works at the Vinyl shop next door—the same one she traded lyrical notes with in class.

Auden Ellis silences the incessant questions in his own head with a steady stream of beats. Despite the unconditional love of his aunt-turned-mother, he can't quit thinking about the loss of his parents—or the possibility he might end up afflicted with his father's issues. Despite his connection with lyric-loving Lark, Auden keeps her at arm's length because letting her in might mean giving her a peek into something dangerous.

When two strangers arrive in town, one carrying a mysterious, dark object and the other playing an eerie flute tune, Lark and Auden find that their painful pasts have enmeshed them in a cursed future. Now, they must come to terms with their budding attraction while helping each other challenge the reflection they see in the mirror. If they fail, they'll be trapped for eternity in a place beyond reality.

Available Now